D0007555

WHAT CAROLINE KNEW

ALSO BY CARYN JAMES
Glorie

WHAT CAROLINE KNEW

caryn james

ST. MARTIN'S PRESS ✿ NEW YORK

This is a work of fiction. All the characters and events portrayed in this novel are either fictitious or are used fictitiously.

WHAT CAROLINE KNEW. Copyright © 2006 by Caryn James. All rights reserved. Printed in the United States of America. No part of this book may be used or reproduced in any manner whatsoever without written permission except in the case of brief quotations embodied in critical articles or reviews. For information, address St. Martin's Press, 175 Fifth Avenue, New York, N.Y. 10010.

www.stmartins.com

Library of Congress Cataloging-in-Publication Data

James, Caryn.
    What Caroline knew : a novel / Caryn James.—1st ed.
        p. cm.
    ISBN 0-312-34312-4
    EAN 978-0-312-34312-5
        1. Scandals—Fiction. 2. Socialites—Fiction. 3. Art museums—Fiction. 4. Museum trustees—Fiction. 5. Man-woman relationships—Fiction. 6. New York (N.Y.)—Fiction. I. Title.

PS3560.A37845W47 2006
813'.54—dc22
                                                            2005052040

First Edition: March 2006

10 9 8 7 6 5 4 3 2 1

Contents

WHAT CAROLINE KNEW

PROLOGUE

Caroline: 1927

I will always remember the way he looked at me and said, "I did all this for you."

And I am still amazed at how many people made it there through the snow, as if they knew they would talk about that night forever.

But I was the only one ruined by it.

At eight o'clock the snow was still falling, dense over the bright streetlamps, but the room was crowded. I had searched all New York for the most elegant exhibition space and had found this: a long, single room with large windows at either end. Now the light shining through those windows was diffused through the snow, beautiful and eerie, unlike any light I had ever seen. I remember thinking that whatever painting Nick had hidden behind that blue velvet drapery, his opening was already a great success.

I begged him again to let me have just a glimpse, but he said, "No, I want to surprise you. I love the look you get when you see something new. It won't be long."

I knew the look on his face, that smile, so playful, so full of promise.

"One quick peek?" I asked and tried to reach around him to pull back a corner of the drapery from the canvas. It was life-size, conspicuous in the center of the wall, and baffling to me. We had spent days together making sure each work was hung to perfection, in just the right place, at just the right height. But after I had left that afternoon, he had somehow hurried this new painting into a place of honor, shuffling a half dozen others in no time. It was so large I had no idea where he could have been hiding it in his studio, when he had found time to paint it, how he had arranged all this without my knowing.

He put his hands on my shoulders and stood in front of me, blocking my way, laughing and handsome, with his golden hair. "Go away. I want a real unveiling," he said, staring at me so intensely that I knew he meant more than he could say in public. His deep blue eyes had never seemed more full of passion, his mustache never more rakish. "I did all this for you. To repay you. Why are you bothering with me anyway? Shouldn't you be greeting your guests and telling them what a genius I am?"

"I stole a minute for you, and you're turning me back into the crowd?" I whispered, but for once he wouldn't be charmed.

He stood there, arms folded, guarding his painting, smiling. "Soon, Caroline," he said.

When I'd arrived a half hour before and seen the strange, midnight blue drapery, I'd been a bit hurt that he had kept something so important from me. We had shared everything about his work, or so I thought. I had seen so many of his paintings take shape, the sketches leading to small oil studies, then the breathtaking canvases that filled the room that night. I had seen the discarded half successes, or what he considered half successes; Nick tossed out work other artists would have thought quite original. I had even seen the failures he ripped up in frustration. He once said, "Patron is too formal a term for what you are to me," and called me his co-creator, his muse. So when he stood in front of that veiled painting and smiled at me, my hurt feelings melted away. I became excited. He had created something—I was sure it was his most brilliant work yet—to surprise me.

There was nothing I could do except wait. I left him standing there and headed into the crush of guests.

It hadn't been easy to get so many different groups of people together: there was the proper social set I had grown up with, though by then I had come to despise their suffocating world of charity balls and each other; there was the last gasp of Mother's Old New York society, family friends I had known since childhood, who had wrapped themselves against the cold and loyally come to support me for her sake; there were all my new artist friends.

My own husband was there under protest.

Harry had come home that evening, fallen into the green leather armchair in his study as if he would never move again, and grumbled the way he always did about my new friends. "I'm paying for this party, isn't that enough?" he said. "Why do I have to go, too? You'd think putting up the money would buy me the right to stay home."

He picked up the cream-colored invitation I had left on his desk as a reminder and propped it on his stomach, which even then was threatening to pop the buttons on his vest.

Mrs. Harrison Stephens
and the Mark Haskell Gallery
request the honor of your presence at an exhibition
of paintings by

NICHOLAS LEONE

| November 17, 1927 | 2 West 13th Street |
| 7 o'clock | New York, New York |

As he looked down at the invitation, I noticed that the hair on top of his head was already getting thin, that he was turning into the image of a self-satisfied businessman long before his time.

"Please don't tease, Harry. Mother has already backed out. You can't let me go alone."

"Where's your perfect little brother?"

"Well, of course, he'll be there."

"With all his perfect little pals from law school?" That might have been the very last time Harry underestimated Will.

"Didn't you see him today?" I asked.

"He stopped by to introduce someone from his firm, someone even greener than he is. Your brother apparently has clients he considers more important than his own family, so he's sent someone else in to help. I had to sit with this new man for hours explaining those old contracts your mother is worried about. Worried for nothing, I keep telling her. I'm worn out." And he yawned, as if I might not believe him otherwise. Harry was so literal.

I sat on the arm of his chair facing him so we could talk as I rubbed his shoulders. "Please, please. Tonight won't be bad, I promise. There will be plenty of people you know. The Woodwards are coming and the Livingstons, and when we get home we can make fun of old Mildred Prescott, you always enjoy that." His shoulders felt looser, and I began softly massaging his neck. "Besides, Davis will be there. What will he think if you're not?" My mother's banker was always a foolproof lure for Harry.

He kept on grumbling. "What's your mother's excuse for canceling? Whatever it is, same for me." I felt like saying, "Old age. Obstinacy. You're almost there," but I didn't.

Mother had telephoned at four. The seamstress was fitting my dress one last time, and I was wearing it when Louis, our butler then, called me to the phone. The silk dress felt so good against my skin that I nearly danced into the next room, the skirt's layer of chiffon grazing my bare legs.

Mother was brisk. "Hello, dear. I assume you have called off this strange event of yours tonight. Look out the window if you haven't."

"It will be fine," I said. "You are still coming?"

"Of course not, how can I? One can't take a motor out in the snow, it's far too dangerous. If we still had the carriage . . ."

I knew better than to press her, so I tried to humor her instead. "You'd rather take a horse and buggy? Be brave, Mother."

"It was a brougham, and I always felt safe in it."

"It was an old-fashioned contraption, practically an antique." Which she had kept until it was a hazard on the street; she had only given it up because the horses were terrified of the car horns honking all around them. I could see her on the other end of the phone, the waves of her gray hair as rigid as they had been for thirty years, feeding remnants of her teatime scones to her lapdogs as she sighed at the foolishness of my generation.

"Perhaps I am an antique myself," she said, "and antiques stay in at night, safely covered."

"You know very well our car is safe, and George is the most cautious driver we've ever had. Why don't you let us call for you and you can pretend it's the old brougham? It would mean so much to me to have you there. It would mean so much to Nick."

With that, I had gone too far. There was never any doubt when you had reached the point at which Mother lost patience. In the imperious voice I had grown up with, a voice carrying the weight of generations of proper society, she said, "Why should I care about a starving artist whom I do not know and have no reason or wish to know? I wonder, why should you care so much, Caroline? Play at being a Medici if you like, but I am not risking my life for this silly game of yours. And you should not be risking yours, either. I'm sorry, dear."

"You are not sorry, you're happy for an excuse to back out. You never wanted to come. You think this is beneath you."

"I don't like using the telephone in this storm, dear, it frightens me, all this electricity running into my ear. Be careful if you do go." And she hung up.

I didn't tell Harry about Mother's foul mood; I just slipped from the arm of his chair to his lap and put my arms around his neck. Like Mother, he thought I was being silly. "Nothing I've ever done has been as important as this," I told him. "It's something I can be proud of, and I want you there beside me. Do I have to beg?" I slid to the floor and squeezed my arms around his legs. "Oh, come on, don't be an old grump. We'll have fun, all night long, I promise. All night."

Even then he hesitated, but finally said, "Well, get dressed then. If we're going we better have George bring the car around soon. The snow was coming down hard when I got here."

It took over an hour to get all the way down to Thirteenth Street. Harry and I sat close together in the back of the car, my arm through his, but we didn't say much. "Is that a dress or a slip?" he'd asked as he helped me on with my cape. "Do you want to freeze to death?" Now I pulled the cape's fur collar up over my nose and tried hard not to shiver.

Harry kept leaning forward and staring out the window, as if looking fierce could help George keep the car from swerving in the snow. I was going over the guest list in my mind, thinking about which of our stuffy friends to introduce to which artists without anyone feeling uncomfortable.

When we finally pulled up in front of the gallery, it was after seven and a few guests had already arrived. As we walked into the room I saw the veiled painting right away—you couldn't miss it—

but I had made such a fuss about this being my party that I refused to let Harry see how surprised I was. I quickly introduced him to Mark Haskell. "Yes, Haskell, you're the man whose business I seem to be backing," he began. There was an edge in his voice I seldom heard, but I had to leave them alone while I searched for Nick.

I saw him on the far side of the room talking to a vaguely familiar couple. I went to them, pretending I had noticed a light glaring on one of the paintings, and led him away toward the veiled work. Even as I did he leaned toward me and whispered, "Don't ask any questions, it's a surprise." We stopped in front of it, and he paused for a few long seconds before he turned to face me. That's when he said, "I did all this for you."

Soon the room was filled with groups of people, as distinct as rival tribes. Men in tailored black clustered with women poised in pale satin and pearls. Women in cotton skirts and colorful shawls mingled with men in rumpled jackets. But it wasn't hard to blend them together; that was what I knew how to do.

I introduced Davis the banker to the most successful dealer in the room (a man Haskell could only envy). I led one of Will's law school friends to meet Anna O'Neil, who painted shrieking expressionist portraits but was demure and soft-spoken in person. I was so grateful all these people had braved the storm that I was even amused by Florence Copley, Mother's oldest friend, though I knew she had been sent to spy on me. "Caroline, what an extraordinary dress. Do turn around. I think the back is as low as the front—that's nothing to you young people, of course. Do turn." I twirled, and as I faced her again she forced a smile. "I must congratulate you on your extremely straight spine, now that I see every vertebra bared."

Even Harry was coming around, blustering with the men, creating that sense they seemed to enjoy so much: that they had been dragged along by their wives and couldn't wait to get home for a last cigar.

I left the art critics alone so they wouldn't feel pressured; there were at least six, from the daily papers and the serious art journals. I hadn't invited anyone from the gossip columns, but a few came anyway, and I thought there were a couple of people off the street. Nick hadn't wanted anyone snobbishly left out and had insisted that this be the official public opening as well. I remember looking around the room and thinking: He will be famous by morning.

I watched him with such pleasure as he moved from group to group, shaking hands and casting his effortless smile. When I was near enough, I could hear him taking in praise modestly, making small talk with the socialites, discussing his work intently with the other artists. One of them, a middle-aged woman we knew casually, had pulled a small pad and pencil out of her purse and was trailing him, sketching as she walked. Well, why wouldn't she? That night he looked more dramatic than usual, in a perfectly tailored suit and a floppy bow tie made of silk that only he could have gotten away with. Someone wrote later that he dressed as if he thought he were the reincarnation of Whistler, but there was nothing ridiculous about the way he looked. He was young and *so* dashing. I was eager for those private moments afterward when we would talk about the evening, our great triumph, laughing and sharing stories as we always did.

Nick and my brother were by far the best-looking men there, though Will was handsome in a quieter way. Nick had a fine, chiseled look, as if every line of his face—firm jaw, straight nose—had been carved by a master sculptor. Will looked like the lamb he was. He had been out of law school for less than a year and still had his baby face, with soft blue eyes and features that became even more handsome as he matured. Nick had flair, but I must say my brother looked more dignified. He was working hard to establish himself then and scarcely had time for a social life, yet he had gotten all his school friends to come to the opening. I looked around and saw Mrs. Copley talking to old Judge Carey, Will talking to Anna O'Neil. I searched for Lawrence Sloane so he and Will could have a nice long chat—it could only help a young lawyer to get to know the district attorney better—but couldn't find him.

By eight the room was bursting, and the snow falling so fast that people began to talk about leaving while they were able to make it home. With flawless timing, when the room was at its fullest, Nick gathered a crowd around him near the veiled painting and called for everyone's attention. "I am touched by your generous compliments. Or should I say your generous, possibly fictitious compliments?" he began. There was a small wave of laughter, and when it died away he turned serious. "I can only hope to improve until one day I deserve that praise. Your encouragement tonight means more to me than I can say. I have one last work to show you. It's the one I consider the truest I have ever done. I dedicate it to Caroline Stephens"—and he gestured toward me, standing not far away—"who made it possible."

As the crowd applauded, he pulled down the blue drapery. I screamed before I could stop myself, "No. Never. I never . . ."

I am told that's when I fainted. I am told I yelled, "You will not get away with this," before I fell to the floor, but I do not remember saying that. It does not sound like anything I would ever say.

I came to consciousness in the car, huddled in Will's arms. He took me home, and all the way he held me and stroked my hair and whispered in my ear that he would take care of me and that everything would be all right. He said that Harry had stayed behind to set things right. He told me that the drapery had been put back at once. "Don't worry, dear," he kept whispering. "I'll take care of everything." Will was my defender, my beloved ally in that awful business from then on. I looked up into his eyes. I had never seen him look sadder.

I lay in a chaise by the fire in the sitting room all that long night, wrapped in a shawl and trembling. It was as if my confusion and betrayal had taken this physical shape, a chill so deep I felt I would never get warm or stop shaking. Will had taken off my thin, wet shoes, sent my maid to bed, wrapped me in the pink cashmere shawl that I often left on the chaise, and brought me tea himself. Whenever I felt overwhelmed by what had happened, I snapped my eyes shut as if I could block it out. You would think that vile painting would be all I could see, but instead when I closed my eyes I saw the way Nick had looked when he said, "I want to surprise you." He had smiled at me with all the tenderness, all the honesty anyone could ever want as he said, "I did all this for you," and now I had no idea why he had done it or what he had meant.

I looked toward the fireplace, with its face of a mermaid carved in dark wood, her flowing hair surrounding the fire; she had once seemed sensuous but now looked like a Medusa. The maroon painted walls, once such a daring backdrop, had turned the color of dried blood.

Hours later I heard Harry thrash through the door and sat up, frantic to explain, but he was too distressed to listen. He stomped around the room and in a rambling speech told Will—he talked only to Will, not to me—what had happened after we left.

Only a few photographers had been in the room, and they were, as Harry put it, "very reasonable." He didn't know if the critics had gotten a good enough look at the painting to say much of anything; he didn't know how our friends would react. But he had done all he could. He had taken "that animal," as he called Nick, by the collar and with the help of some other men tossed him into the storm. The room had emptied quickly. The gossip columnists had dashed out, and everyone else had left quietly. What could they say? And with the painting covered, there was nothing left to see.

Harry had stayed at the gallery making telephone calls. "I managed to get a few private detectives to guard the building. No one can sneak back in and steal it or photograph it during the night," he said, pacing around in a fury as I lay there, still speaking to Will as if this didn't concern me at all. "I convinced Haskell not to open tomorrow. I told him to do nothing until I speak to him in the morning." I suspected that Harry was waiting for the bank to open before dealing with Haskell; I guessed those very reasonable photographers had emptied his pockets, but I didn't interrupt to ask.

He said he had wanted to take the painting home for safekeeping, but it was too large for any car. I couldn't help muttering, "You needed Mother's brougham after all," and the sudden thought of her almost made me ill. "Will," I said, sitting up, "Mother will hear about this."

"I'll handle her. I'll tell her myself."

"It will have to be destroyed, of course," Harry said, ignoring both of us now, pacing in circles and talking about the painting as if it were one of his father's racehorses.

Will mumbled something about how we didn't own it, so destroying it could be a problem, but he seemed to be talking to himself. I had my own secret fear. I knew how Nick worked, making sketch after sketch, study after study. I was sure there must be more.

At midnight Harry went out into the dying storm to get the morning papers. We were hoping, against all reason, that the incident would be overlooked. "Maybe there's been some tragedy we don't know about that might overshadow it," Will said. "A fire or a murder. If we're lucky."

"No newspaper will care about a woman fainting, will they?"

Harry asked as he was leaving. I was horrified at his simplicity; he was so willfully blind.

"I was the woman in that painting, Harry, you can't deny that," I yelled, with more energy than I knew I had left. "*These* are the earrings in the portrait," I said, grabbing the small gold filigrees that dangled from my ears and had been passed down from my grandmother. "People are talking about it this minute, they'll talk about it tomorrow over breakfast. The way we planned to laugh at Mildred Prescott, they are laughing at me right now. And the papers haven't even come out yet."

"How could they even describe it?" he asked. He seemed subdued and suddenly confused. "What could they say? It looked like you were doing something . . . I can't even think how to say it." I could see him convincing himself. "They can't print that. It's something no lady would ever do. No one would believe it of you."

"I wonder."

He left, but the storm had delayed the papers, and he had to go out twice more before he found any. It must have been nearly 4:00 A.M. when he came home with an armful of newspapers, walked into the sitting room trailing snow from his overshoes, took a small sculpture from the table, and threw it against a wall. It was the figure of a woman, and as he grabbed her by the neck I shuddered.

Every paper had covered the story, as news or as gossip and in one case as art. The *News* was one of the least painful. It began: "Mrs. Harrison Stephens, socialite and benefactor of the arts, collapsed last night at the sight of a lewd portrait of herself at the opening of an exhibition by an unknown artist, Nicholas Leone."

Others were much worse. The *World* wrote, "Mrs. Harrison (Caroline Holbrooke) Stephens, wife of one of the city's most prominent businessmen, created a scandal last night by inviting her friends to view a nude portrait of herself in a deviant act. One witness, a woman who knows Mrs. Stephens well, said, 'I think Caroline has come under evil influences. Why else would she go out of her way to upset her friends and humiliate herself?'"

A large headline on page 3 of the *Journal* read, "Society Gal's Indecent Pose." They printed a rough drawing of the painting, a re-creation they said had been "cleansed for publication."

We read silently, passing the papers among the three of us. At first, we pretended it wasn't so bad. After all, Thomas McLaughlin from the *Chronicle*, one of the most respected critics in the country, had rushed his review into print because he had seen great art in Nick's painting. "The centerpiece and possibly the masterpiece of the exhibition, quickly unveiled and then shrouded again, was a life size nude oil painting of the art patroness and collector Mrs. Harrison Stephens. With one arm bent behind her neck and the other reaching down languorously before her, the image was life-like yet stylized, evoking both Botticelli's *Birth of Venus* in all its delicate beauty and Picasso's *Demoiselles d'Avignon* in all its brash sexuality. In the momentary glimpse this critic was allowed, the painting appeared to have an originality of composition, a visceral pull, and a visual power that might well redefine portraiture for our age. It was worlds apart from the other works by Mr. Leone, derivative landscapes with green suns and purple moons that are faint echoes of his betters, Hartley and Dove. Even a glance revealed the Stephens portrait to be a significant work. It is lamentable that it was so quickly hidden away."

But soon we could see there was no hope. "A pornographic portrait of Caroline Stephens, who threw the party for Leone and is known as his 'patron,' was the talk of the evening," the *Mirror* gossip columnist wrote. "When Leone unveiled the painting, which he dedicated to his beautiful hostess, the upper-crust guests gasped in shock. Mrs. Stephens fell to the floor in a swoon, but not before vowing revenge. 'You can't do this to me,' she screamed. To describe the painting in a family newspaper isn't easy, but here goes. She is wearing gold earrings, nothing else. Her long hair is down and is tickling one bosom. One hand is in front of her, tickling her private parts. You can say this for her society crowd, they know how to entertain themselves."

I made myself read every terrible word. I had to know what I'd be facing. I knew there was more to come. By the time I finished I was sobbing, Harry was ranting, Will was staring solemnly into the fire. If Harry had known how, I think he would have broken into the gallery then and torn the painting apart with his bare hands. As usual, his heart was in the right place, but his brain was God knows where. "I'll take it to the country and start a bonfire, so they'll never be able to find the pieces," he yelled. "I'll set fire to the whole building if I have to."

"You don't understand at all, do you?" I said, crying and feeling dizzy but getting more impatient with him by the minute. I threw off my shawl, stood up to face him, and tossed the papers at him. "Look at these. All my friends and all those strangers will believe I posed that way. They'll believe it." I didn't know why Nick had betrayed me, and my soul had been torn to shreds by it, but I knew I had not posed for that painting.

"I can take care of that," Harry said. "I'll call Gardiner and Robertson and the other publishers first thing and make sure their papers never mention it again."

"It's too late. Besides, you can't control the gossip rags, those men don't belong to your clubs. And don't think you can buy them off, there are too many of them and they don't want your money. We are more valuable to them as dirty linen."

"Then I'll buy the damned newspapers."

"Be realistic," I cried. "We don't have time for nonsense."

"Nonsense? You think I'm kidding? He isn't fit to live. He should be drawn and quartered. He should be tortured. He should be bankrupted. I'd sue him for every penny he's got, if he had a cent."

I sat down, exhausted. Of course Harry would reduce it to money. "Go ahead, sue him," I mumbled, so tired I hardly knew I was speaking at all.

"That's impossible, Caroline, what are you saying? You can't sue," he exploded, as if I had meant it any more than he had. "That's public. We want to make this whole thing disappear as if it never happened, not make it worse."

"Never happened?" I said. "It happened. In public." I barely had the strength to speak and felt as if I were in a trance. We had all seemed to be talking gibberish, but as I spoke I slowly began to see things more clearly, as if I had spotted some distant star that had broken through the darkness, a small but saving light I could only reach toward. "It did, it happened in public, I need to fix it in public. That painting is a lie. People need to know."

Harry was calm now. "Need to know what? It's your word against his," he said, his voice turning bitter as he glared at me.

"I did not pose for that painting," I told him just as calmly. "I wish you would believe me."

He said nothing.

"I wish you would believe me, but if you don't it doesn't matter now. Right now I need you to be practical."

"I am being practical, dear," and the word 'dear' was as icy as I have ever heard it said. "It is your word against his."

I turned to Will.

My good, idealistic Will. He seemed to be in his own thoughts, sitting absolutely still on the edge of the big armchair by the fire. I went to him and put a hand on his shoulder, but he didn't move. He sat staring into the flames as if he wanted to fling himself in, never to face the world again. "Let me sit with you," I said, taking his hand. I nudged my body next to his on the edge of the seat. I took his chin gently in my hand and turned his head away from the fire toward me. "You do believe I never posed that way, don't you? I never could."

His words were perfect, though his voice was lifeless. "Of course I believe you, Caroline, you don't need to ask that. I'm just wondering what to do next."

Philip: 2002

$\mathcal{M}$y Grandfather Will called me to his bedside when he was very ill, very near the end. He had taken care of everything, set up every detail of every trust, left precise instructions about running the foundation, made bequests to even the newest servants. He had been grooming me to take over for years by then, and I was sure there was nothing left to say. You can imagine how unprepared I was for what I heard."

As he spoke, Philip slowly led his old but now distant friend Alessio up the grand staircase in the Great Hall of the Metropolitan Museum.

"I can still see him propped up on his pillows in the big mahogany bed. He looked terribly weak, but his voice was as firm as ever. Grandfather said, 'I'm going to tell you where to find that old portrait of your Great-Aunt Caroline. Try not to judge her. It makes her look like a whore.'

" 'Aunt Caroline's portrait?' I babbled like an idiot. 'It exists? It can't.'

" 'If it had been up to me, I would have destroyed it long ago,' Grandfather said. 'But it wasn't my choice to make.' "

Now Philip was taking Alessio to see that portrait, through crowds of tourists in running shoes and shorts, all heading to see

Caroline too. A rose-colored banner floating outside the museum announced: "Nicholas Leone and the Stephens Circle—April 5 to September 15, 2002." As the men walked straight up that imposing staircase, out of place in their gray business suits, Philip took every teasing curve his story allowed. They would not arrive before he had explained how the painting had gotten there, before he had enticed Alessio to accept his offer.

"Grandfather dozed off suddenly in those last weeks. He seemed to be drifting then and closed his eyes. There was no point in asking more, and we didn't discuss it again until two weeks later, after he had been taken to the hospital.

"Of course I had known about Aunt Caroline's portrait since I was a boy, more than anyone thought I knew. The adults whispered about it when I was small, and it was obviously some dark family secret not fit for children's ears. When I was old enough to ask, my father brushed it aside. He said it was buried in the past and was so painful for Aunt Caroline that no one dared speak of it in her presence—that would have been unforgivable—even though everyone who mattered said she came out of it just fine in the end. He made me promise never to mention it to Grandfather Will. Then when Father died so suddenly—I'm sorry you never got to know him—well, I couldn't break the only promise he had ever asked me to make. Grandfather and I talked nearly every day for many years after that, and he never so much as hinted at it."

"I would have written when your grandfather died, if I had known," Alessio said. "He treated me like his own son when we were in school."

Philip paused on the staircase and turned to look back down. He seemed to be surveying an empire below, or maybe he was only stopping to catch his breath. Either way, his face was discreetly turned away from Alessio as he said in a tone of utter sincerity, "Oh, no, I wouldn't expect you to have heard. We had lost touch."

He would not think of calling attention to the way his college friend had reappeared after nearly twenty years, along with so many other long-lost friends and colleagues, simply because the portrait had reappeared too. Philip wasn't the most high-powered intellect in the Holbrooke family, but his innate politeness would never fail him. The old money in his bearing and his speech came wrapped in an endearing, transparent charm. He needed so much to be liked, was so guileless in his appeal for compliments, that the charm worked. His dealings with men were smooth, and with women it was entirely a matter of which of them would begin to flirt first. He wasn't clever enough to fool women, at least not the ones who were clever themselves, but he was so handsome, so flattering in his attention, that it didn't matter.

He had been genuinely pleased to hear from Alessio again and was reassured by the way they fell back in step with each other as they walked side by side up the staircase. They had been as close as brothers at Dartmouth, partly because Alessio, the Italian exchange student, was too new and confused to realize that Philip was the richest of the rich boys, either toadied to or resented by the others. It was a relief to Philip, so soon after his father's death, not to be treated as the young master and heir. Even then, it was easy to predict how their paths would one day separate. They had stayed friends for a time after college, when Alessio went home to graduate school, then started a small art gallery in Milan, and Philip took his place running the family businesses and philanthropies.

In truth, Philip merely looked over the shoulders of the astute and trusted executives who ran the companies—the most lucrative were the old shipping and railroad lines that had been transformed into air-freight carriers—and who guided them through diversification, dot-com nightmares, and other treacherous passages he observed from a leisurely distance. He spent most of his time on the family foundation, built on the profits from refineries that were sold at the right time to guarantee a seemingly bottomless fortune. Giving away money as a career played to his social strengths. Like his great-aunt Caroline, he had even become a trustee of the Met, a position he considered his most substantial professional achievement.

Philip realized that in the last decade or so Alessio must have been slipping in and out of New York to visit galleries and collectors without calling him. That was how life and friendship went, he told himself. He also knew that for years he had been regarded as a lightweight, the Holbrooke family factotum (though he would never let the world see that he knew).

But in the privacy of his own thoughts, he had no false modesty. Why shouldn't I take some credit? he asked himself. None of this would have happened without me. I am the one who rediscovered the portrait after more than seventy years. I am the one who decided it should be displayed. I have become a great benefactor of the arts.

When the Met mounted a small exhibition around the portrait, every major critic in the country and many from abroad had come, and every one of them had left dazzled. Such a huge response to so small a show was astonishing, but Aunt Caroline deserved it.

The art world didn't see it quite that way; it was mesmerized by Caroline but thought Leone deserved the praise. A rapturous essay in a little-known art blog was e-mailed around and set the tone early: "As I stood before Caroline I experienced what I imagine the first viewers of the *Mona Lisa* must have felt. I had never seen such a mysterious smile. I could have stared at the portrait for hours without exhausting the enigma of its character or cracking the code of its form." It ended with a clumsy expression of what turned out to be the most haunting and persistent of Caroline-related questions: "The painting is the only known Leone in existence, which has set museums and galleries on something of a safari for more. Dealers around the world are asking, 'What others might survive and where?' "

Philip had actually memorized the review from *The Times* of London, whose critic called the painting "the missing link between Picasso and photorealism." He wrote, "We can only speculate about the new heights that portraiture, and Leone, might have reached had this iconoclastic, reinvigorating painting been allowed to see the light all those decades ago."

The scholarly journals were still weighing in; art historians were making pilgrimages; ordinary people were cleaning out their attics hoping that some grimy painting they had picked up at a flea market might turn out to be a missing Leone.

After the first extraordinary flurry of publicity, even Philip's wife, who ordinarily left him alone, had something to say. "Everyone will try to take advantage of you now," she told him gently. "Remember what your grandfather would have wanted. Please don't get carried away."

"Olivia, give me some credit," he said. "I am every bit as skeptical about all this attention as I should be. Don't worry." And she retreated into docility again. She had done her duty by warning him.

She didn't know how carefully he had planned his next steps. He had secrets to tell. He would cooperate with the dozens of magazine writers and television interviewers pleading for family memories. But why should he give them the best material, then fade into powerless obscurity again? He would be shrewd. He would leak his most cherished, most valuable secrets to someone he trusted, someone who would put them to the right use, someone who would treat them with the respect Aunt Caroline deserved. He was encouraged when Alessio had turned up.

If I can't share this magnificence with one of my oldest friends, he thought (to his credit, he told himself he was being ironic when he thought it), what kind of benefactor am I?

Alessio's family had its own peculiarities. The ancient aristocratic strain had given way to fierce Marxist grandfathers, and he had inherited vestiges of both. He was a connoisseur who never compromised his fine taste and standards in art; perhaps that was why he was still scrambling for his first major success. Yet he refused Philip's offer of a private viewing of Caroline's portrait, insisting that to get the true effect he needed to see it as any tourist would. Philip played along, amused that Alessio had kept his boyish ideals along with his boyish looks—the dark skin, deep brown eyes, and thick black hair that had always made him look like some generic Italian movie star, Philip thought, the kind whose name no one could ever remember.

As they continued up the wide granite steps, Alessio struggled to keep pace with his much taller friend and noticed that the two of them appeared more than ever like opposites, despite their nearly identical suits. Philip had grown into his heritage well. The patrician air, the slight formality that had made him seem like a misplaced nineteenth-century gentleman at Dartmouth in the seventies now made him seem the most civilized man on earth.

Even the worst reproductions of Caroline's portrait showed that Philip had inherited the Holbrooke looks, those perfectly proportioned features that made the family seem unfairly blessed, beautiful as well as rich. His light brown hair had receded and thinned, and he wore it too long in back to compensate (Alessio wondered why even the most confident American men did that). But instead of diminishing his looks, the receding hairline only made his perfect features more evident. He had the soft blue Holbrooke eyes that sent out an irresistible warmth. His version of their nearly identical suits was impeccably tailored, its fabric of a quality Alessio could never dream of owning. He took comfort in the fact that his own manner cried out "serious" while Philip's emphatically did not.

"I think you look like your aunt. There's a family similarity," Alessio said.

"I was always told I looked like Grandfather, and he and Aunt Caroline were like twins. I'm afraid I'm just a shadow of them, though, something's been lost in translation. She was *so* beautiful, especially when she was young. I've seen dozens, maybe hundreds of photographs of her from that time. She was exquisite. Sometimes she was surrounded by scruffy artists and women who always make me think of the word vamps; she looked totally modern and comfortable among them but never tacky. She wore her hair rolled up softly somehow, so it looked like a bob, but it wasn't. Her clothes were stylish, up-to-the-minute, but more elegant than anyone else's. Her flapper dresses were made in Paris. Have you ever seen photographs from the night of the opening? She was ravishing. She wore a white dress with little straps and one of those ragged, pointed, whatever-you-call-them long chiffon hems floating over a short skirt. Sexy but completely covered and proper. It was cut audaciously low in back—a fraction of an inch more and it would have been vulgar, but it wasn't. She was an old woman when I knew her, but even then her voice was seductive, as lyrical as music." Philip stopped. "I'm getting carried away, aren't I?"

Of course he's getting carried away, Alessio thought; that's what I've come for.

"I heard the name Caroline Stephens over the years in Rome and Milan, and knew she was a great collector and an even greater patron of the arts," he said, perhaps overstating the reach of Caroline's taste and influence. "But I never knew she was your aunt and I never heard of Nicholas Leone."

"Hardly anyone had. There was that brief burst of interest back in the sixties, but he was forgotten again right away. As he should have been. I've seen some photographs of his earlier paintings, mostly bad black-and-white photographs taken in his studio, and they don't come close to Aunt Caroline's portrait."

"I've seen those pictures too. It's difficult to judge, but I agree, the lost works seem to be minor. Still, there is a market for them. Anything of his that is found will be worth a lot. And who knows, there may be important work that hasn't been attributed yet."

"You have no idea how many people have been after me about that," Philip said, his tone suggesting he was sharing a confidence with a friend rather than turning away one more overeager dealer. "This is the only Leone I know of, truly. We've hunted for others for years. And this is the one that matters, isn't it? You're the expert, but I think the critics are right, this was a spectacular breakthrough, one of those moments of genius that can happen to an artist once and never again. I feel disloyal saying that, because Leone was a reprehensible human being, but he *was* an artist, at least this once. He used Aunt Caroline very badly in life, though. You have no idea. She deserves at least as much credit as he does." Philip glanced at Alessio to see how he would react.

"Because she supported his work?" Alessio asked.

"I mean we wouldn't be here without her. She did much more than give him money."

"Are you saying she posed for the portrait?"

"Absolutely not!" Philip said quickly. "She denied that to her dying day."

He stopped at the top of the stairs and turned to face his old friend. "I know what really happened," he said, in that tone of casual charm. "I know everything, and I can tell you if you like. Aunt Caroline told me the story the year before she died."

"She talked to you about the portrait?"

"She did. During Christmas break our sophomore year. It was

one of the high points of my life, I knew it even then, when I thought the portrait had been destroyed."

"You never mentioned it. I thought we told each other everything in those days."

"I didn't tell anyone. It was too intimate to share. She had told me something she had never told anyone else. She was handing down the truth that only she knew, and she was handing it to *me*, to me alone. I don't know, maybe she simply needed someone to know, anyone. I can't say why she chose me, but she did. She talked about a lot of other things she had kept hidden, too. Of course, she could never have anticipated all this," Philip said, sweeping a hand grandly to take in the staircase, the tourists in the lobby below, the signs pointing toward Caroline's exhibition. "Frankly it's just as well she didn't live to see it. But you should hear her story before you see the portrait. You'll be able to appreciate it better afterward. Let's not pretend you're the average tourist anymore. Your opinion is too valuable to me."

"There's more than I've read in print?"

"Much more. Follow me, let's have a drink on the roof."

Philip turned left, and they took an elevator down to the basement, where they switched to a different elevator, the only one leading to the roof. Alessio suspected that the slow climb up the grand staircase had been for dramatic effect; they could have come straight to this elevator if Philip had been heading for the roof all along. But maybe Philip had changed his mind on the way. No matter. Alessio thought the least he could do was give Philip a few more minutes as the center of attention, and Philip was pleased that Alessio was falling into line so easily.

Already, at midmorning, the sun was unbearably hot as it beat down on the roof, and Philip led Alessio toward a shaded bench under a vine-covered trellis. Looking to the right as they passed,

Alessio glimpsed Central Park, lavish and peaceful, a luxurious green blanket of trees that gave no hint of people, much less urban grit. But the bench Philip had chosen offered a different view, facing the terraces and penthouses on Fifth Avenue, and beyond them the ugly, boxy stone buildings on Madison. He left Alessio sitting there while he went to buy drinks.

"You said you didn't want special treatment. What could be more appropriate than cheap champagne in plastic glasses?" he said as he returned. "To Caroline," and he raised his glass.

"To your Aunt Caroline," said Alessio, clinking plastic. "Were you close to her?"

"No, oddly enough. She and my grandfather were part of the same world, and they both seemed remote from us when I was small. I've never asked, but when I was a boy there may have been a rift between my mother and grandfather about Aunt Caroline. I remember hearing Mother mention something about her at a dinner party. She was defending her, something along the lines of 'She led a blameless life after the scandal,' and Grandfather Will stood up and said, 'She led a blameless life *before* the scandal too.' He tossed his napkin on the table and walked out. I think he never forgave Mother for talking about it in front of strangers, and there may have been some lingering resentment that attached itself to us children for a time. So, no, I was never close to her. But every Christmas she would send my sisters and me checks to buy whatever we liked, and we would visit her to say thank you. She still lived in the town house off Park Avenue, the one she and Uncle Harry lived in back in 'twenty-seven, when everything happened. Look there," he said, pointing across Fifth Avenue and slightly south. "You can't see it from here, but that's about where it is, Caroline's house."

All Alessio could see were slabs of gray high-rises obstructing the view. But he could imagine, if he turned slightly to look over the park, the graceful world Caroline had known.

"My sister Anne and her family live there now," Philip said. "I'll take you there if you like. It would be crucial for your research."

"Of course I would like to see it." Alessio knew he was meant to ask "What research?" but he was not willing to let Philip manipulate him that far. He sat quietly sipping the sticky sweet champagne, the last thing he wanted in such heat.

Finally Philip went on. "I'm getting ahead of myself, aren't I? As I said, I'm the only one who knows everything. But I'm no writer, I need help telling the story. I trust you as a friend; you're trained as a scholar; you know the art world. You might write Aunt Caroline's story, a full-blown biography."

"But I haven't done scholarly research in years, and I haven't written in English since college, nothing more than letters."

"We'll get you help with the language, not that you need it. I'd give you access to all Aunt Caroline's papers, things no one has seen. There are boxes of them, and they are extraordinary, I've been through them. The Brancusi letters alone are invaluable. I'd put you in touch with people who knew her and tell them to cooperate. You would have complete access to her art collection; there's quite a lot we've kept in the family, more than you might guess." He paused, then added quickly, "And I'd pay for expenses, of course," as if he were embarrassed to mention such a crass detail.

"I'm grateful, truly. But why? You know the most important critics, you could get any scholar, I know they've been chasing after you. Why come to me after all these years?"

"Because you are my friend and my brother and I trust you," Philip said, putting a hand on Alessio's shoulder. "You're like family. I know you'll understand Aunt Caroline and tell the world the truth." He paused a few seconds before he took his hand away and became more businesslike. "I can give you a more practical reason if you want. You don't have the biases of the American critics, and you won't get caught up in all the rivalries these museum people have with each other. The curators are in a constant state of civil war here, you know. The academics are even worse."

"Yes, that's true everywhere," Alessio said.

He knew Philip was offering a priceless opportunity. At the very least it would bring the professional stature he had longed for. It might even lead to the missing Leones and the unimaginable fame and wealth they promised. Philip was practically handing him a fortune. Even with the heat and champagne, though, Alessio realized he should not give in too easily. He turned in his seat and shifted to look over the green treetops of the park, as if he were thinking for a moment. Then turning back to Philip, he asked, "Would I be what you call a ghost writer?"

"No, no, you would be entirely independent, we wouldn't try to tell you what to say at all. As if we could. I need you because you're qualified and you'll be taken seriously. I intend this to be legitimate. You'll do a fantastic job. And an honest one, which matters more than anything. I want the best for Aunt Caroline."

"I should hear more," Alessio said, and Philip pointed once again over the skyline toward Caroline's house.

"That's where she told me the story," he said, and as he went on he continued to stare in her direction, as if she were there and he could see her through all the brick and concrete that came between.

"She told it as if it had happened to her the day before. I had gone to her house late one afternoon to thank her for the Christmas present as I always did. My sisters were away skiing, so I was alone. I was shown into her sitting room. She had changed it since the twenties, naturally, but it still had some touches from that time. There was a remarkable Art Nouveau carved fireplace, a woman's face in the middle of huge, sensuous waves of hair. But the rest of the room was restrained and elegant, with pale gray fabric on the walls. There was very little art hanging, but what I saw was exceptional: a small Rembrandt of an old woman's face, a couple of other Old Masters in heavy wooden frames.

"It was a frigid day, and we sat close to the fire. I remember Aunt Caroline sitting up very straight in a small ivory velvet side chair, smiling shyly but beautifully at me. She never looked her age, though she was seventy-six by then. She was wearing a rose-colored suit and a long, long rope of pearls. I realized later she was wearing those same pearls in most of the pictures from the twenties. She still had soft brown hair. By then it was bobbed, but it looked like it wasn't.

"I sat facing her and thanked her for the Christmas present. We talked about school a little. She asked why I wasn't skiing, and I said I preferred sailing, so we talked about that for a while. After her butler had served tea, she told him that we should not be disturbed, not even to bring more tea or tend the fire. 'I want a nice private chat with Philip,' she said, something she had never said before.

"When the door was closed, she smiled more beautifully than ever, leaned forward, took my hand in both of hers, and held it tight. Her hands were trembling the tiniest bit, as if she were nervous, and it seemed that clasping mine helped steady hers. But her voice was calm and lovely as she said, 'I am going to tell you a true story, and that will be your present to me, a great gift if you'll allow it, my dear. I trust you completely, and I want you to hear what happened to me long ago. Your grandfather will never tell you. There was a scandalous painting you may have heard of . . .'

"She sat back but kept looking into my eyes almost the whole time she was talking, for hours and hours. Sometimes she would lean forward again and touch my hand or my knee; sometimes she seemed near tears. There was a large folder of papers on a table by her side; now and then she would reach into it and read from an old newspaper clipping or letter. It grew dark outside and the fire slowly burned itself out, but I didn't notice the cold or the darkness, I didn't move. I lived in her soft, enchanting voice.

"She began, 'I will tell you how it came to be, how I tried to put the affair behind me, how it would never let me go.' "

ONE

Caroline: The Scandal

People thought all Harry and I had in common was family money, but it was more than that. Harry kidnapped me one day, and I was thrilled.

I hardly noticed him at first. He was one of Mother's business advisers and came to meet with her once a month—he was no more to me than a faceless figure in a dark suit walking down the hall. At the time I was wildly in love with Spencer Leggett. Mother was terrified I would become engaged to Spencer; I was terrified I would not.

I had met him at a friend's debutante ball not long after my own. Don't believe what you hear about the twenties; they were not roaring for all of us. I was out in society barely two months before I realized that the men I was likely to meet in this proper way, anyone Mother thought acceptable, were as similar to each other as their white ties and tails. They all blended into one deadly bore, and I was mad with disappointment. Oh, they drank and talked about their sports cars and played jazz records, but it meant nothing. Beneath the surface they were conventional young men who had been through their supposedly wild days at college and were ready to settle into their fathers' lives alongside women as prim and meek as their mothers. They already looked as if they had left every bit of spontaneity behind at Princeton or Yale, where they thought such things belonged. They had sown their wild oats and gotten that out of the way, as if they had survived chicken pox; now they were immune.

I watched them as they chose among the rows of young women in white gowns and gloves, all of us identical too. My own dress was flouncy and frilled, appropriate and hideous. I looked like a walking carnation. How could I have known any better? How could I have been alluring, when I was so sheltered and Mother so strict? So I smiled as I had been taught, and danced every dance, and made perfect polite conversation, and no one seemed to notice how bored I was. For a year I had been dreaming that my life was about to change. Sometimes as I dozed off at night I could actually see it: two grand, heavy doors, white with gilt trim, stretched to the ceiling. They would slowly open before me. I would step across the threshold and walk into . . . Well, I didn't know quite what, but certainly not this.

When I first set eyes on Spencer, he seemed like all the others. Even Mother considered him suitable because her father and his grandfather had been boyhood friends. Spencer's father was an amateur Egyptologist who had endowed a chair at Princeton. Spencer had not inherited his father's high-mindedness, but he did get his flair for adventure.

You wouldn't know that to look at him. He had straight brown hair, brown eyes, a pleasant, pale face; he was tall and solidly built—absolutely unremarkable and wholesome. When he put his name on my dance card for a waltz, I hadn't yet noticed the reckless look in his eye.

As we began to dance he asked, "What do you think of this ball?"

"It's lovely," I said, without thinking—half the time my mind was somewhere else. As I went on reciting the usual polite lines, he cut me off.

"No, honestly, what does it remind you of? Doesn't it make you feel like you're back in your first dancing class? Remember those lessons, when some gray-haired old lady would force you to dance with the other children? And you only wanted to run back to the nursery and play?"

Well, I had enjoyed dancing lessons—I was always the good little girl—but suddenly it seemed that he had expressed, that he must actually share, the stifling disappointment I was feeling at all these tedious balls. "You're right," I said, and I laughed for the first time that night. "You're brilliant! That's just what it is, it feels like we're back in our nursery days."

He grinned, and I saw—or thought I saw—a hint of daring in his eyes that I had not found in anyone else. "I've noticed you before," he said. "You're the most beautiful girl in the room, and you always have the perfect smile, but I can't help thinking that none of this interests you much. Are you engaged?"

"No."

"So you're on the prowl for a husband."

"I'm not on the prowl for anything!"

"But that's the only reason to be here. Why come otherwise?"

"Mother insisted," I said, blurting out the truth—as if I had ever thought to question her.

"So your mother made you come," he said with the slightest trace of sarcasm, as if I were, in fact, a child. And at once I insisted on being a grown-up.

"Oh, I've decided this is my last ball. I'm not coming to another," I said, making it all up on the spot. "They're too dull for words, aren't they? Why should we be in here dancing this waltz when there's a whole world out there that's infinitely more exciting?" I had no idea what I was talking about. I was simply desperate to sound sophisticated, to say anything I thought he might like, something he would not expect from a girl as tame and proper as me. It probably came out sounding more petulant than enticing, but something worked, because as the waltz ended he said, "If you stop coming to dances, how will we see each other again?" Then he nodded good-bye and stepped away without another word. I didn't see him for the rest of the evening, though I looked. My next partners must have been mystified by the way my eyes kept darting across the room.

We did meet at other dances, of course, and soon Spencer began to escort me to friends' dinners and parties, the kind that were so acceptable that if someone played a Charleston everyone congratulated themselves on being so modern. He was unfailingly attentive to Mother. I was starting to think the reckless look had been one of my silly dreams.

The night I saw the real Spencer—the fearless, unconventional Spencer—was the night I fell in love with him. His older sister and her husband were our chaperones. His family was obviously more open-minded than mine, because they took me to a dark little club that was, even to my innocent eyes, illegal.

Everyone we knew had been drinking in private for years, of course, ever since Prohibition started; it was possible to get quite good liquor from abroad. But this place was different, on a quiet street far uptown near the East River. It looked like the library of any gentlemen's club, with dark wooden shelves behind the bar and small, round tables. But there were overdone touches of red velvet on the chairs and gold tassels on the curtains that gave it, intentionally I can see now, the aura of being tawdry and dangerous.

The club was full of smoke and so noisy I could hardly hear the music, but I could feel by the way the room vibrated that it was furiously fast. The tables were crowded in a circle around a tiny dance floor, where couples shimmied and kicked and sometimes crashed into a table. The four of us sat around a small table drinking gin. I sipped at mine; I never got used to the burning taste. I danced with Spencer and once or twice with his brother-in-law—a highly unattractive, corpulent, older man as I recall. Deep into the night, I remember Spencer nudging his brother-in-law and pointing across the room at a woman with bright, smeared red lipstick. She had bleached blond hair that might have been neat earlier in the evening but was now frizzed and sticking out messily from a silver band across her forehead. Her face looked flushed and sweaty.

"How many do you suppose she's had tonight?" Spencer asked. "Six? Seven?"

"At least."

Spencer's sister leaned over to me and whispered, "They're not talking about how many drinks she's had. They're talking about men." I didn't know whether to laugh or not—she *was* joking, wasn't she?—and I must have looked shocked, because she patted my hand to reassure me. "You're such an adorable baby! Don't be alarmed, we don't mix with people like her," she said. "But isn't it fun to watch?"

I may have been shocked but I wasn't afraid, because Spencer made me feel so safe that night, as if he were my guide through some exotic country. He kept his arm tightly around me as we sat close at the table. When we heard angry voices raised on the other side of the room, he pulled me closer and whispered, "Don't worry. No one will touch you. You're with me." Then we would dance across the floor so fast that by the time we stopped my breath was short, my heart racing, my body throbbing. His solid, wholesome looks seemed exceptionally, irresistibly handsome. We stayed until the place closed.

That evening everything was bliss. It was worth dealing with the fuss when I arrived home near dawn and had to ring and wake our butler to let me in. Spencer walked me to the door and offered to come in and apologize to Mother. "I'll say my sister's car broke down."

I told him it wasn't necessary. I didn't say that in his state he would probably make things worse. As I crept up the stairs to my room, clinging to the banister, Mother came to her door, drowsy and angry. I blurted, "Spencer's sister's car broke down." I offered a million apologies and promised it would never happen again. She looked fierce and skeptical—as she should have—and silently closed the door.

I missed breakfast, and she hardly spoke to me at lunch. I was abashed and felt genuinely awful—I *was* still her good little girl and hated to disappoint her—but that afternoon I snuck into the pantry, borrowed a spare key to the front door, and had a copy made. From then on I took it with me whenever I went out with Spencer.

I would tell Mother he was taking me to the theater or the opera, and we would dash off to clubs all over the city, in Harlem and Times Square and Greenwich Village, laughing and drinking and dancing all night. We heard blues and jazz, mostly by musicians long forgotten. We drank what we could get—well, it seems such an ordinary thing to do now. Maybe it was ordinary then; I suppose it was, but that didn't make it less forbidden or exhilarating for someone like me. Spencer seemed to be the center of a strange world where a sense of abandon was a virtue. I had never had a sense of abandon.

And it was more than an attraction of opposites. Spencer was the first man who ever truly understood me. The night he took me to that dark, disreputable club, it was as if he were testing me to see how far proper little Caroline would go. From then on he had a way of knowing just when I was ready to go further. Before long I would have followed him into the desert and lived with him in a tent if he had asked.

As long as I was home in my bed by morning, and didn't wake Mother when I came in, it was easy to keep my nighttime life a secret from her. "Edith, take your nose out of your teacup and look around," my Aunt Martha had told her years before, frustrated by Mother's refusal to see beyond her own refined nose. The phrase became a family joke but didn't affect Mother a bit.

Keeping a secret from Will was another story. When he came home from Harvard for spring break that year, he could tell I had changed and I could tell that he had not. He was so serious it was endearing, a beautiful little lamb with a world-weary expression on his face.

Even though he was two years younger, he called me his little sister. He had always been my protector, ever since Father died when I was eight, and I loved him for it. He and his friends were a brilliant group, and even among them he was known for having the fastest, sharpest mind. I could never have hidden anything from Will, so I didn't try. Or not very hard.

He sometimes asked where I was going as I headed out, and I would truthfully say, "Dancing with Spencer, I don't know where." Then he would settle in for the night with his books; he did get to law school a year early.

He had been home for several days that spring when I crept in at two in the morning looking terribly rumpled—I didn't think it mattered, I expected the entire household to be asleep. Will was standing in the doorway of the front sitting room, fully dressed. I wondered if he had pulled back the drapes and noticed how long Spencer and I had been parked in his car outside, but I didn't ask. I waved good night as I breezed up the stairs, but he wouldn't let me off so easily. He ran after me and caught my arm. He sniffed at my face, pretending to be a dog, and said, "Liquor on your breath? On my little sister?" He was trying so hard to sound lighthearted.

"Of course, dear little brother," I said. "I told you I was going to a club with Spencer. It's such fun, it makes all our friends' dances seem as dull as Mother's. Please come with us next time. I would love for you to come. You're always studying so hard, it will do you good."

Will would never scold me, so he dropped his jaw in fake shock again, as if he were making a joke. "I'm going to be a lawyer, and you're asking me to break the law?" His comic, wide-eyed expression didn't fool me. I saw how concerned he was, and I was touched.

Still, there was no need for him to worry. "Think of it as research," I said, deciding that he *should* come along, for his own good.

"Caroline . . ."

"Do it for me, please? Come along and see if I need protecting."

He did join us a few times that spring and summer for my sake, and sweetly tried to fit in. But he never seemed to relax. He sat nursing one drink all night, smiling stiffly and trying to be part of the conversation, shouting uncomfortably over the music and noise. Sometimes I would catch him staring into space or sneaking a look at the door, as if he expected the police to break in, arrest him, and ruin his future—even though no one we knew had ever had the least trouble.

Spencer once tried to tease him into asking some women in the club to dance. "If you're waiting for a formal introduction, you'll be waiting a long time in this place," he said. But while Will studied the women who were dancing alone or slinking around the floor with their drinks—he was obviously intrigued and attracted—he never approached one. I didn't know whether it was because he was too shy or too embarrassed by their cheapness, or maybe—it's a wonder it didn't occur to me then—because I was there and he didn't want me to see him with that kind of woman.

What I knew was that he was more loyal than I could have hoped. As much as he disapproved of Spencer, he would never have betrayed me to Mother. Once as he was leaving to go back to school, he wagged his finger at me in that stiff, endearing, fake-jokey way he had and said, "Be careful, little sister." As always, I took his good, loving advice. I was very cautious.

Then Spencer's name appeared in a gossip column in the Mirror—not in the Times's society pages, where we were accustomed to being, but in a lurid scandal sheet—and my life became chaos. The column was ludicrous, full of innuendo, written in such a higgledy-piggledy style that no one could take it seriously. But they did. What it said frightened me in so many ways that I didn't know which of them should scare me the most.

Man-about-town Spencer Leggett almost got into a fistfight at a shady nightspot on Tuesday when a stranger tried to crash his party and made a crude remark to a young lady at his table. We hear the drunken stranger complimented his date's buxom figure. Gallant gentleman that he is, Leggett jumped to her defense and had to be restrained by two other men in his group, all members of his fast young crowd. Lucky for her, the lady's prominent family thought she was snugly tucked in bed at the time, alone.

I had spent the evening with Mother in her box at the opera and at a supper afterward, a dreary night. It was quite late when we got home and yawned our way to bed. While I was still asleep the next morning, Mother came into my bedroom and tossed the paper in my direction, folded to the gossip column. After I read it I didn't wonder or care who had given her such a rag. My stomach was in knots. Who was the "young lady"? What "shady nightspot" had they been discovered at? Was it a place I had been to? On an unlucky night, could that well-bred woman have been me?

While I was agonizing in bed, the blankets drawn over my head, Mother was telephoning Will in Cambridge, and in minutes he was telephoning me. Without asking how I was or what I thought, he jumped in. "She's on the warpath and wants me to come home to chastise you," he said, not unkindly but without much patience either. He wasn't trying to sound playful anymore. "You know I hate to agree with her, and I would never lecture you, but you have to admit he hasn't treated you well. If nothing else he hasn't thought about your reputation. I think you know that already. Anyway, that's not what I phoned to tell you."

Even Will was against me. I could hardly speak. "Are you there?" he asked.

"I'm here," I said, as meek as I had ever been.

"Well, pay attention because she's had enough. She has decided that you should marry Harrison Stephens. That's what I called to tell you."

"What? That stuffy man who does her accounts and fawns over her? Him? She can't mean it. I hardly know who he *is*."

"That's all I know. And I'm going to be late for my next class."

"She can't make me!"

"She can try. You've been warned, little sister. Warned again. I have to go now." And he hung up.

I crawled back into bed but couldn't think about anything as silly as Mother's pathetic attempts at matchmaking. I could only add Will's disappointment to all the horrors swirling through my mind. We were bound to hear soon enough who the mystery woman was. I desperately wanted to know and didn't want to know at all. I tortured myself with more questions that I couldn't begin to answer. If I had been there in her place, what would I have done? Was Spencer my fearless protector and guide on our wild adventure, or was he the man who could drag me down to the gutter of the gossip columns? Could he possibly be both? Had he been sleeping with her?

I waited all day to hear from him and didn't. I pretended to be sick and had toast and tea brought to me in bed for lunch and dinner so I wouldn't have to face Mother. For the next two days, without a word from Spencer, I rehearsed how I would lay down the law when I saw him. I would be stern and find out the truth. I would let him know how unhappy I was. I would make him swear never to take me to that place, wherever it was. In my fantasies he would beg my forgiveness, swearing to love only me.

But on the night he finally arrived to pick me up for a friend's dinner party, a date we had planned weeks before, I was so relieved to see him that I never dreamt of letting my doubts or anger show. As he helped me on with my coat, it was all I could do to even mention the gossip column, and I did it as lightly as I could.

"So I hear the Mirror thinks you're a gallant gentleman," I said, as if it were all too ridiculous.

"You don't believe what you read in the papers, do you?" he said.

"Not always. But what could they have meant?"

"You know they make up most of what they print in those columns."

"But . . ."

"There's nothing to it, the story was completely exaggerated," he said. "I think it's sort of funny, don't you? Now, where shall I carry you off to tonight, my most beautiful girl?" (Most beautiful? Were there others, less beautiful but more daring?) He stood behind me with his hands on my shoulders and started marching me toward the door, then stopped. He turned me to face him, leaned over to kiss my neck, and whispered, "We'll change our plans. Forget the dinner. Imagine your perfect evening and I'll snap my fingers and make it come true."

Then he did what he so often did: took me in his arms and started dancing me around the room as he hummed into my ear. He would take some bit of music we had heard together, and however bluesy or jazzy it had been, he slowed it down until it became a soft, romantic love song. When we were dancing in public he would remind me of those private moments, whispering, "We're alone. There's no one else in the world."

I let him dance me away that night, as if there were no one else in the world and never would be. We phoned our excuses to the party and drove all the way to his sister's empty cottage in Southampton, where we built a fire, stretched out on the carpet, and kept each other warm all night.

In the harsh light of home, my love for Spencer was not so simple. From the day of what she referred to as Spencer's "disgrace," Mother began her relentless campaign for Harry.

She started by inviting him to join us for lunch the next week; he was waiting with her in the dining room when I walked in, a surprise to me. I had become so wrapped up in my life with Spencer—planning when to see him and what to wear, scouring the gossip columns to make sure he wasn't mentioned—that I had forgotten Will's warning. Finding Harry at lunch was more than annoying. It was a clear sign of Mother's determination. Well, I was determined too.

Although I had met Harry in passing during his business visits, I had never thought of him as my contemporary. He was agreeable looking in those days, with a small mustache that gave him a slightly roguish air, or at least made it look as if he were trying to be roguish. Hard to imagine now. He had a full face that—actually, it was beginning to be a little jowly even then, but it gave him an air of openness and honesty. He was staid, though, so staid. I was astonished when I learned he was only five years older than I was; he seemed so at home with Mother's generation.

All through lunch she prodded his conversation. "I've always told Harrison that I trust him with my affairs because he knows about family interests firsthand," she said. A consommé was brought out, and I almost laughed into my soup when I noticed it was the same pallid color and thin consistency as Harry's little mustache.

"Tell Caroline about your grandfather the pirate," Mother prompted him.

"He wasn't really a pirate," Harry explained sensibly, as if I would have misunderstood her minor attempt at wit. "My great-great-great-grandfather was a merchant seaman who eventually owned a fleet of ships."

"He brought the family from England generations ago," Mother went on. "How is it our two families have never crossed paths? What a pity."

"My great-great-great-grandfather settled in Boston. It was my father who came to New York."

"But you'd think we would have met in Newport."

"Our summer place is in Saratoga."

"Then you must know the Bradfords."

"Very well."

Mother's efforts to draw him out meant that Harry was talking, to the extent that he was talking at all, more to her than to me, which suited me just fine.

"Harrison studied economics and business at the Wharton School in Philadelphia, Caroline, isn't that interesting?" she tried again.

"Fascinating beyond belief," I said and asked the closest thing to a rude question I could manage. "It doesn't sound as if you need to be in business, Mr. Stephens, with a whole fleet in your family," I said. "Why do you work so hard? Why work at all?"

Harry appeared to take no offense. Coming from almost anyone else, I would have seen that reaction as generous and polite in the extreme; from him I took it to mean he was too obtuse to be insulted.

"I've always been interested in how money operates," he told me earnestly. "There are economic principles most people don't understand, and when they try to oversee their own affairs they only make things worse. After studying economics and business, I thought, Why waste all that knowledge on my own family's firm—they get along well enough with my father and brother at the top. Why not use my knowledge to improve other people's circumstances?"

"So this is your way of dispensing charity to the less fortunate?"

"I think your reasons are admirable," Mother broke in. "Don't you agree, Caroline?"

"Virtuous," I said. "Saintly."

Harry so blithely refused to be insulted that, intentionally or not—and I don't think he could have meant to do it—he shamed me into being well-behaved through the roast beef and even the ice cream.

By the end of lunch, Mother was inviting him to join us for dinner the following week. "Caroline will be here, and we'll both be happy to receive you again. Won't we, dear?"

What could I say? Even I felt bad about the way I'd treated him. "We'd be delighted, Mr. Stephens, truly. Please come," I said, finally putting some warmth in my voice.

Of course, I was still trying to work my way back into Mother's good graces. Every time she heard my beloved Spencer's name, she would shake her head and mutter, "Disgrace, disgrace." She had not forbidden me to see him—she must have realized that would do no good—but she glowered whenever he arrived at the door, and I was worried she would deny her blessing when he proposed. So when Harry asked me out, I accepted, to prove to Mother that I was not "foolishly obsessed with that black sheep Leggett boy" as she put it. I saw Harry to keep Mother quiet and Spencer to please myself. I thought I was being quite clever.

Whenever I was with Harry—at extravagant but stuffy restaurants, at the opera because Mother had given us her tickets—my mind was with Spencer, wondering what delicious night he had dreamed up for us next, how he was amusing himself while I was out with another man, what other woman he might be with.

After a few weeks I decided I could gently start turning down Harry's invitations. Mother couldn't say I hadn't given him a chance. But she was far ahead of me.

She had insisted on accepting a weekend invitation for both of us to join a large party visiting Harry's family in Saratoga when his father's horses were racing. The Stephenses had hired a private railroad car for their guests, and since Harry had gone ahead of us, I was the youngest person in the car by decades. I stared out the window as we left the city behind, telling myself I had only to get through the next two days and I would be free. I spent part of the trip planning how to tell Mother that my future would be with Spencer.

I considered saying, "I know you disapprove, but he will convince you he deserves your trust." That seemed too risky, though, an invitation for her to set impossible terms for him to meet—slay a dragon, stop going to nightclubs.

I thought of telling her, "It will mean all my happiness." But if she were concerned with my happiness, she wouldn't be trying to force drab old Harry on me, would she?

I could try saying, "If you don't give us your blessing we'll elope," but she'd think I was bluffing.

Or maybe I would just stop seeing Harry and wait for her to notice. As the train carried me toward the Stephenses', I gave up rehearsing for Mother and went on staring out the window at the passing fields, all the while envisioning myself dancing in Spencer's arms as he whispered that I was the only woman he would ever love.

That evening I endured an endless formal dinner with the weekend guests—the women even grayer than the men—which at least saved me from having to see Harry alone. I slept late on Saturday and that afternoon was sitting on my own at the back of the Stephenses' box at the races, trying not to doze off from heat and boredom. The race with his father's strongest horse in it was about to begin when I felt a hand over my mouth. Harry had crept up behind me and whispered, "I think you need to be rescued." He put his arms around my waist and half-carried me away before anyone could notice, before I could say a word. I didn't try to resist. Next to the rest of the company, even Harry seemed exciting.

When we got outside, he proudly led me to his new car: a two-seat Pierce-Arrow that was entirely unlike him. In fact, the car was suspiciously like Spencer's, even a similar pale yellow. I wondered whether Mother had told him what I seemed to like, but he was so happy and I was so desperate to escape that I stopped worrying about his motives and decided to enjoy the afternoon. He had, after all, rescued me.

He drove for half an hour, the wind cooling us in the open car, until we got to a broad, grassy field—I found out later that his uncle owned the land—where he unpacked a blanket, and champagne and foie gras from France. It was a cliché, but such a lovely one. The day was gorgeous and bright, and we sat there under a tree so at ease with each other that there wasn't much need to talk. We watched the clouds and the butterflies, pointing out especially brilliant ones; the odd car passed by; we drank more champagne and ate strawberries. By the end of the afternoon he kissed me, a real kiss.

I had always imagined that one day poor old Harry would stand outside our door, his hands behind his back, and politely ask, "May I kiss you good night?" But now he simply leaned over, took my face in his hands and kissed me—a slow, languorous kiss, a kiss that made me forget he was the man of my mother's dreams. His lips parted and I felt Harry's tongue reach toward mine. My own mouth opened and that's when I thought: Maybe he'll do. Suddenly I saw a different Harry, had discovered something in him Mother hadn't. I could see he had been acting for her benefit, behaving like the ideal, staid son-in-law when in truth he was someone far more exciting. I would let her think he was dull, predictable Harry; I would know better.

"Where did you children disappear to?" Mother asked when we joined them at dinner, slightly sunburned and cheerful. I must say she didn't seem upset or even surprised, but I was. And confused. Back among his parents' guests, Harry seemed to revert to his stiff old self. But every now and then he would catch my eye and wink. I thought I saw him wink at Mother once, but I may have been imagining that.

We left Saratoga early Sunday morning, and I spent the train ride home asking questions very different from the ones I had asked myself going up. Had Harry simply *seemed* interesting next to the fossils at his parents'? Had I been suffering from sunstroke in that field? I was so confused that instead of turning Harry down the next time he called, I gave him another chance. At the very least I wanted to know if I had simply spent a delusional afternoon in the too-hot sun.

I began to suggest places to go and new things for us to do— nothing outrageous, none of Spencer's haunts, but Broadway shows and Chinese restaurants, places where we wouldn't meet our parents' friends. Harry always agreed. And sometimes, not always, as he walked me to the door afterward, he would find a dark shadow on the path, and stop, and quickly but passionately kiss me good night.

Still, he was not Spencer, who seemed to become more devoted when he learned—we traveled in a fairly small circle, after all—that he had competition. He had a knack for discovering clubs and musicians minutes before they became popular, and now seemed to go out of his way to find ever more obscure spots.

The two of us were alone the night he took me to a club he promised was the most astonishing yet. "It has the best jazz and whiskey in the city," he said. "You may not care about the whiskey, but it's dark and incredibly sexy—you'll like that part. It will be our secret hideaway." As we drove far downtown, racing nearly to Wall Street, every now and then he reached for my hand and squeezed it, and we laughed whenever he had to put both hands back on the wheel again, always at the last possible second. The reckless gleam in his eye came out in his driving too, but I never minded. He parked, and we walked a block or so, then turned into a narrow side street and down concrete steps to a basement.

He was right about one thing, the place was dark. When my eyes adjusted I saw the strangest mix of people; a few looked like foreign royalty, others like they had slept in their clothes. The tables were so close that my bare arm brushed against the jacket of the man sitting at the next table, and I felt the greasy filth of the fabric. There were no waiters, so Spencer left me alone while he went to the bar to get drinks, and until he returned I stared down at the empty tabletop so no one would try to talk to me. The basement smelled so musty, even the cigarette smoke couldn't mask it.

The music, though, was as incredible as Spencer had promised. There was a man playing a saxophone, music so beautiful, so aching, that it seemed to exist in a world all its own. As soon as it began, the seedy atmosphere faded away. Years later, when I heard Sonny Rollins, that musty basement came back to me so vividly I wondered if he were that man's son; I'm sure he wasn't.

We were immersed in his music when there was a scuffle behind us near the entrance, too loud and ugly to ignore. I turned and saw several policemen in uniforms and other men in suits pushing their way in and yelling. Men and women were tumbling to the floor, some knocked down by the police, others trampling each other as they raced toward the front door. Spencer grabbed my hand and ran in the other direction, into a small back room near the stage, apparently someone's office. He opened a closet door that led down a few steps to a dark passage through adjoining basements. Dim lightbulbs were strung up at great distances and I could hardly see as I stumbled after Spencer, clutching his hand. I could hear other people running behind us, and an hysterical woman sobbing in panic. I turned my ankle and nearly fell as we dashed across the rutted dirt floor, through open doorways and around odd corners, but Spencer still had my hand and almost dragged me as we kept moving forward. We climbed a flight of stairs to ground level, and he made me wait while he peered into the night to make sure no one was there. Then he pulled me out after him. We were on the street, a few blocks from the car. "Look calm and walk slowly, as if we're out for a stroll," he said as he put his arm around me; we were still alone when we reached the car.

He drove away quickly and didn't slow down or speak until we were halfway uptown. "Are you okay?" he finally asked. I nodded yes without looking at him, although I was trembling with fear and anger and some deeper, more ominous dread. I saw that he was heading home; we said nothing the rest of the way. I just kept looking down at my pink satin shoes, covered in dirt, and I remember thinking, as silly as it sounds now, that those ruined shoes were a symbol that I hadn't left that place untouched. When he parked in front of my door, he put his arms around me and said, "Oh, my beautiful girl, you're shaking. Well, you're safe now. I told you I'd always take care of you, didn't I?"

"How can you say that?" I cried, pulling away. "Why were we in that place? Why would you take me there?"

"It's no different from any other place," he said calmly.

"It obviously is."

"We ran into some bad luck, that's all," he said, as if he had done nothing more serious than drop a glass or a plate—accidents happen, no real damage.

"How did you know the way out of there?"

"I'd heard."

"You'd been there? You knew they'd had trouble before?"

"No trouble that I know of, Caroline, or I would never have taken you there. You hear about precautions at certain places, that's all. Don't worry your beautiful head anymore, everything's fine."

But it wasn't. He was so cavalier that every word he spoke upset me more. He tried to pull me back toward him but I jumped out of the car and ran to the door.

I bathed and went straight to bed but of course couldn't sleep. And even after all that, I'm sorry to say, I found myself wondering if Spencer was angry at me for running off, though he was the one who had been wrong and selfish and careless. What should I have said? What should he have done? What could I ever expect from him? Through that long, sleepless night, the one thing I knew without doubt was that I wanted him, wanted him still, wanted him to make it all right.

The next morning I assumed he would call or turn up at the door to apologize and try to make it up to me. I ran when I was called to the phone, but it was only Harry, saying he would pick me up for dinner that night at 7:45 as we'd planned. And I went because I thought I'd go mad sitting around.

It wasn't nearly our best date. I was even more preoccupied than usual. If Spencer was my hero, my guide, my knight, why hadn't he called? I was so quiet that Harry actually asked what was wrong, but I couldn't tell him, couldn't admit I'd been to such a disreputable place.

"Nothing. I'm just tired. I slept badly."

"Have I done something to upset you?" he asked, concerned and full of practical resolve, as if he were tackling some problem he could surely fix if only he knew what it was. He looked at me, solid and unblinking.

"Dear Harry," I said, reaching across the table to put my hand on his but speaking half to myself. "You would never drag me through an underground tunnel, would you?"

"What in the world are you talking about? Of course not," he said. "Why would you ask that? I've never suggested such a thing. If I did, if I ever gave you reason to think I would, I'm so sorry, Caroline."

"No, of course you didn't, I'm just being silly tonight," I said. "You've never done anything to upset me." He seemed tremendously relieved.

As the days passed and I waited for Spencer's call, I kept thinking about that gossip column Mother had found so disastrous. I could imagine a new one that began, "Spencer Leggett and Caroline Holbrooke, heirs to two of the city's most established families, were arrested last night while trying to escape from a downtown speakeasy." Let Spencer stay away; I was better off without him. That's what I told myself. And yet I kept wondering if I had done something to offend him. Maybe I should have explained why I was so upset instead of running away. Maybe he really didn't understand—how could he if I hadn't told him?

A week went by and I nearly called him dozens of times, but whenever I picked up the phone I could see the imaginary headline floating before my eyes—by then it had become "Holbrooke Heiress Arrested"—and I couldn't go through with it. I never called because at the end of that week, with the best timing of his life, Harry proposed and I accepted.

I didn't accept at once. I asked for a week to think it over, and so gave Spencer another week to call, hardly knowing what I would say if he did. As I counted off each day, and fell asleep each night to a dream that I was dancing in Spencer's arms, I reminded myself about my secret Harry, the dynamic man I had glimpsed at our picnic in Saratoga, the one who knew how to kiss and would never drag me through a tunnel, the one who cared so much about my happiness. Maybe recklessness was overrated, something I should banish to my dreams.

At the end of that week, I sat staring at the phone while waiting for Harry to arrive. When he was announced, I went downstairs and said I would marry him. Mother was deliriously happy. I let her think I was giving in to her wise advice, while I smiled at the thought of the other Harry, the one only I knew.

Spencer did phone a few weeks later, and I left word I was not at home; I told the staff I would not ever be at home for Mr. Leggett again, although I couldn't resist sending him an invitation to our engagement party.

For months, the party and the wedding preparations kept me on a cloud. Looking back it was more like being in a fog.

I should have known on the night Harry and I went to the theater to see Eleonora Duse in *Ghosts*. She wasn't young by then, and even I might not have chosen Ibsen, but seeing her was an event. At intermission Harry said, "I don't know what's older, the play or the actress."

"You aren't enjoying this, are you?"

"We can leave and take a drive, there's a nice breeze tonight. Let's not waste any more of our time here."

He had come so far, I took this to mean we belonged at a more avant-garde play, the two of us. Or that we should settle into his cozy little car and share our most private thoughts. And so we left. And we drove. I was so naïve.

Will knew better before I did. On the night of the engagement party, Mother was in my room helping me dress. She clasped the waist-length string of pearls Harry had sent as my present and said, "I'm so happy you made the right choice, Harry will never disappoint you. And you look beautiful after all. I was wrong about the dress. The pearls are exquisite against it." She had tried to convince me to wear a flowing organza gown, but I had found one in pale pink silk, chic and straight and simple. "I know you will have every happiness, my dear." And she left to check on the arrangements downstairs one last time before the guests arrived.

Alone, I looked around my room and found it hopelessly girlish, with its ruffled skirts on the bed and dressing table, its tiny red rosebuds on the ivory wallpaper. I was eager for my adult life to begin. Harry had found several town houses where we might live and asked me to choose which he should buy. I chose the one off Park because I felt at home the minute I walked into it. Harry liked it because it was large; I liked it because it was graceful. He left the decorating entirely to my taste, and I was busy at it. It all gave me an immense sense of possibility.

Even so, with nothing left to do except wait for the guests to arrive, I was beginning to feel anxious about the evening. When Will knocked on the door, I was happy for his company.

"Harry and the Stephenses are here. They're downstairs waiting for you," he said.

"Does he look handsome?"

"He looks like Harry in a dinner jacket," Will said flatly.

"Well, you look handsome in your dinner jacket," I told him.

"And you look beautiful," he said, although he sounded as if he were telling me someone had died.

"Thank you, but you're not very convincing. Are you all right?"

Will walked to the window and looked out. I heard him take a deep breath before he turned back to me and said, "I've been around in circles about whether to say anything to you, but if I don't I won't be able to live with myself, so I'll just tell you straight out. You can't go through with this, Caroline. You can't marry Harry."

I stared at him and let out a nervous laugh, but I could see at once this was no joke. I sat on the edge of the bed and prepared myself to hear about other women, an illegitimate child, gambling debts, any horror short of murder. Will looked so grim, murder might not have surprised me. I wondered which of those terrible problems I could live with, which would be bad enough to call things off. "What is it you know about him?" I asked.

"Don't worry, there are no skeletons in his closet. If there were I would have found them."

"What then?"

"It's just that he's not good enough for you. Don't laugh, it's true. He's ordinary, he's anyone at all. He's not smart enough or interesting enough. You'll wake up married to a cipher, and I know you, Caroline, you'll be miserable."

I was reassured but a bit indignant now that I knew Will was concerned simply because Harry was Harry.

"Harry is wonderful," I said.

"Do you believe that?"

"Of course I do. Besides, you don't know him the way I do. He is wonderful. He's good, he's . . . he's . . . mature, he's . . ."

Will laughed. "You can't even find three wonderful things to say about him. Listen to you. You're kidding yourself, little sister."

"Don't call me little sister when you're trying to bully me."

"I am not bullying you. You've convinced yourself you love him for some reason, but you can't delude yourself forever."

"Why are you telling me this now? Do you expect me to walk downstairs and tell two hundred people, 'I've changed my mind, sorry.' "

"Don't go through with this, you don't have to. I know it will be embarrassing to break it off now, but you'll get past that. You'll survive the embarrassment, but you won't survive marriage to Harry."

I sat on the bed while he paced back and forth, as logical as if he were making an argument in court. "The rules have changed, you know that better than I do. You won't be an outcast for breaking an engagement. And this is practically an arranged marriage anyway; it was Mother's idea, it's archaic."

His tone softened. "I didn't want to upset you, but it's better to hear it from me now than from everyone else later. You can't marry him, you'll die of boredom. You would have realized it yourself soon enough."

"You're wrong. I love Harry," I insisted. "I know things about him you don't, wild, exciting things."

He froze in place, his jaw clenched, his hands tightened into fists. "I find that hard to believe."

"It's true."

"Why are you saying this? Are you trying to hurt me?"

"Hurt you? Are you trying to hurt me by ruining my engagement?"

"I would never hurt you! You are about to ruin your life! Have you already? Are you and Harry lovers?"

"Of course not, that's not what I meant."

"Then it's not too late."

He was emotional now, not the lawyer anymore but my distraught little brother. "Don't you understand, I'm trying to save you from your own unhappiness. You can't even see how unhappy you are. Don't go, Caroline, don't go down there, you can't go." Suddenly he sank to the floor and sat on the carpet at my feet, looking up like a lost child.

"Don't be jealous, dearest," I told him. I knelt by his side and put my arms around him to comfort him. "I'm still your little sister. I always will be."

He looked as if he were about to cry. "You think this is about me, but it's not, it's about you, I'm trying to protect you," he said. "You think I don't know anything, but I do."

"Please be happy for me, Will. I need you more than anyone to be happy for me."

He rested his head against my shoulder for a second and closed his eyes. "I *want* you to be happy," he mumbled. "That's what this is about."

I stroked his head as he sat there, quietly, for what seemed a long time. When he looked up at me again, I could tell he had decided to stop fighting. He had gone as far as he could. He stood and gave me his hand. As he helped me up, he forced a smile and said in his old fake-jokey way, "I have one more reason, what about this? If you marry Harry you will turn into Mother."

I laughed and joked back. "Now you've scared me."

We stared at each other for a few seconds.

"If it makes you feel better I can always divorce Harry later," I said, as cheerfully as I could. "Things *have* changed. I wouldn't be a complete social outcast."

He said nothing and just kept smiling. He must have known I would never do such a thing, though at the time I thought I meant it.

"Let's go downstairs," I said. We walked out of that innocent, rosebud-covered room and down the staircase, my hand grasping Will's strong arm. I really did think he was just feeling lonely.

Harry beamed at me as I walked into what we called the ballroom, as my grandmother had, though no one had held a ball there in my lifetime. It was mid-December, and the room looked festive, with a huge Christmas tree in one corner and candles, garlands, and ribbons everywhere. A string quartet was tuning up. Harry kissed me lightly on the cheek, then turned to his parents and said, "Look what Santa Claus brought me." The words made me cringe, but that was a small thing.

Soon the room was filled, mostly with friends of Mother's and the Stephenses' but also with younger couples who were becoming the friends Harry and I would share. I greeted them happily in the receiving line; later we would eat pheasant and lobster and drink champagne, and I would dance into my new life.

Just after the receiving line had broken up, as I was mingling among the guests before dinner, I turned and through the crowd saw Spencer standing in the doorway. As soon as he spotted me he walked quickly in my direction, as serious and determined as I had ever seen him. He stopped me as I was moving from one group of guests to another, took my arm as if he were leading me to greet someone on the other side of the room, and said in a voice so low no one else could hear, "We have to see each other alone. Right now. Slip outside with me and we'll drive away."

I stared at him as we walked, and he said, "It's important. Let's leave, at least for a few minutes."

"Don't be insane. You know I can't do that. And it's the last thing in the world I want to do."

By then he had led me through the ballroom into the front hall, and kept walking. "Then come upstairs with me where no one will find us," he said, turning left and starting up the staircase, still gripping my arm. When I resisted he stopped and said, "I have something to tell you and I can't do it here. It's private. If you ever cared for me, please give me these few minutes alone with you." I hadn't spoken to him in all those months—it hadn't taken him long to stop calling—and I was furious at his timing, but I couldn't live the rest of my life wondering what secret he was prepared to share. I took his hand, and we hurried to one of the guest rooms on the third floor, where no one would think to look for us.

We were barely behind closed doors when Spencer put his hands on my waist, looked down at me, and said blithely, "So, my most beautiful girl, you're going through with it?"

"Of course I am." I stood stiffly, with my arms by my side. I could not have this conversation twice in one night, and certainly not with him. "Are you conspiring with Will? What are you two trying to do?" He was close enough so I could see and smell that he was not drunk, but he was acting so strangely.

"What does Will have to do with anything? I'm trying to make you run off with me. Is he trying to do the same thing?" he said, putting both arms around me and nuzzling my neck.

"You never did have anything to tell me, it was a cheap trick." I sounded angry but hadn't moved an inch.

"Don't be annoyed," he said. "Here's what I have to tell you: I can make everything all right again." Suddenly he stood back, gave a huge, comic, courtly bow, and began humming "The Blue Danube Waltz" as he took my waist and started to dance. I laughed without wanting to; the melody was so unlike anything he had ever hummed before, I couldn't help it. He held me lightly and at arm's length as we swirled around the room over and over. He hummed faster and faster, more and more comically, until I was dizzy and giddy.

"Why are you singing that?" I asked.

"Isn't this the respectable, fussy way to dance at an engagement party?"

"What do you want?"

"This," he said. He stopped moving but still held me around the waist, one hand in his.

"Our last dance?"

"I hope it's not the last. It can't be. Please don't let it be."

He pulled me closer and began swirling me around again more slowly, not humming now, until we collapsed backward onto the bed, half-lying, half-standing, with my feet still on the floor and Spencer on top of me. Instinctively, I put my hand around the back of his neck as I had so often before.

"My beautiful Caroline, did you think I'd abandoned you?" he said, looking down at me. "Is that why you're doing this?"

I knew what I should say. I could hear the words "I love Harry" in my head. Instead I said coolly, "I thought I had abandoned you."

"This is what I love," he whispered, "being alone with you, with the rest of the world just outside the door, never guessing." He moved my legs so I was stretched out on the bed, then lay next to me and began kissing my neck. "I do have something important to tell you. You're the best dancer I've ever known."

"This can't happen," I told him.

"Oh, you love danger, you know you do," he teased.

"Not anymore."

"Oh, yes," he said, kissing my neck again. "You do, you do," he whispered in my ear. "You always have," he said as he looked into my eyes and went on kissing me until I felt I was drifting through every glorious place I had ever been with Spencer—a rowboat on the lake, his sister's country house, the dark backseat of a taxi, always, always in his arms. I let the rest of the world slip away as if I were sailing out to sea on the longest, laziest day I had ever known, safely in his arms. I was his, only his, and I did feel beautiful. After a while he gave a grunt, then a great, familiar sigh, and was still as he nestled his head against my neck. I stroked his hair and said, "I wish we could stop time. I wish we could stay here forever."

"We can," he said. "Don't get married." I thought of what Will had said. I began to imagine a life as Spencer's wife instead of Harry's, living as recklessly as we liked, dashing off to parties with whomever we pleased, gossip columns be damned. I heard Will's voice saying, "The rules have changed." Then Spencer mumbled sleepily, "Why do you want to marry so soon? We're just beginning to have fun. Marriage is for cowards." And at once I saw myself running through those dark basements with him again, stumbling and scared and more heartbroken than ever.

He nestled against me more comfortably, but I calmly pushed him off, stood and straightened my dress. "You *have* been fun, but that's over," I said, trying so hard to sound aloof and dismissive, and not to cry. "Now you have to go down to the party ahead of me so no one will see us together. I'm sure I must have been missed."

He looked at his watch. "It's hardly been fifteen minutes," he said, and he put his arms around me again. "Run away with me, Caroline. I'll carry you off into the night where no one will ever find us. I'll have you back before dawn."

"You think marriage is for cowards?" I asked, pushing him away again, and then I *was* furious. "You're the coward, not Harry. Now go."

"What's happened to you? You're not yourself tonight, my most beautif—"

"Go," I said.

"Come with me."

"Go."

"How can I make it up—"

"Go."

And he turned and walked away without looking back, closing the door behind him.

I smoothed the bedspread the best I could and hoped no one would notice the difference. I rushed to my own room to fix my hair and lipstick, and turned in front of the mirror to make sure I looked the same as I had when I'd left. I smiled as I walked back into the ballroom, taking deep breaths to disguise how out of breath I really was, trying to look fresh, as if I had stepped out for a minute to powder my nose. And why shouldn't I smile? I had a perfectly lovely future ahead of me.

I didn't have to search the room to know that Spencer was gone. I walked straight to Harry and put my arm through his. He beamed as if he didn't have a care in the world or a thought in his head.

And I did not allow a single thought of Spencer to cross my mind until after the last guest had left, Mother had declared the party a spectacular success, and Will and I were saying good night.

I took Will's arm as we climbed the stairs together. "Don't worry about your little sister," I told him as we parted on the landing. "I am not making a mistake. I love Harry."

I did love Harry always, even when he grew old and fat and dispirited. It wasn't his fault I had misjudged him. And I think he was always faithful to me. But Will was right. Harry bored me almost at once. He bored me on our honeymoon.

Our first night together, at the Plaza, was sweet and reassuring. He kept asking me if I were all right, as if I might break, which I took to be very considerate. He still knew how to kiss, and I was sure that when he realized the rest of my body wouldn't break I would see the passionate, secret Harry I had glimpsed in Saratoga, the Harry I knew was hiding inside, perhaps too shy or insecure to come out. But he never turned up. Not on the ship to Venice (Harry's idea, a magnificent romantic gesture); not in our suite at the Danieli, overlooking the canal, in a large, romantic bed that did not allow me to make excuses for his lethargy, as the sometimes swaying stateroom had during the crossing.

I kept waiting for Harry's roguish twin, and by the time I realized he was a phantom, it was too late. I came to think of the Harry I had seen at that picnic as an illusion he had created out of sheer competitive will, an alter ego meant to enchant me and win me over. After he had me, the real, stolid Harry could give up the ghost of the passionate suitor.

Of course that came to me much later. At first I spent my nights wide awake and baffled that any man could be so physically tepid—not uninterested, not incompetent, just tepid, like lukewarm water. Daylight only made things worse. In those first weeks, the reality of our life together began to register with a great pall.

All through the honeymoon trip he read his Baedeker and worried about translating menus. He carried lists of Italian words for food, and whenever we left the hotel would draw careful little maps of our route on slips of paper that he carried in his pockets. I was surprised he walked as far as the hotel lobby without his guidebook. "It's easy to get lost in Venice," he said over and over until one day I snapped at him. "That's what happens, you get lost. You're *supposed* to get lost in Venice. It's fun. It's what makes it Venice!"

He looked at me as if I were a madwoman.

"Why did you want to come here?" I asked.

"Because people come to Venice on their honeymoon. It's what they do," he said patiently. "You liked the idea."

Well in theory, I had.

I tried to inspire him. We took a gondola ride by moonlight despite the cold, and when I leaned over and dipped my hand in the water, he practically wrestled me back to my seat for fear I'd fall in. I ran my wet fingers down the side of his cheek and began to kiss him, but he glanced toward the gondolier. "We're not alone," he said, pulling back.

"Let's pretend we are."

"But we're not."

So I tried in private. On our last night in Italy, I came into the living room of our suite dressed for dinner and found him looking out the window at the canal—so glittering, so magical. I took his hand, turned him away from the window, and said, "Dance with me."

"Here? Without music?"

"We'll sing."

He looked puzzled, then said as if he'd had a brainstorm, "Maybe I can get the concierge to bring up a radio," and was out the door before I could stop him. So I sat there by myself humming "O Mio Bambino Caro" as I looked at the canal in the moonlight. Twenty minutes later he came back, empty-handed and dejected, shaking his head. I knew he was trying to do something to please me, something he thought I'd like; I felt bad that it made him look ridiculous. But that, I soon realized, was Harry. It was useless to leave anything to his imagination.

It was in Venice that I learned to appreciate the profound meaning of the phrase "sleeping like a log." When it was time for bed— and he required a great deal of sleep all through our life together—Harry would lose consciousness almost before his head hit the pillow and would not be roused. He lay there like a huge fallen tree trunk.

When we came home and he was put in charge of all Mother's business affairs—he was part of the family now—he slept more. Even awake dear Harry sometimes reminded me of a log, solid and dense. He was lovable in his best waking moments, but they were so rare.

So we settled into our large, elegant house, and I gave dinner parties for the bankers and lawyers and businessmen who belonged to Harry's clubs and their tedious wives. Sometimes he would invite newer colleagues, men who had become fabulously rich supplying concrete or steel for the bridges and skyscrapers going up all around, but the new-money men were every bit as dreary as the old. I think they aspired to dullness as a sign they had arrived, and most of the time I helped them along.

Our dining room was pretty in the most conventional way, with our glistening ivory-and-gold wedding china and heavy Waterford crystal. At each party I made sure the most important man sat at my right, and I played the dutiful, charming hostess. I would act fascinated as some construction magnate explained infinitesimal differences in the quality of concrete. "It's not visible to the eye, but in later years it will show in the building," he'd say, then lean toward me as if we were conspirators. "I can always tell which buildings have been put up on the cheap." I would smile and nod in silent amazement at his wisdom, and he would later say that I was a fascinating conversationalist. It was a breathtakingly mindless thing to do.

My world was so narrow that I could actually amuse myself by tossing some mildly mischievous remark into the dinner conversation—pathetic but true. Sometimes I was the only one who noticed. Then I discovered I could count on Larry Sloane to help.

Harry claimed to loathe politicians but for some reason didn't consider Lawrence Sloane to be one, even after he became the district attorney. Larry had been in private practice when they met, so I suspect Harry never thought to put him in any other pigeonhole.

I was always taken aback when I set eyes on Larry. He was not especially attractive, lanky with a long face and horsey features. But he became animated when he talked, and his looks improved. By the end of a conversation he seemed positively handsome—even his enemies said he was one of the smartest men around—and the next time we met I would be surprised all over again that he wasn't better looking.

Barbara Sloane was the meekest, mousiest wife imaginable, and it was apparent Larry had outgrown her, although he was devoted to his son and daughter—they were barely out of diapers then. He was such a relief from all the self-important braggarts I was used to.

The first time he was seated by my side I began with the usual chatter. I always tried to learn some flattering bit of information about each guest beforehand, and I told him, "I heard that you gave the most wonderful talk at Harvard the other night."

"Where did you hear about that?"

"My brother was there, he's a student at the law school, and he raved about your speech. He said you were especially insightful about the need for strong municipal laws. I so wish I'd been there."

"Oh, it was a lot of hot air," he said. "I've given that speech so often I can give it in my sleep. You would have been as bored as everyone else." He *was* famous for his honesty, but until then I'd thought that was just a campaign slogan.

"No, I wouldn't have been! The subject may seem obvious to you, but it wouldn't have been to me. I do wish I'd been able to hear you."

"I'll give that speech again, I'm sure, there will be plenty of opportunities," he said. "But it would have been good to see your face in the audience." And his looks were transformed.

Now I may not have been invited into Harry and the other men's political discussions, but I could read and I could eavesdrop and I knew as well as anyone that Larry and the mayor were deadly enemies. The mayor was as corrupt as Larry was incorruptible, and Larry had been quietly threatening to run against him.

One night when Larry was among our dinner guests, I mentioned the mayor in the most innocent way. The papers said he had adopted a stray dog. "Was it really a stray or was it a gift?" I wondered. "Or was it— Oh, I've heard that the mayor has a special word for the gifts he receives from businessmen. What does he call them? 'Beneficences,' is that right?"

"Beneficences, yes, a clever word for bribes," Larry muttered.

I could count on Harry's friends to take the wrong side of any issue, and before long Larry and one of the self-important guests were caught in a prolonged, politely heated debate about whether the police actually delivered the mayor's "gifts" to him or simply turned their backs when they were paraded into his office. As the men carried on, I sat back and smiled, enjoying my own party at last. Such small pleasures!

Whenever I did such a thing, Harry would rant afterward, but it was worth it. "Why didn't you stop them? I thought they were going to throttle each other," he'd yell with vast exaggeration. "Our dinner table is not the place for a political brawl."

"What could I have done? They're opinionated men."

"I *heard* you mention the mayor."

Harry thought I should be content to spend my days with his colleagues' wives or the daughters of Mother's friends, girls I had known since we were learning to say "Bonjour, Mademoiselle" together in our first French class. At these dinners one of the other women would always leap in and do what Harry thought I should have done—break up the so-called political brawl, offering the most innocuous comment she could think of.

Some red-faced businessman would be braying at Larry, "I'd pay higher taxes and consider it a bargain," and some Barbara-like wife would abruptly say, "Caroline, I hope you haven't forgotten the committee meeting to discuss the opera benefit next week? Don't you think ancient Egypt is a heavenly theme for *Aïda*?" And the table would turn to her as if she had just said, "Caroline, did I mention I have the secret to eternal life?" I felt trapped in eternal tedium.

Will did what he could to free me. Whenever he was home from school he would spend more time at our house than at Mother's. He never breathed an unkind word about Harry after the night of the engagement party, and Harry regarded him as a well-bred dilettante. I was grateful they tolerated each other for my sake, but when Will was at one of our dinners, the difference between them was more evident than ever. As Harry and his friends blustered about how to reshape the world in their image, Will would catch my eye. Our faces were perfectly still, but we could see each other howling with laughter at the inane discussion all around us. And though I laughed with him, I couldn't ignore the distressing truth beneath it: this preposterous scene was my home, my dinner table, my life.

When we had been married about a year, I thought I was pregnant. I could hardly stand to see how puffed up Harry acted at the news, how insufferably self-satisfied; I didn't like thinking he was ludicrous. But it was even harder to see him sad and deflated when we learned I was mistaken. I never told him how relieved I was to be wrong; it would have meant the end of youth, the end of everything.

Our circle seemed as tiny as if we lived in a small town, so I expected the familiar dullness on a night we went to the Stoddards'. Milly was an old but not terribly close or remarkable school friend whose husband was now a friend of Harry's. We arrived at the door at the same time as a woman who introduced herself as Milly's cousin, Susan Leggett. I knew immediately that this was Spencer's wife. I'd heard about their wedding, which surprised everyone when it took place just six months after ours. I knew that she was from an old banking family in Philadelphia, and that they had settled there and had a child within a year. I had never even heard her name during all the time I'd spent with Spencer, though, and would have expected someone quite different from this pale blonde, so slight and pallid she seemed to fade into the wallpaper. I did not envy her.

I *was* curious to see Spencer for the first time since he had turned his back and so casually walked out of the guest room. "Spencer is already here," Milly said as she greeted us. "Let's go into the drawing room."

He looked heavier than before, his face fuller than I had ever seen it. Oddly, that helped brush away whatever lingering anger I felt; he had not thrived without me. But he had held on to his easy charm. Milly, who must have known that I'd dated Spencer, thoughtfully offered introductions as if she hadn't. He smiled warmly at both Harry and me and said, "Oh, we've met, good to see you both again," as if we were a couple he had always liked and never gotten to know well enough. It was a very smooth act; I did envy that.

During dinner I learned that Spencer and Susan had moved back to New York, that their infant daughter was named Emmeline ("A family name," Susan explained), and that Spencer was as spirited as ever. He teased Milly by asking whether she had the latest Bessie Smith recording—Milly, who liked nothing better than to be coaxed by her guests to play Chopin after dinner. It was her great and well-known vanity.

"We prefer live music," she said.

"You mean Bessie is dead? Don't tell me!"

"You know what I mean," Milly answered with barely veiled exasperation, as if she couldn't believe that her sweet cousin Susan had married this lout.

"Oh, Milly, did I tell you I have the perfect centerpiece idea for the *Aïda* benefit?" one of the interchangeable wives at the table said. "Tiny mummy cases in the center of every table. You don't think that's too morbid, do you? They are coffins, after all. We could do pyramids instead. But, oh dear, there are bodies in them, too, aren't there?"

Trying desperately to avoid the mummy conversation, I glanced around the table and saw Spencer looking my way. As he caught my gaze, he ever so briefly let his eyes glaze over in a sign of shared boredom and amusement, just as Will might have done. How could I not forgive him the past—it seemed so, so long ago? And at least he wasn't boring.

Soon he and Susan had become part of our set; Susan's family was so important in the financial world that Harry actually encouraged me to include them. Once, Spencer snuck up behind me as we were leaving someone else's house and began to hum "The Blue Danube Waltz," but I ignored it and he never did anything else the least bit suggestive.

We were chatting with them during intermission at Carnegie Hall one night when Spencer horrified Harry by suggesting that the four of us go to the opening of an art gallery in Greenwich Village later that week. He must have known that Harry would balk and that I would not. In fact, I was delighted.

Naturally I expected Susan to be with him when he arrived to pick me up. I'd never known Spencer to be interested in art, so I suppose I thought it was one of her interests, though she never did seem to have any. But he turned up alone, with no explanation. As he helped me into my coat, I wondered if this was a date—there was no humming to give me a clue—and whether I wanted it to be. Either way, Harry was in his study, and I had no intention of telling him that Susan was missing. Before I had a chance to see what was on Spencer's mind, Will turned up unexpectedly, as if he'd had a premonition about this evening and appeared when I needed him most.

"I thought you were taking Jenny or somebody to the theater tonight," I said.

"Her name's Janey and she has a cold, so I came to see if you'd like to join me instead." The invitation hung there even though Spencer was standing by my side.

"We're going to a new gallery, you come with us," I said, and he agreed at once. I'm not sure what would have happened if I had gone off alone with Spencer. Maybe I would have had an affair with him; but I did not, no matter what anyone said or thought later. Will's arrival snapped me to my senses, startling me out of any fantasies or warped memories about Spencer, and the three of us drove away in his car—not a little sports car anymore—the best of friends, or so I hoped.

"There will be 'artistic' women there tonight, Will, don't miss an opportunity," Spencer said as he drove, teasing just as he had in the old days.

But my little brother was learning to defend himself. "You're still the expert on those things, aren't you?" he asked. "You can point me in the right direction."

When we got to Tenth Street, so far west in the Village that we were almost at the river, Spencer found a parking space in front of an elegant building with large bow windows and an enormous limestone seashell over the doorway. I should have known that wasn't where we were heading. We walked into a nondescript brick tenement nearby, then up a steep flight of stairs, and followed the noise to the gallery, which was hardly a gallery at all.

It was no more than the living room of someone's apartment. The furniture had been cleared away, and burlap lined the walls. Abstract iron sculptures on wooden pedestals were arranged in a row down the middle of the room; some looked like piles of metal rocks, and others soared toward the ceiling. Paper collages hung on the walls, and a smattering of people stood in front of every piece, if only because the room was so tiny. As I took this in, Spencer disappeared into the crowd.

I flitted around trying to get my social bearings while Will did his best to stay at my elbow. I stopped in front of a collage so thick with scraps of newspapers and brown paper bags that it reminded me of a grocery sack that had fallen apart in the rain. A dour looking man with gray hair and paint-splattered shoes came up to me and asked, "What do you think?"

I nearly told him, "It's very brown," but said, "I haven't decided yet. What do you think?" This was not merely one of my reliable hostess tricks. I expected this conspicuously artistic man to reveal the work's genius.

"Junk," he said. "All his work is junk. There he is now, preening around as if he's Picasso." He pointed to a pudgy man in a bright blue shirt and a smug grin. "Though I hear women like him, so maybe he's partly right."

The gray-haired man was as blustery as any of Harry's friends, so I assumed the people in this room were a shabbier version of our circle, all thinking alike, as if they had taken a blood oath not to disagree. But as I walked through the crowd I discovered that while everyone thought the artist was acting like a buffoon, they could not agree about his work. I heard that it was ambitious and derivative, that it had textural depth and was muddy. "It does look like grocery bags that have fallen apart in the rain," I said almost to myself, and the group I had wandered into laughed as if I were extremely witty.

Not everyone was arguing about art; some people were gossiping about each other.

I overheard a middle-aged woman say, "I'm not surprised. Alfred would be much too jealous to show up tonight." Her black, well-cut dress made her seem as polished and out of place as I did, and she was talking to a sweet-looking young woman in a beige linen dress so faded its yellow daisies seemed to be disappearing before our eyes.

"But if he's avoiding us, that means he takes us seriously, doesn't it?" the younger woman said. It was clear that this Alfred had slighted her by not showing up and she was trying to put the best face on it, but the well-dressed woman wouldn't let her. "Oh no, it's simple pettiness on his part," she answered.

As in our circle, everyone seemed to know everyone else. But when they talked about charity here, the conversation was evidently about how to get money, not how to give it away. "Paul and Dolly were about to be on the street when Gerty came through and paid the back rent. She bought a few small pieces too."

"Bought him. Jesus, that makes him seem better than he is. Why not just give him the money? That burns me. Why won't she buy me?"

"You're not destitute enough."

"How did she know he needed it? Who got to her?"

"Oh, you know Lady Bountiful, she has her spies, even if she pretends to be one of us."

"I'd let her think she's Rodin if she'd buy something of mine."

I had never heard such things.

They were all terribly nice and eager to meet me. Of course, even then I knew that some people would be attracted to me for my money. I obviously had some. But I was so happy to be in this atmosphere—so new to me, so charged with energy—that I didn't care. The room became more crowded and hot, the air thick with smoke, but by the end of that night it seemed like the freshest air I had ever breathed.

Will and I lingered for hours until Spencer reappeared to drive us home. I never knew where he had disappeared, or with whom. "The art wasn't much, but sometimes all you need is a little fun," he said, and all of a sudden he seemed painfully glib, just a boy from my distant past. We rode uptown silently. Will looked exhausted and fearful because Spencer had been drinking and was shaky at the wheel. I was quietly ecstatic.

That was the small, inauspicious beginning of my passion for art. The work at that show, I came to realize, had been dreadful. But the future the night promised was entrancing.

I had met the owner of the so-called gallery—that is, I had met the wiry young man whose living room we were in, and his wife, the sweet woman with the fading daisies on her dress. I'm sure he could see that I had never bought a picture in my life, but that I was enthusiastic and possibly rich. He introduced me to several artists that night; he took my address and said he would make sure every dealer who mattered knew I was to be invited to their shows. "I'm not important, look around," he said, gesturing toward his chaotic apartment. "But I know people who are." He was right about both. He left New York a few months later. But I began receiving invitations to more shows than I could ever have seen, everything from Duchamp to clumsy landscapes by Sunday painters.

I had been raised to think that fine art ended with Sargent's portrait of Mother. It had been commissioned by my grandmother as a wedding present and was tucked away in a corner of our sitting room. Mother was reluctant to have it hanging at all. "One of his least successful portraits," she always sighed with disappointment, but I thought he had captured her to perfection.

Sargent had posed her standing beside a fireplace, in a lacy white dress with a pink sash around her waist, her hands folded on the mantelpiece. It was a completely unnatural pose, however graceful the composition, and she seemed to be leaning stiffly against the mantel. But what Mother saw as an awkward mistake I thought was a revelation. That very stiffness conveyed her personality. There was a rumor in the family that she had given Sargent such a hard time he had threatened to quit.

More than that, the portrait captured her eyes, the fierce, unwavering look she'd apparently had even as a young woman and that only intensified as she aged. When we were little, Will and I would joke that Mother's portrait could spy on us when she wasn't home, as if she were hiding inside it like a ghost. We must have half-believed it because we never did anything naughty within the portrait's range of vision. When Mother died, she left it jointly to Will and me, and we donated it to the Met as fast as we could.

By the time I was in my teens, I knew that the last thing I wanted to be was one of those women in a Sargent portrait, always ramrod stiff. Then I saw one that spoke to me as nothing else had.

Not long before Harry and I were married, I went to Boston to a cousin's wedding and was taken to a Sargent exhibition there. Everything seemed graceful and familiar until I came to a painting of a young woman sprawled on a sofa, enclosed in the folds of a luxurious wrap, her head flung back, eyes closed, her long hair loose and fanned out around her. I stood before it, stunned and unsettled. It seemed extremely sensuous to me, suggesting she was spent from some afternoon tryst. It hinted at all kinds of abandon. I noticed that the title was *Repose* and realized, "Of course, she's only sleeping." But even then, I wondered why she slept and if she would wake to a secret, wild life or simply pin up her hair and be good.

It is still one of my favorite paintings. I suppose if I had been in a different state of mind that day in Boston it might have opened my eyes to art then, but I saw it so soon before my marriage that all I could do was impose my own obsessions on that languid image.

By the time Spencer took me to the downtown opening, I was ready to see everything, everything in my world, more clearly.

When I began collecting, dealers swarmed to advise me. I listened to all opinions, from dealers and artists and other collectors, then made my own choices. I bought whatever I liked: photographs, sculptures, and especially paintings. I never concentrated on one artist or style. I simply bought work that showed me the world in a way I could not have imagined it, much less created. The image of a hand, a block of bright color, a tangle of metal—it was all so stimulating that often I lay awake at night, unable to sleep because my body was still excited from the rush of ideas going through my mind. As I read and studied, I came to know good art from bad, originality from artistic theft, people who genuinely appreciated me from those who were trying to use me—or so I thought.

It's easy now for people who come to see the collection to write that I was prescient—that's their favorite word—in buying all those Hartleys and Sheelers and Demuths. They forget about the mistakes, the no-name artists who deserve to be forgotten, all the work I sold or stored long ago. But I never regretted a penny I spent. It gave me a purpose. As I gained confidence, I began to help some artists with gifts of money for supplies or for rent on studio space. Suddenly, having money meant something.

Harry was almost as fussy about the art he allowed in our house as he was about the guests at our dinner table. He had his way in any room that a visitor might see, and it took no time to gauge what he would accept: you had to be able to identify the objects in the painting. Anything else belonged in my own suite of rooms, which began to look like a private, eclectic museum. I redesigned the rooms to be as simple as possible, to highlight the art, and adored spending time there. My favorite place was my personal sitting room, with its ivory carpet, black velvet settee, and graceful Brancusi bronzes, his birds that looked like flames; my bedroom was white, but two large Hartleys made the walls burst with color; there was a soothing Marin seascape in the tiny dressing room.

I didn't want to antagonize Harry; he was, after all, not complaining about a thing. But I did want to include my new friends in our life together, and I tried. It was a disaster.

I gave a few dinners that made everyone uneasy, the artists staring at the silver before tentatively picking up a fork, and Harry's friends smiling tightly. I was trying so hard to convince Harry to accept my friends that I didn't dare throw a grenade into one of *those* conversations. Finally I made a terrible blunder. I invited an artist—long forgotten now but known as a minor Dadaist then— who was not at all concerned about using the correct fork. He played with his food, arranging it on the plate in colorful shapes around a tower of bread; he called for ketchup to be brought to the table, quickly, because he needed more red. He was obviously trying to provoke the other guests, who were sophisticated enough to see through it. Everyone remained unflappable, watching him build his little bread tower. When he was through he stood, pointed to his plate, and announced, "A man's bread is his castle!" Someone at the table began polite applause.

Harry sat fuming through this juvenile performance. And before the door had closed completely on the last guest he roared, "Never again, Caroline! Do you hear me?"

Harry rarely put his foot down, but he did then.

I was on my own, my life split in two. I can't say I minded.

It was at Mark Haskell's old storefront gallery near Washington Square that I met Nick one fall afternoon.

Haskell had an uneven list of artists, and I wasn't interested in any of the paintings he showed me that day, but I can recall them even now: forest scenes in garish colors. I suppose I remember because so much changed after that.

Haskell had gone to a back room to get some drawings and was walking out again when the door opened and a young man dashed in, his blond hair disheveled from the wind, a package about a foot long wrapped in brown paper under his arm. He raced toward Haskell, tearing the paper off as he went, without stopping or noticing that anyone else was there, as if the wind itself had carried him in.

His back was to me as he held up a small painting and said in a rush, "Here it is. You remember the problem? I think I've fixed it."

Haskell was annoyed and terse. "Mrs. Stephens," he said, "this is Nicholas Leone. Nick, Mrs. Harrison Stephens. I was about to show her some drawings."

Now Nick turned to face me, obviously surprised. "I'm sorry, Mrs. Stephens, I'm not usually this rude, believe me," he said. I had never seen such lucid blue eyes. His smile was effortless, his voice warm and amusing as he shook my hand and asked, "How can I convince you I'm civilized?"

I laughed, but Haskell said, "Maybe you can come back tomorrow. Or next week."

Nick looked embarrassed. Haskell hadn't even glanced at his painting, so I asked to see it, and when I did I realized at once that his golden looks were the merest reflection of his talent. The painting was an abstract sunrise in concentric circles of gold and orange and yellow, so delicate it might have been a mirage yet so vibrant it seemed about to burst off that small canvas.

"It's a study for a larger work," he said, as if apologizing that it wasn't better.

"Oh, but it's beautiful," I told him. "I love the lightness of it. And I would very much like to see the finished work."

That small oil study *was* beautiful, and I was tempted to buy it on the spot, but I had learned not to seem too eager. I did, however, rescue Nick from Haskell's insults; I stole him from under Haskell's nose.

"I was just leaving, Mr. Leone. Would you mind walking me to my car? May I have my driver drop you somewhere?" I said.

"Mrs. Stephens, can't I show you these last drawings?" Haskell asked.

"Not today, thank you, I really must go." And I headed for the door.

"Thank you for coming then, I hope to see you again soon." As he held the door open, he turned and said to Nick, "I might as well look at what you have now." But Nick had quickly slipped the painting back in its wrapping and was following me out.

"I'll come back tomorrow," he told Haskell. "Or next week."

When we got to the car and I asked where the driver should go, Nick gave an address so close by he could easily have walked, yet he wasn't at all sheepish about using this transparent ploy to talk to me.

I knew he couldn't be terribly successful or I would have heard his name, and I could see as much. The dark suit he wore, with a white shirt and no tie, was crisp but not new, the clothing of a man who has good taste but can rarely afford it. He was clearly a struggling artist, and struggling artists had *so* many reactions to me. I had come to expect groveling and flattery, as well as supreme arrogance meant to put me in my place as the lowly servant of art, not its creator. I never knew which to expect. But Nick did none of those things, not ever. He looked at me with those clear blue eyes and treated me as a woman, always, not as the walking embodiment of a checkbook.

"Please don't give Haskell another thought," I said. "I'm sure you can do better than that gallery."

"He's not so bad, he runs hot and cold. If I catch him when he isn't trying to sell something, he can be encouraging. I shouldn't have barged in like that."

"I was relieved you did. He was showing me the most hideous work."

"Not Sandler's purple trees?"

"Yes, how did you know?"

"He's always trying to unload those." He laughed. "I don't think he's sold one yet."

We had turned onto Thompson, a narrow street full of closely spaced tenement buildings, and suddenly we were at his address. "Is this where you work?" I asked.

"Yes. I rent a room from a family and live and work in it."

"There can't be much light with the buildings so close."

"That's the worst of it, but I manage."

How could he possibly manage?

I hesitated, but something in his easy manner told me to go on. "I hope you don't mind my asking, but do you earn your living from painting?"

"Not this kind of painting. I do commercial illustrations when I'm lucky, newspaper and catalog advertisements mostly. I'm becoming known for lifelike men's hats," he said, with immense good humor. "And that's a step up. Last winter I got more experience as a sign painter than I ever wanted."

"But you should be painting all the time."

"This keeps me modest," he said, still smiling brilliantly.

We were blocking the street, and a car behind us honked. "Thank you for the ride and the company, Mrs. Stephens," he said, taking my hand. He held it for a flash of a second and looked as if he were about to kiss it, then changed his mind and shook it again. "I'd really like to know what you think of my work." He raised the half-wrapped package in his hand. "Lightness was exactly what I was aiming for in this. I have a feeling you'd understand what I'm trying to do."

"I'd like that. Where can I see it? Does Haskell have more?"

"I can show you. Tell me when and where, and I'll bring some things around."

It couldn't have been more proper.

I tried to tell myself there was nothing unusual about Nick's bringing work to show me; other artists had done it often enough. But having seen that first small painting of the sun, I knew there was something exceptional about his art, and I must have sensed there would be something more intense about my dealings with him too. I did change my dress several times before he arrived.

He was friendly but professional as he walked into the sitting room that morning, loaded down with a portfolio and several canvases tied together with rope. "It's good to see you again," he said as he walked straight to the windows and asked if he could move the draperies back to let in more light. He stood near the windows, holding up his works one by one so the full light shone on them, saying nothing. He had about a dozen sketches and oil paintings, and as he silently showed them to me, I moved closer and stood in front of them in awe. I don't want to exaggerate, not all of it was genius, but even the failures were marked by true originality and boundless ambition.

And here is the strange thing in view of what happened later: he never painted human figures. He made glorious paintings of nature, so real you felt you could walk through one of his wheat fields or gardens, yet in tones more jewel-like and beautiful than nature had created. He turned empty buildings into eerie palaces, shimmering as if they were mosaics but solid enough to endure for centuries. He created landscapes in various stages of abstraction, shaped by dazzling colors. But never did I know him to draw or paint a person.

I bought two pieces that day and asked to see more. "I've shown you the best," he said. "I'm not sure the rest is worth it, but I'm working on some new things you might like." We drank coffee and talked about how to frame the paintings I had chosen. One was a hauntingly beautiful house, no more than a shack really, of iridescent silvery blue. It stood alone in the middle of a field at night. The windows were dark, but the walls of the house itself seemed to glow with otherworldly light.

"This house, it's eloquent, as if it's speaking to me," I told him. "I don't know what it's saying, but I feel as if it's telling me something." I felt foolish as soon as I said the words; it seemed such an amateurish response, as if I were asking him to explain his work. I knew better than to ask an artist that. But he looked startled and pleased.

"That's the house where I was born," he said. "Of course it looks nothing like that, and there were neighbors crowded all around us, but that's what it is."

"Where is it?"

"Pennsylvania, where I grew up. My father is a carpenter, and I got a scholarship to study at the Art Students League. After I finished a few years ago I stayed on."

"Does you family still live in the house?"

"They do. It would be hard for me to go back and look at it now, after painting this. I suppose I've turned it into something else, whatever that is."

"You've turned it into something full of light and beauty, you've absolutely done that. But there's another quality—I wouldn't call it sad exactly, but something—"

"Maybe I've turned it into what I wish it had been when I was a boy. The brightness and beauty anyway, that was missing." Then he laughed and seemed surprised at himself. "I can't believe I'm telling you this. I never talk about these things."

I didn't know at the time whether "these things" meant his work or his life—I soon found it meant both—but I felt so happy, honored really, that he could talk to me about them.

"I adore that house, your vision of the house," I told him. "I think I'll put it in my bedroom so I can see it in my dreams."

"I almost didn't bring it today. Something made me pack it at the last minute."

I didn't stop encouraging other artists when I met Nick, but he was so extraordinary that from then on he always came first. I helped with money to rent a studio, which he desperately needed. There was nothing secret about any of this. I had made the same gifts to many others.

He scouted around for the studio, and one afternoon called to say he had found a few and would like me to see them before he chose. That wasn't necessary; I had offered him a flat amount to use as he wanted. But he said, "I'd like you to see them. I have an idea which is best, and I'll feel better about the whole arrangement if you agree." So the next day my driver took Nick and me to look at several places, all modest but with excellent light. He gave no hint about which he preferred and didn't have to; there was no doubt which he should have.

It was farther downtown than any of the others, on a remote side street on the Lower East Side—not far from Washington Square but a world away socially. The studio was on the top floor of a strangely designed wooden building slightly taller than the others on the street. Although I could see people through the front windows, the building looked desolate. Aging gray paint peeled off the clapboard sides, and the concrete steps leading to the front porch were pitted and broken. A dirt path overgrown with weeds led us around the side of the building to the back, where there was a separate entrance: an unpainted wooden stairway zigzagged up the side of the building to the top floor, stopping nowhere else. As we crossed a shadowy landing at the top, I wondered why Nick was even considering such a depressing place, but when he opened the door we emerged from the gloom into a room transformed by a skylight. It was a garret but it felt wide open, close to the heavens, a tower that left the earthbound world behind.

"This is it," I said, instinctively tilting my face toward the light. "This is the most luxurious room I've ever seen."

"I'm glad you like it," he said. "I thought you would, but I was worried about dragging you to a neighborhood like this. I know it's not what you're used to. This is a remarkable place, though, isn't it? I'm told it was built for an artist about thirty years ago, and the outside staircase was added so it would be easy to carry things up and down. There's no hot water, so it's even cheaper than the others we saw."

"You must take it," I told him. "And I'm so happy you let me see it. Now I can imagine you working here." Even that much seemed a privilege, more than I'd expected.

"Well, you can imagine it. Or you can visit me here. To check on my progress, I mean. I hope you will." Lightly, tentatively, he put his hand on my arm. "You know, I would give up this place in a second if I thought the neighborhood would stop you from coming. That's why I wanted you to see it first. I hope you'll come here as often as you like."

We had chatted so easily and excitedly all day—about artists we admired, buildings we drove past, his grand ambition to create paintings like none the world had ever seen—that I didn't hesitate. "I'll come, as long as I don't disturb your work."

"You could never do that." He had taken his hand away, and we stood there staring at each other, astonished that we had fallen into this shared adventure, these shared thoughts. Standing there, it was as if the disreputable street and everything outside vanished; it was always that way whenever I was in the studio, even that first time, as if we possessed this private place together. Spencer—and every other man I'd ever known—became a pale shadow next to Nick.

And his work flourished there. It gave me so much pleasure to see that, to feel I was making some tiny contribution by giving him the chance his talent deserved.

He arrived early every day to catch the morning light, and by four or so had done his best work. I loved to stop by in the late afternoons, nearly every day when I could, when Mother and Harry thought I should be gossiping with the opera guild ladies.

We had furnished the room with a small tea table and a daybed he could nap on. It would never be a pretty room; it had pale green wainscoting and a checkered linoleum floor, but that didn't matter. We had made it comfortable, casual and lived in, with cups and spoons scattered across the table next to paintbrushes, and a rumple of blankets on the daybed. Sometimes I would arrive to find Nick himself rumpled on the bed and would gently touch his shoulder or hair to wake him. He would stir slowly and begin to mumble before opening his eyes and smiling up at me. Sometimes he was dreaming and talking restlessly about work in his sleep. Sometimes he would wake calmly, open one eye and say in a sly tone, "Why, Caroline, how nice of you to join me."

At first he was shy about letting me see what he was working on, as if that would be too intimate. But before long he was showing me whatever he had done that day, however rough. If he was still at work when I arrived, he went on quietly while I watched. Sometimes I went down the hall for water and made tea while he talked through what he was trying to do. "It's not balanced, I think I need to make this blue patch brighter" or "You shouldn't be able to see any lines here, it should seem like a ball of light."

There were times when I heard anguished self-doubts. "This is so ordinary I can't stand to look at it," he'd say, throwing a sketch or a canvas on the floor in disgust. It was never as conventional as he thought. But some works were better than others, and I didn't automatically praise everything, as much as I might have wanted to. He came to trust my judgment, he said, because I understood him so completely. It was as if we had known each other always, as if there were no social distance between us, no distance of any kind.

I didn't mind the coffee-stained spoons and his rumpled sheets on the daybed. He didn't mind that I had to carve out fragments of my time to give him, that my life wasn't really my own. In our private world, we talked about art and music, politics and books, and could pick up a conversation from the day before as if no time had passed since then. We did not talk about Harry or my other world, the one that seemed so much less real to me.

Even now I believe I was a help in his work. He always said that I had a better sense than he did of when he was wasting his time and when he was breaking new ground. I'm not sure about that. But I do know he never painted people and he never asked me to pose.

In the spring of 1927, when I saw his newest work, I had the idea of organizing his first show, of bringing together everyone who mattered: the collectors, the critics, Mother's Old New York set, all my new friends, anyone who could help him. I thought I could do something valuable by showing them my Nick, my discovery. Maybe that was grandiose; maybe I was obsessed; or maybe I just hadn't learned my lesson from those misbegotten dinner parties Harry had banned. But I don't think so. I wanted the world to see his genius.

The exhibit took months to prepare. We chose Haskell to present the show, not because he was an important dealer; he wasn't. But he had, in the end, encouraged Nick. And frankly, we knew we could control him better than anyone else. A dealer would give the show legitimacy, but with Haskell the project would be ours.

We helped him find a better space for his gallery. Together, Nick and I chose the paintings, including the ones I had bought from him that first day, and others he had given me since. We supervised the hanging and gave the iridescent silver-blue house a prominent place. Until then I had kept it in my bedroom to remind me of

Nick. It had become a symbol of our bond, reassuringly beautiful, the last thing I saw at night and my first, glorious vision in the morning.

I used every charm I had to get all those people to come to the opening. That night I was in heaven. Nick and I were like one.

Of course, I've never entirely trusted myself as a judge of character since.

TWO

Caroline: The Trial

Toward dawn on that horrible night of the opening, we had all been quiet for some time. I was lying on the chaise again wrapped tighter than ever in my shawl, my hair down now, my head back, but my eyes wide as I stared toward the drapes waiting for first light to creep in. I felt delirious with fatigue; once, I saw the image of Nick, translucent as if he were some watery apparition, standing before the window holding up one harmless canvas after another as he had on the day he'd first come to see me. I snapped myself awake; I was afraid to keep my eyes closed for long, afraid that if I slept I would wake up a different person—banished, disgraced, accused of shameless behavior that only Nick and I knew for certain had been invented out of malice.

Harry lay sprawled on the sofa, his back to Will and me, but what he'd said still seemed to echo through the room. He had never spoken so angrily, yet his hurtful words were easier to dismiss than his naïve ones: "We want to make this whole thing disappear as if it never happened." The uselessness of that idea, of his entire response, was maddening. Harry and Will had even used the newspapers to keep the fire burning, as if destroying them would make the stories themselves go up in flames. I knew we had to fight what Nick had done to me, but I didn't have the slightest idea how.

Finally Will said, "There's no point in sitting here. At least go to bed and try to get some rest," and I agreed. He helped me to my suite and waited in my sitting room while I went to the dressing room to change. When I caught sight of myself in the mirror, I was shocked that I looked like the same person. I think I expected to see some grotesque, mauled version of myself, some bloodied reflection of what I was feeling inside, evidence that Nick had changed the way people would look at me forever.

Will tucked me into bed. He was exhausted too, but instead of sending him to the guest room that had become his, I asked him to sit by my side and talk. If I could look into his innocent eyes, I wouldn't be tempted to stare at the empty space on the wall where Nick's shimmering house had stood.

I was sitting up against the pillows like an invalid and in fact had never felt more helpless. Will sat on the side of the bed facing me and rubbed my hands.

"This will seem better in the morning," he said, then shook his head. "I don't know why I said that. I don't know why it would be better."

"It *is* morning, and it's not better," I said. I sank back into the pillows and fought to stay awake. "Remember when Spencer's name appeared in that gossip column? That seems so trivial now."

"Oh, it was pretty trivial then," he said kindly. "Maybe it's true these things pass."

"No. This won't pass. Who will ever believe me?"

"I will."

"Who else? It means *everything* to me that you believe me. But who else?"

"People who know you."

"People will believe anything. I've believed things myself. No, I have to prove it's all a lie, it's the only way."

Our conversation was rambling, broken by long stretches of silence; our voices were weak, but we couldn't let it go.

"Harry will talk to some publisher friends tomorrow. It will quiet down," Will said.

"Harry can't take care of this," I told him, my voice breaking with exhaustion. "He can't. He'll mean well and he'll think he's being helpful, but he won't know what to do."

"He'll make sure no one ever sees that painting again. He'll know how to handle that, that's only about money. Maybe that was Leone's intention all along—paint something we'd pay any price for."

I felt tortured by why Nick had done this, but I didn't think it was for money. He only cared about money because it bought him the freedom to paint, and I'd already given him that. "I don't think so," I told Will.

"Maybe we should try to buy it anyway. I hate to see him gain anything from this, but the most important thing now is protecting you. If we buy it, we can make sure no one sees it again."

"It's been seen."

Will had moved to the chair by my bedside, but we kept talking, desperate enough to suggest any far-fetched possibility, saying anything that entered our worn-out minds.

"Do you think you'd like to take a trip?" Will asked.

"Run away? I'd love to, but that would make it seem as if I have something to be ashamed of."

"Right. I was only thinking it would be easier on you until the attention dies down."

"I can't run. What *can* I do?"

For one deluded moment I thought it must all be a mistake, that I could talk to Nick and make it right. He would explain everything publicly: that he thought he was creating a work of art, that he had no idea I'd be upset, that it was done entirely from his imagination. One of Harry's newspaper friends could arrange an interview with him.

"Do you think it's worth trying to get Nick to say I never posed? Get him to give an interview to the papers?"

Will thought for a while. "I'm not sure anyone would believe him now." Minutes passed before he went on. "Why would he do that anyway? Take it back?"

"Because it's true?"

"That didn't stop him from painting it in the first place."

"Because we'd pay him to say it?"

"Didn't you say he wasn't after money? You're not making sense anymore."

"None of this makes sense." We were both half-asleep and babbling.

"He has no money without me," I said. "Not a cent, that's why Harry won't sue, remember? We might as well sue, we have nothing to lose and there's nothing else to do."

"You'd have a lot to lose. Don't dismiss what Harry says just because he's the one who said it. He's right, it's a bad idea to go after Leone. Your name would be dragged through the mud in court and in the papers. That's pointless."

"Do you have a better idea?"

"Not at the moment."

"We won't sue for money, we'll sue for an apology. Can we do that?"

"Give this up," he mumbled, very close to dozing off. "Your reputation would still suffer. Some people would still take his side."

Suddenly I was wide awake, frantic at the thought that anyone could believe Nick—that some people always would.

"No! No one can take his side, I can't stand it!" I said. I was leaning forward, grabbing Will's shoulders, practically shaking him awake. "We can't wait, we can't give anyone even a day to think such awful things about me. I don't deserve it! Harry is just afraid of more scandal if we sue, but you're a lawyer, you could do it for me, you'd know how."

"Caroline, Caroline," he said, holding me tight, rocking me in his arms to soothe me, then settling me back against the pillows. He drew the comforter up under my chin as if he were tucking in a five-year-old and nuzzled his nose against mine for a second. "I understand how upset you are, but we need to think this through."

But I wouldn't be calmed, and kept ranting. "Everyone has to see that Nick betrayed me, I was trying to help and he took advantage. It's as if he stole my soul. It's worse than if he broke in here and stole everything valuable to me, like a common criminal. Why does he want to destroy me? I wish he had just stolen things, I could live with that." And out of this delirious raving two words came crashing through. "Common criminal," I said, "he is a criminal, he belongs in jail. Can't Larry Sloane have him arrested? Can you call him right now?"

"It's five o'clock in the morning; you're so tired you've lost track of time."

"Call him before he gets to his office, please. Tell him I need to see him urgently, today, now."

"And tell him what? We want him to charge Leone with stealing your soul?"

"Harry's right, suing him would be petty and public and awful. He's a criminal. Larry sends criminals to prison, he can help."

"It's more complicated than that, dear."

"No, it's not. It's that simple. Please call Larry."

"Let's talk about it later. You have to calm down and get some rest, you're hysterical."

"But I have to see him first thing, before anyone else gets to his office. I have to go to him myself, but no one can know."

Will looked at me tenderly. I could see he wasn't taking any of this seriously. But, as if a fog had abruptly lifted, I now meant every word. I lay back and spoke calmly. "Please listen, because I need you to be on my side more than anything I've ever needed. I know I'm right about this. It's better than suing. People are calling *me* lewd and indecent, but *he's* the one who made an indecent painting and is pretending it's a portrait of me. Aren't there laws against that?"

"The district attorney might not interpret the law precisely the way you do."

"We can try. Please, please, Will. If I get some sleep now and ask you to call him again in the morning, will you do it?"

"If you sleep, I'll do whatever you want."

"Thank you. My lamb. What would I do without you?"

I closed my eyes and turned my head the other way, though of course I couldn't sleep. Will sat there in the chair, feigning sleep too, I'm sure. He must have thought I'd wake restored to reason.

At six, I sat up and turned toward him. His eyes were closed. "Are you awake?"

"Yes."

"Would you please call Larry now?"

He looked at me. "You haven't slept, you haven't kept your part of the bargain."

"This is bigger than any bargain and you know it. You're all I've ever had, dear, the only person I can count on."

"What about Harry? You can count on him."

I reached for Will's hand. "It's not the same. I can never love Harry as I do you. You were right about that after all. Please help me. Please don't make me do this alone."

"You know I'll never leave you alone," he said, taking my hand in both of his. He thought for a bit longer, then said, "If it makes you feel better, I'll call Sloane, but don't be surprised if he doesn't agree with you."

I dressed quickly while Will went to Harry's study to make the call. I was sure Larry would have come to me if I'd asked, but how could I when I was about to beg him for such a huge favor?

Will returned to say through the dressing room door that we should leave right away. "Sloane sounded baffled, but he agreed. He'll meet us at his office at seven. I only said we needed to see him urgently, I didn't explain why. Do you want me to wake Harry?"

"No, don't, I need to do this myself."

"Shouldn't he know? Maybe you should let Harry or me talk to Sloane. You're so upset and tired. Besides, he may pay more attention to a man's opinion."

"You don't know Larry the way I do. He'll pay attention to my opinion, I know he will." I knew no such thing, but I believed he was an open-minded man, a man who could be persuaded.

"I'm going to shave. I'll meet you downstairs in ten minutes," Will said.

I was waiting with my coat on in five, and we snuck out while Harry was still asleep—or at least we didn't hear any sound coming from his rooms. Will drove me downtown to the district attorney's office himself, so that even George, whom we trusted thoroughly, wouldn't know where I was going. The main streets had been cleared of snow overnight but were still icy and nearly deserted. Will hardly said a word as the car crept and swerved along.

"We should have waited," he told me as he slowed for a stop sign. "I should have gone to my office and done some research so we'd know if he can be charged with anything. The law has to be behind us, and I'm not sure what it says about this."

"Larry will know. He'll find something."

Will was concentrating hard on keeping the car from skidding, which made him sound more annoyed when he finally said, "It's not matter of finding something. The law isn't there to be twisted."

"Is it twisting the law to punish someone who has been vile to me?"

"It doesn't work that way."

"Well it should."

He shook his head. "You're too tired for this."

"No, I'm not."

"You are," he said. Then he switched from his curt tone to the teasing, singsong voice of our childhood. "Yes you a-are."

"Am not," I answered.

"Then why do you sound like a baby?" He laughed. Only Will could have found a way to tease me and make me smile at such a moment.

"I may be a baby, but I'm a wide-awake baby, I promise you."

We didn't say much more until we arrived at Larry's building and entered an unlocked side entrance as Will had arranged. I asked him to wait there, in the downstairs hall. "I need to talk to Larry alone," I said, unbuttoning my coat.

"You can't, you don't know what you're doing, you're too exhausted."

"I told you, I'm perfectly lucid now."

He held my coat open in front of me and said, "If you're so lucid, why are you wearing the same clothes you wore last night?"

It was true. I had rushed to wash my face and pin up my hair, then had simply picked up the clothes I had dropped on the floor. Under my warm cashmere coat I was wearing the bare white silk and chiffon dress that had made me feel so sensuous the night before.

So that is how I went to see Larry.

The outer offices were empty, and the heavy wooden door to his private office was ajar. I tapped lightly and pushed it open, thinking that if he seemed the least bit embarrassed, if I caught a glimmer of suspicion or doubt in his eyes, it would signal how easily my friends would turn their backs on me. But Larry was a dream. He got up from behind his desk, walked toward me, took both my hands in his, and said, "What a night you've had. And you don't look any the worse for it."

I almost cried with relief. "You're being very kind. And I do need a friend, someone I can trust. That's why I came to you. I'm so grateful to you already, Larry."

"Let me take your coat," he said, and I was left standing there in my filmy, inappropriate little dress.

"You are an apparition," he said.

I must have been an apparition of pure frivolity in my party clothes, surrounded by dark wooden bookcases and brown leather chairs and the lingering smell of cigars. "I'm sorry about the way I look. I was so distraught I threw on my dress from last night."

"It's not like you to apologize for being beautiful," he said. "Sit down." And we sat side by side in armchairs facing his desk. "I planned to be there last night, but Barbara has been in bed with a cough and was afraid to go out in the storm."

"I'm glad you weren't there to see it. But you've read the newspapers?"

"Yes," he said and looked at the carpet. "I assume Will's call had something to do with that."

"Everyone has seen the papers, and everyone saw that awful painting," I said. "The papers called me pornographic and indecent, and I can't bear it. I don't know why Nick did it, but I never posed for that painting, I swear to you, I had no idea it existed. It's pure malice, it's all a lie, and I want to clear my name."

"I don't blame you for that. What can I do to help?"

"Well, Nick is the indecent one, isn't he?"

"I suppose so."

"And . . . you can do something about that, can't you?"

"I'm not sure I see what you're asking."

"I probably sound like a fool, but can't you have him arrested and sent to prison? Will thinks you can."

Larry's horsey face looked startled. "He does? On what charge?"

"Oh, I don't know what you call it legally. He didn't say exactly and I'm not the lawyer. I said I was sure you'd know what to do."

"Has this man Leone defrauded you in some way? Stolen money, or extorted it?"

"Oh, no, it's not about money."

"Forgive me for asking, but I think we can talk honestly. Has he blackmailed you in some way, my dear?"

"No, not at all, nothing like that. He's stolen my good name, he's lied about me."

"By painting the picture?"

"Exactly."

"And suggesting it was taken from life?"

"Yes."

"I see." He didn't look as if he did.

"I suppose you might sue for defamation of character, but it would be an extraordinarily hard case to make. It is possible, though. You'd have to give a deposition and testify against him in court, which would make it apparent that he's a cad and that you've been badly used, you'd gain that. But really, I don't know that suing is the best course."

"Oh, you're right, I don't want to sue. That seems too petty, as if I want personal revenge."

"Don't you?"

"No, not at all. I want it established that I did nothing wrong, that Nick is the one who's vile, that he invented all of this. Isn't that justice? I want the law to clear me, I need you to clear me. Everyone knows you're the most honest man there is. I so need you on my side, you're the only one who can help. It would mean everything to me."

He looked thoughtful, his face longer and more serious than ever. "Maybe you should let this all die down. Going to law, one way or another, is not the only way to win. Harry has powerful connections. I'm speaking as a personal friend now, giving you his best advice. I think that's the way to handle it; the results would be more certain than with the law."

"What could Harry do to help me now? He's not like you. He's not nearly as smart or sophisticated."

"I can talk to him."

"Oh, no, please don't," I said, clutching Larry's hand. I leaned forward so I could look straight into his eyes, so he would see that I meant every word. I drew our clasped hands toward my heart and said, "Please don't tell him about this. He'll be very jealous that I came to you. He wants to see himself as my protector, but he can't help or understand me the way you can. He can't begin to know how."

Larry came to sit on the arm of my chair, keeping one hand on my heart and putting the other strong arm around me. "You're shivering, my dear. And I'm not sure I know how to help you out of this."

I looked at him in despair. "But I had such faith in you," I said sadly. "Don't you think what Nick did to me was obscene?"

"Of course I do."

"If it's obscene, isn't that illegal?"

"Sometimes."

I sank my head against him, lost. "You are my only hope, my only friend," I whispered. I was tired and closed my eyes briefly—maybe half a minute or so—and might have dozed off if I hadn't heard Larry's voice, calm, measured, reluctant. "There is an option, but a tough one."

I looked up at him. "What?"

"A charge of public obscenity. The law exists, but there are no guarantees. Leone would undoubtedly argue that this painting is a work of art."

"But it's not, it's a vicious lie," I said, so unnerved by the very idea that I leapt up and began to pace. I walked to the windows, I walked toward the door, hardly knowing where I was going, rubbing my bare, freezing arms. I could feel the hem of my dress brushing against my knees as it had the night before.

Larry sounded just as agitated as he followed me to the door. "Don't leave, Caroline," he said as he locked it.

"I wasn't leaving, I don't know what I'm doing anymore."

And before I knew what was happening I was sobbing on his shoulder. He put his arms around me to keep me warm and whispered, "Oh, I hate to hear you like this, my poor dear, you don't deserve it."

I pulled myself together after a minute and he asked, "Are you all right?"

"Yes, I'm so sorry. I didn't mean to be this way. I don't want you to think I'm weak."

"Weak?" he said, rubbing my back. "You're soft, but you're not weak. And you'd have to be extremely strong to get through this if we did prosecute Leone. It could turn into an ugly public display."

"I'll be as strong as you need me to be," I said, looking up at him and still leaning into him for support. "If you'll help me, I'll be whatever you need me to be. I'll do *anything* you want."

He just held me and looked at me silently, as if running things over in his mind.

"I can't go through this alone," I told him.

"You won't have to," he promised.

"Then you'll help me?"

He looked down at me for another minute, then nodded. "I'll do everything I can."

He stroked my arm reassuringly again, looked at his watch, and said, "We should get down to business."

He led me back to the chair and sat behind his desk, taking notes. "I have to ask you a few questions before anyone else gets here. The party last night, was it open to the public?"

"Yes, that was the official opening. Almost all the guests had been personally invited, though."

"Did you or Harry sign a lease for the gallery?"

"No, I gave a check to Mark Haskell, the gallery owner. He signed and paid for the lease. I never signed it, and Harry never knew any of the details."

"Good. I wouldn't want you or Harry implicated if we charge Haskell and Leone. And the painting is still there?"

"Yes, Harry arranged that. And he got Haskell to agree not to open this morning."

"Does Leone have other paintings of this sort anywhere?"

"I've never seen any. I'd never seen that one. I guess he must, that's how he works—he makes sketches, then some studies, then a larger painting. I never saw anything like it in the studio, though. Oh, I don't know anything anymore. I never saw anything like it at all. It's so confusing."

"I'm sorry to upset you, I can see that I have. We're almost through. A few more questions, if you can."

"Of course."

"Were you ever alone with Leone? His studio, his apartment?"

"In his studio, yes, but never his apartment. He rents a room in a family's house on Thompson Street. I've never been inside."

"Who are his friends and associates? If I were to charge him with obscenity, who would support him besides Haskell? Who might claim it was art?"

"I don't know, I wasn't looking at it that way. The point is, it's a lie about me, he's trying to humiliate me. Art is the truth, and that painting is a lie."

I noticed him write and underscore "Art is the truth, and that painting is a lie."

"But who would take his side?" he asked. "Does he have influential friends?"

"I think I was the only one."

"Good."

"Will can help," I reminded him. "Will has influential friends, or at least he'll know where to find them. He'll give you every resource his firm has, I'm sure. He could be a tremendous help."

"Our office doesn't really work that way," he said, echoing Will. I felt unimaginably naïve.

"Another thing—and I apologize again if this is indelicate. Will can advise you legally, but you might want to talk to another lawyer, someone outside the family, someone you're able to confide in fully."

"I have nothing to hide. And I can confide in you, can't I?"

"Yes, of course you can, and I'm glad of it." He looked at his watch again. "Are Will and Harry with you?"

"Will is waiting downstairs."

"I'll walk you down. I need to talk to him."

As he helped me on with my coat he said, "We should arrange a meeting soon, just the two of us. I'll need your help and maybe a great deal of your time."

"Happily," I said, turning to him and feeling secure for the first time in what seemed like years. "As much as you need." His horsey face had never seemed so handsome.

Downstairs, a few people were rubbing their hands and shaking the snow from their boots as they arrived for work. Larry glanced at them as we quickly passed, then pulled Will aside and whispered something. All I heard was "Talk to Harry immediately. Make sure he lets Haskell open this morning as usual. I'll call you later."

Then Larry was gone before I could say a thing. As Will took my arm and walked me to the car, I asked, "What's going on, why is he letting the gallery open? That's the one thing Harry did right."

"I don't know. I can only guess."

"Well guess."

"Maybe he doesn't feel like knocking the door down or getting a warrant. Or maybe last night wasn't public enough. If you're going to charge someone with a public display of obscenity, there has to be a public display. He must be making sure he's got the evidence."

"But more people will see it."

"Probably not for long."

"Then everything will be okay?"

"I can't imagine how."

When we were settled in the car, I expected him to ask all sorts of questions, but he sat there brooding. "I told Larry you would help him," I said. "You will, won't you?"

"You got me a job in the district attorney's office?"

"Be serious. He mentioned something about Harry's influential friends. You have influence too. I think we have to count on every friend we have, all of us."

He stared straight ahead. "I guess you're right." Then he laughed but without any real humor. "And to think I was worried about being caught in a speakeasy."

By the time we got home, Harry had already left, we assumed to go to the gallery. Will drove off after him, and I didn't hear a word from either of them all day. I didn't hear from any of our friends either, and was grateful for that—what could I have said to them? I couldn't bear their feeling sorry for me and I felt ill at the thought of discussing Nick's lies. So I spent the day restlessly peering out from behind the closed drapes. A few reporters were lurking on the sidewalk; a few others huddled inside a car to stay warm. Now and then one of them would ring the doorbell and the servants would turn him away. They had given up by the time Harry returned, alone, near dusk. By then I was frantic and ran to meet him at the door.

"What happened?" I asked. "Is the painting still up?"

"No," he snapped, as if I had no right to know. "Don't ask questions, I'm handling this. Haven't you done enough?" He didn't even pause as he headed toward the stairs.

"Where is Will?" I asked, following him.

He didn't look back as he climbed the stairs, still wearing his coat. "He went to see your mother. I didn't want to be part of that conversation." His valet told me later that Harry went straight to bed and fell into a sleep so deep he didn't wake until ten the next morning. He woke with a dreadful cold that kept him in bed for a week.

I was picking at my solitary dinner that night when Will returned, looking drawn and somber, carrying the evening papers. We went into the sitting room, which now seemed haunted by the shadows of the night before.

"Harry won't tell me what's happening, he won't even speak to me. Please don't keep things from me. Where have you both been?"

"I've just come from Grand Central, sending Mother and the servants off to Newport."

"She didn't send them ahead to open the house? She must be furious."

"Not so furious at the moment. I'd say she's more concerned with not running into anyone she knows. She'll be furious later."

"What did she say?"

"She didn't send you a message."

Then Will told me what had happened that morning. He had

raced to the gallery and pounded on the locked door until Mark Haskell let him in.

"I saw that Harry and Haskell had taken down the painting, still veiled, so I pulled Harry aside and told him they had to put it back up, unveil it, and open the doors on schedule. He thought I'd lost my mind."

"How did you convince him?"

"Would you argue with an order from the district attorney? Do you want to hear the rest of the story or not?"

"Sorry, go on."

"We made up something for Haskell about not wanting to interfere with his business and helped him put the painting back. The drapery was still on when we did; we let him take care of that. Then Harry and I left and stood freezing on a street corner for half an hour until the place opened at ten."

"What did Harry say?"

"Nothing. Not a word. By ten, a handful of people were outside the door, waiting. We guessed they were reporters. Who else would be there so early in that weather? And I was pretty sure I saw at least one person with a camera, but there was nothing we could do at that point, nothing that wouldn't make things worse."

"Reporters?" I said slowly, in horror. "Photographers? Are you certain?"

"Oh, don't worry. A minute before the door opened we noticed a police wagon heading toward the rear entrance of the building." Will shook his head. "I've never seen anything like it. We ran to the back, and by the time we got there the police had Haskell and were loading the painting into the wagon, completely covered again. The whole thing couldn't have taken three minutes. Whoever made it into the gallery couldn't have seen much, if anything at all. We went around to the front again and saw some of the same people who had been outside, walking away. The police must have been in the gallery all along, before the doors opened. I don't know whether to be impressed or appalled. Whatever you said to your friend Sloane obviously worked."

"What will happen to Haskell?"

"Oh, he'll probably get off. He's already made bail. It's Leone they want. Here." And he handed me the evening papers, opened to the pages about Nick. "Artist Jailed on Obscenity Charge." That was what they all said more or less. "Lewd Painting Leads to Arrests."

The story wasn't front-page news even in the scandal sheets, and the respectable papers barely mentioned it. But there it was, complete with photographs of Nick being led away in handcuffs, between two policemen. When the police had found him in his room that morning, reporters and photographers had been waiting on the street, and for once I was glad they were. Those pictures showed Nick as he really was: the vicious smirk on his face revealed the monster who had so deceived me. I must say, in the middle of all that pain those smirking photographs gave me some satisfaction.

Still, the stories were upsetting. They said that Nick had yelled as he was taken away, "I am an artist! I am being persecuted!" In one paper the caption under his picture asked: "Artist or pornographer?"

"Artist or pornographer?" I yelled, outraged to think that anyone would believe him.

"You'd better get used to it," Will said, so abruptly that I flinched at his harsh words and he became more reassuring. "Don't panic, this is all going better than you think, better than I would have predicted. The police yelled back so reporters didn't hear what Leone said next. It's a good thing too. He said, 'Let them come after me with all their money and power. Let's see who wins.' It wouldn't have helped us if that had gotten into print."

"How do you know what he said? Were you and Harry there?"

"No, but I was told. Now you know everything I do."

"Who told you?"

"It doesn't matter. Are you all right? If you are, I think I'll slip out while I can and go home."

"Yes, I'll be fine. Are you? I can see this has been hard on you too." My dear Will had bags under his eyes and deep lines around his mouth. He looked as if he hadn't slept in weeks; he looked old, as if decades of experience had descended on him overnight.

"No good choices," he mumbled to himself, shaking his head.

"Are you sure you don't want to stay here?" I asked, although I couldn't imagine why he would. Our house seemed more like a mausoleum than Mother's. "Or at least let George drive you home?"

"I think George should drive me if you don't mind, I'm too tired. I'll get my car tomorrow."

"I'll call him right away."

"Yes, I've had a busy day," he said sarcastically, in a tone so unlike him. "I've rid society of a vicious pornographer and made the streets safe for the upright, chauffeured likes of us."

"You are tired, I'm worried about you. Can you take the day off tomorrow?"

He laughed bitterly. "I do believe you are an innocent, Caroline. Good night, little sister," he said, and he kissed me on the cheek as he walked out, leaving the papers behind. I looked at Nick's sneering face and read his words in print.

I thought of the words he had yelled that had not gotten into print. He was wrong about our money and power. As I had hoped, the arrest took things entirely out of our hands.

When Harry finally woke up, he was surprisingly useful.

During the week he spent in bed recovering from his cold, he slept and slept, which was just as well. The first afternoon, I tried to take him some soup and realized at once that I should leave the tray and go. He could hardly bear to look at me, much less have a conversation. I let the servants tiptoe in and out. I left him to himself. But I was aching to explain things.

And since he wouldn't let me near, I wrote him a love letter.

My darling Harry,

There will be time, so much time I hope in our long lives together, for me to convince you that I was innocent of any acts that might have embarrassed either of us. For now I simply want to tell you how dear you have always been to me, how blessed I am that you chose me, how I have treasured every minute of our married life. No other man could have made me as happy as you have, and whatever you are thinking now, you must know *that* much is true and can never change. My greatest joy has been in your arms.

I am yours, my beloved Harry, only yours, and always have been.

My deepest, undying love,

Caroline

I asked his valet to leave it under his pillow. Harry never mentioned the letter to me; for all I know he tore it up in a rage. But when he came out of his room a few days later, he wasn't glaring anymore. He didn't have much to say to me, but then he never had.

Will had rested and returned as his old lamblike self.

The three of us banded together. We needed to; in those next weeks the press went mad.

A photographer broke into Nick's studio soon after the arrest, and his paper ran a story under the headline "Artist's Love Nest: Exclusive Photos." There was a picture of the rumpled daybed, sheets tangled, two pillows next to each other. The story played up the most lurid lies, but there was just a passing mention of the most important news: when the police had searched Nick's studio and room for evidence, there was not a single painting or sketch, not a scrap of paper to be found in either place. No one seemed to know where his work had gone or why.

The police suspected a reporter or photographer had somehow gotten there first and stolen everything, but couldn't prove it. Frankly, I never thought that made sense. Wouldn't any paper have printed photographs of the work if they could? Nick might be hiding it all with a friend—he must have had some—but the landlords at both the studio and the house claimed they had seen no one coming or going overnight, no one skulking around. The police had taken the paintings from Haskell's gallery as evidence—all Nick's work that I owned was there, too—and that's what was left of his art. The papers called it "the mystery of the disappearing Leones."

That puzzle obviously didn't inspire their creativity nearly as much as the sex scandal. "The artist and his married, blue-blooded model trysted in this room, where he painted the sexually titillating portrait," one of them said. But the mystery of the artwork was what terrified me. The disappearance was so swift, so complete that it seemed to me Nick's paintings and sketches must have been taken by a very efficient person for a reason. The works were bound to turn up. Who could guess what new horrors would arrive when they did?

"We must find out what happened to them," I told Harry and Will, who calmly assured me, as they would again and again over the next months, that they were already looking into it, that I shouldn't worry, that they would take care of everything.

I knew they were trying to spare me. "You think you're protecting me by not discussing this," I told them one night at dinner. "But that only makes me worry more."

Harry may have stopped glowering, but he was still easily annoyed. "There's no point in discussing anything, Caroline. I said we'll take care of it and we will. Now leave it alone."

Evening after evening Will would join us for dinner, then he and Harry would go to his study to talk privately. I was never allowed to join them as they sat there thrashing out their plans to save my reputation.

I would knock on the door and bring whiskey or coffee, and they'd stop talking until I left. So I would take the Queen Anne side chair we had placed in the hall by a small table and quietly move it close to the study door. Sitting there, with my ear to the door, a book open on my lap, I learned a great deal.

Sometimes they veered away from the subject and didn't talk about my case at all; they discussed business and current events and sports, as if they were Victorian gents who'd retired for brandy and cigars after dinner.

But I did hear that Haskell insisted he had known nothing about the veiled painting, that Nick had somehow carried it in when Haskell had gone home to change clothes that night. He was willing to testify that he thought the work was salacious, and if he did that Larry was inclined not to prosecute him.

I heard Will coaching Harry on what to say to the publishers and editors who could be so useful to us. Harry should meet Gardiner and Robertson and his other friends for lunch at the club and make sure they understood that we had no control over Larry Sloane's prosecution. I heard Harry repeat after Will, "The district attorney has made his decision. We would have preferred that he let it rest and spare us any more notoriety. God knows, my wife has suffered enough already. But this is Lawrence Sloane's battle, not ours."

I overheard Harry ask, "Should we warn them against this Leone character too?"

"That's good," Will encouraged him. "If they give the story too much attention, they're falling into Leone's trap, giving him exactly what he wants. You can say something like 'I know you're too smart to be manipulated by him.' You're not telling them what to do, remember, you're dropping the idea into the conversation as if it's their idea, you're flattering them into doing what we want. And remind them that if they print anything sympathetic to Leone, they might antagonize the district attorney. That's even more important, Harry, don't forget to mention that. Sloane might be the next mayor, and your friends wouldn't want to cross him for the sake of some no-name artist trying to further his career. That's good, let's work on that." I was quite proud of my little brother's political instincts. He was learning so fast.

Without Will's script, it's difficult to imagine that Harry could have made anyone understand. He was good at hardheaded business deals, not subtle persuasion. And it wasn't as if these publishers could be bribed. But somehow dear Harry came through. The respectable papers were straightforward about the story as it went on. Even the friendly ones couldn't ignore it, but the headline in the *World*, Frank Gardiner's paper, read "Artist to Stand Trial for Obscenity." No mention of "trysts" or "society sex shenanigans" as there was in the tabloids. The *World* described the portrait as a "suggestive painting of a nude woman" without mentioning my name. And that was as it should have been. After all, the issue was pornography, not the model's identity.

Still, the gutter press was beyond hope. They assumed that I had posed shamelessly, that I had betrayed Harry and my family and my own good name. It was the only attitude that sold papers, so they had no interest in discovering the truth. And because there were no photographs of the portrait, the descriptions of it became more and more lurid. You'd have thought I was rolling in the mud with men, women, and sheep by the time some papers were finished with me. I half-expected to see a drawing of me doing just that, mud dripping off my gold-filigreed earrings.

I was amazed that the gossips had the nerve to go after me, their own lives were so shocking. Or maybe it was their low characters that made them turn to gossip in the first place. Either way, I learned a lot about them sitting outside Harry's study too. As it happened, Will's firm was handling a suit against a columnist known in print only as Samson—can you imagine a more ludicrous name?—who had been very hard on me. The suit had nothing to do with his column, it was a minor real estate issue, but the firm had hired a private detective who learned that Samson had been married three times and that each wife had suffered black eyes and broken bones. "It's irrelevant to the case, but it gives us some leverage," I heard Will say through the study door. "*They* know that *we* know." Will had never been much interested in scandalous rumors, but now scandal seemed to be everywhere.

Harry changed too. He suddenly showed a passionate interest in politics. He courted the people he had scorned, contributed to their campaigns, offered to support their favorite causes. Oh, I knew part of this was a way to shore up our damaged reputations, but even in his private conversations with Will he seemed obsessed with politics now. When I heard the two of them complaining about city corruption, as Larry had at that long-ago dinner party, I almost wept—those dreaded dinners seemed like paradise now. "Do you know what I learned today?" Will said, astonished. "For ten thousand dollars you can buy a judge. It's done all the time."

Harry whistled. "Stiff price. But I guess the going rate is the going rate." He may have grown more interested in politics, but he would always be a businessman first.

Sometimes I would grasp a single word—"statute" or "witness," "consultant" or "destroy"—and have no idea what they were referring to. It was frustrating to be left out, but I was pleased that Harry and Will were getting on so well. Harry, it seemed, was even confiding in Will about buying a racehorse. That may seem frivolous, but I could see that in this dark moment Harry was becoming more like his father. That was his version of reaching for a life preserver, and I found it strangely reassuring, a sign that there was a future. Will, who knew nothing about horses, was for once Harry's student.

"So no one in the racing world would think it's odd for you to buy this horse?" Will asked.

"Not at all. A horse is always a risk, and this one comes from a pretty good line."

"And what you're paying, that's what the whole thing should cost? No one will think you're overpaying?"

"It's a little high, but within reason."

"Okay, you know what you're doing, I say go ahead."

In those months, while we were waiting for Nick's trial to begin, we made a show of life going on as usual. Harry and Will went to their offices every day, and Harry was busier than ever managing Mother's companies; he wanted to make certain there would be no repercussions from the scandal.

Will took on new clients and had his first great success. He was named executor of the estate of a man who owned acres and acres of rich forestland, a huge vote of trust in someone so young. He seemed almost as proud of his smaller clients, though. One was a former bank robber who had served his time in prison and gone on to an honest life; now his three brothers were trying to deny him his share of the modest family house their father had left them. A onetime thief was not the kind of client I had envisioned for my brilliant brother, and I worried that my problems were hurting his career, but my ever-idealistic Will explained that he was happy about the case. "The man reformed. And even if he hadn't, he deserves to be treated fairly; it's his childhood home as much as theirs. Besides, he's paying us very well, and he's paying on time, which makes me look good with the firm."

The holidays came and went like bothersome obligations. Mother stayed in Newport out of season, refusing to take my call;

her embarrassed silence wasn't making it any easier for me. The Stephenses had fled the day after the opening too and planned to roam Europe for as long as they had to. Harry, Will, and I had a cheerless Christmas dinner and a New Year's Eve toast at home.

And with the New Year I decided to leave the house and go on with my life. That was my plan for survival. I resented the way Nick's betrayal had taken control of everything, and I refused to let him win by hiding any longer. I needed to feel I could hold my head up in the world.

Harry forbade me to go near what he called my "bad Bohemian influences," and Will cautioned me that I had to be more respectable than ever now. Well, I wasn't in a very social mood, so that wasn't hard. But I *did* have to leave the house, and I thought it was important to show that supporting artists hadn't been wrong. So I began visiting galleries quietly.

It was terribly unpleasant at first. I dressed demurely, in the dullest clothes I had, so no one would notice me. I had trouble finding such drab things in my closet. I retired from my wardrobe my favorite peacock blue coat and my purple cape with the fox trim, and had the seamstress copy a few old suits in the plainest brown and gray. Still, many people in the art world had known me before, and I could sense them pointing me out to those who hadn't. The first time a stranger in a gallery asked me about Nick's painting I was so unprepared I turned and ran out the door. But soon I became stronger.

Some people couldn't resist asking what the painting had really looked like. I learned to answer honestly, "I'm afraid I can't talk about it, it's too upsetting."

Even sympathetic strangers didn't know what to say. "All the great artists painted nudes," one dealer said. "You have nothing to be ashamed of."

"I have nothing against nudes, unless they misrepresent *me*," I told him. "But thank you."

"At least he didn't paint you with two noses and three breasts," he said, trying to recover.

"If only he had."

I went on buying whatever I liked, and sometimes bought work I didn't, just to help an artist who needed it. I gave more gifts than ever. But I made one new rule: I would never buy anything from anyone who was prepared to testify that what Nick had done was art. Those were the terms of the sale, and I made certain they were clear before I signed the check. I hired a business agent, at Will's suggestion, who negotiated for me. I had always done that myself; after all, I knew what art was worth. But it would have been impossible for me to speak Nick's name out loud, and just as impossible to think of supporting someone who might help him. The agent discreetly took care of that.

I had to step in only once. A moderately successful sculptor was indignant when my agent raised the question of whether he might testify for Nick and balked at this condition of the sale. I knew him slightly: pompous, middle-aged, the type that condescended to me, but genuinely talented. I arranged to meet him at his gallery without the agent to look at the piece I wanted to buy, a small, round bronze with a rough texture, like a distorted globe of the world. We looked at it together, and I told him how much I admired it, how strongly I felt that it belonged in my collection. "I have the perfect place for it, between two Brancusi Birds."

"But you would like me to say that Leone's painting is not art," he said angrily. "I cannot say that because unfortunately I have not been permitted to see it. I do not prejudge things. I cannot be told what to say. And I will not be censored under any circumstances. Even if I never sell another piece." Unlike most artists, he was suc-

cessful enough so he could afford that position, although he culti-
vated the untrimmed beard and shabby clothing of the impover-
ished.

"I'm very sorry if you've misunderstood," I said, trying to ignore my personal distaste for him. "I'm afraid my agent can be
clumsy sometimes. I'm not asking you to say anything. I simply
want some assurance that you will not appear in court or in the
newspapers saying the painting is art, that you won't speak out in
his favor. I'll be happy if you say nothing at all." I could see he was
about to argue, so I jumped in and explained what I rarely did.
"You see, I've been so betrayed," I told him. "To me it isn't about
the painting but about the deception and the malice. He did deceive
and use me. I'm sure you agree that's not what an artist should do."

"That doesn't mean the artist should be silenced."

"No one is being silenced, or not by me. I have nothing to say
about what happens to him, he's being prosecuted by the district
attorney. Please understand, it's just that I couldn't bear it if someone I had supported—a true artist whose work I admire as much as
I do yours—if that person took the side of a man who has treated
me so shabbily and hurt me so deeply. Who has betrayed his own
art as far as I'm concerned. This is very personal for me. And I do so
want you in my collection." I took his arm and walked him in a circle around the bronze globe on its pedestal. "I want to be able to
look at this every day. My agent has made some very good deals for
me, but I won't try to bargain with you. I know this work is un-
derpriced and its value is sure to increase quickly. Your reputation is
growing every minute." I offered him more money.

"You've never been interested in my work before," he said.

"That was my mistake. I am still learning, I hope. If you let me
have this piece, would you come and see it among the Brancusis?"

He asked for a bit more money, not much, just enough to make
him feel he had gotten the better of me. "Who can say what is art

and what is not?" he concluded as he shook my hand. I was quite happy with the deal and sent my agent around with the contract and a check the next day.

My collection grew enormously in those months; I didn't have much to do with my time except put on my drab clothes and go to galleries. I bought some things too rashly and sold many of them later for far less than I had paid. I'm not sure what ever happened to that distorted bronze globe. But the simple act of going ahead with my life was worth whatever it cost.

I made exquisite, valuable purchases then, too, on some good advice. I thought it might be useful to know a few critics, men who could point me in new directions. I was shy about approaching them, but they seemed happy to meet me. No one refused my invitation to lunch. We always met publicly, in a restaurant, because I worried someone might misunderstand a private invitation to my house—that is how cautious I had become, how concerned that I might be seen as a scarlet woman. I may have resented what the scandal had done to me, but I was realistic.

After lunch we might go to a gallery together. The critics opened my eyes as I'd hoped they would, and I bought work by many of their favorites. A few of them even became friends, often strange but delightful friends. One confided in me about his affair with an unhappily married woman. Everyone in the art world had known about the affair for years, but he had convinced himself no one knew a thing. I could only wonder if he'd told me this so-called secret because he assumed I was an unfaithful wife myself.

Another critic known for his savage reviews was such a teddy bear in person that he even looked like one—a balding teddy bear, with pudgy, rosy cheeks and round spectacles sliding down a button nose. He had a wealth of harmless gossip about the tangled romances of artists.

The one critic I could never bring myself to meet was Thomas

McLaughlin, who had praised Nick's painting and called it art. How could he look me in the eye?

I didn't mention the scandal to any of them—artists, critics, or dealers—and if someone brought it up, I replied with the simple truth. As time went on I was reassured by their kindness in treating me as if nothing had happened. I felt they had come to see that Nick had maligned and used me. The most influential people in the art world, at least, could see that.

If Nick had any supporters, they were so insignificant they couldn't even raise his bail. Since the works in his studio had vanished and the paintings in the Haskell exhibit were being held as evidence, he had nothing left to sell. So for five months Nick sat in the Tombs waiting for his trial to begin while his family in Pennsylvania tried to scrape together money for a cut-rate lawyer to defend him.

Even though we had nothing to do with the prosecution or trial, Larry was as good a friend to me as he had promised, and he kept me informed about his case against Nick. We didn't want there to be any mistaken hint of favoritism—he was as principled and independent in this case as in any other—so he would sneak into the house for our talks late at night, when the servants were in bed and Harry deep into his implacable sleep. Larry was generous with his time, but I don't think he minded. He was working enormously hard and seemed to enjoy relaxing and telling me about his day.

I would have the cook leave a cold midnight snack in my private sitting room. She must have known I wasn't eating and drinking all that alone, but I've always been generous to the staff—and kind, I hope—and they've been loyal. Still, we were so discreet that I would creep down the back stairs and open the door for Larry myself. In my rooms he would take off his jacket and shoes, loosen his tie, and stretch out on the black velvet settee while I brought him a drink. He was so tall his legs fell over the edge. I often wished I could paint or draw so I could have captured that comic image, I found it so cheerful and masculine and appealing in my little room.

Sometimes we didn't mention the case at all. At other times he would tell me what I was sure Will already knew: that Larry's office was lining up strong witnesses against Nick, including experts who saw no artistic value in the painting. They would discredit it, placing it in a completely different category from Ulysses or any other true work of art that had been dragged into court.

"And when do you expect I'll have to testify?" I asked one night as I was pouring him more champagne.

Larry sat straight up, his stockinged feet back on the floor, and looked at me in shock. "Why in the world would you testify? I thought you wanted to stay out of it."

"But I have to get up there and tell my story. That's the point."

"It is? Have you discussed this with Will and Harry?"

"It isn't up to them. I know what I'm doing. It's very important to me to do this."

"It would be a circus, darling. You can't want that."

"We can't help the circus part, can we? I have to be heard, in court under oath. I want all the papers there, I need them to hear that I didn't pose for that painting. It's the only way to correct all the horrible lies they've written about me. I thought you understood that."

"But there's no need for you to testify, Caroline. In fact, it's better if you don't. We need the issue to be obscenity, not you. I thought we agreed on that."

He looked confused, and I was dismayed. "I can't believe how we've misunderstood each other," I said, sitting by his side without touching him. We stared at each other, and the space between us seemed cavernous.

"Surely you can see why I need to do this," I told him.

"I can see what you're saying, but I think you're wrong. And there's no legal reason."

"There must be one. Besides," I said, as I stood and walked to the window, "why would you even come here to tell me what's going on if it has nothing to do with me?" I stood looking out the window for long minutes. He knew how much this mattered to me. He knew about the empty space where Nick's silvery painting of his house had stood, a space I superstitiously refused to fill until the trial was over. Hanging another work there now would be like putting a tiny bandage on a gaping wound.

Finally I heard him put his champagne glass on the table. Then he was standing behind me, his hands on my shoulders as he whispered in my ear, "We'll think of something if it's that important to you."

"It is," I said, turning to face him. "I knew you wouldn't let me down."

Because I had seen the portrait, if only for a flash, Larry decided I could testify that it had been publicly displayed and had caused great distress to those who had seen it. My guests and I, upstanding pillars of the community, considered it obscene, a blatant and shocking affront to our moral standards. That was what the law cared about, he warned me; the fact that I had not posed for Nick would be harder to get in.

"But he said it was the truest work he'd ever done, he dedicated it to me, everyone heard him."

"He's not charged with defamation, he's charged with obscenity. If you talk about whether you posed or not, the judge may well decide it's not relevant—or worse, decide you're involved. At the very least he might prevent more questions on the subject and strike what you say from the record."

"Then I'll have to talk fast. I don't care about the court record, I just have to let the reporters hear me say it." It wasn't a perfect plan, but I felt I could make it work.

Larry himself helped prepare me during our comforting nights in my sitting room.

I had moved the Queen Anne chair from the hall and sat there as if on the witness stand while he paced back and forth, playing the parts of all the attorneys. At first I was a disaster, talking more to my loyal friend than to a courtroom of strangers.

"How do you feel about Nicholas Leone?" he asked, playing Nick's lawyer.

"I despise him, I feel betrayed by him," I said honestly.

"No," Larry corrected me. "You mustn't sound angry. You have no personal feelings for him at all, you never did."

"Of course not. I see."

"You must be as calm as I am now," he said evenly. "You're baffled by his ungrateful response to a patron. Now: What were your feelings for Nicholas Leone on the night of the opening?"

"Are they really going to ask me that?"

"Maybe, who knows? If they're smart they'll try to suggest you're testifying to get back at him—not an absurd possibility, if you don't mind my saying so. Most of all, I want you to be prepared for anything. If you're going to say the wrong things, I want it to be now, not later. Understood?"

"Yes, thank you for that. You're a dear."

"And try to forget I'm Larry for a minute."

"Now why would I want to do that?"

"Caroline."

"I'm sorry. I'll be serious."

He walked away, then turned to face me again, and I wondered if the lawyers could possibly look into my eyes as fiercely as he did when he asked, "What was your relationship with Nicholas Leone?"

"I was his patron," I said calmly.

"That's better, but it's too vague. You have to say something like 'I helped him with small gifts of money to support his work, as I had for many other artists.' Will can help you with the precise language. Memorize it. I don't want you to be thrown by anything."

I took a deep breath and tried to stay calm, but as he went on my stomach became more knotted; every one of his questions seemed to cloak some nasty accusation.

"Have you ever posed nude for Leone?"

"No."

"Seminude?"

"No."

"Have you ever posed nude for anyone else?"

"Anyone else? What do you mean?"

"Anyone *else?*"

"No! No one! And I never posed for Nick. He doesn't even paint people!"

Larry smiled. "That's true, he doesn't."

"And I thought you weren't Larry anymore?"

I got up from the Queen Anne witness stand and walked toward him. "This will be all right, won't it?" How could I have been so rattled?

"It will be fine, we're just beginning. We'll have to meet often in the next weeks to get you ready, though. Once the trial starts it will be too risky for me to sneak in here, even late at night."

"Not at all?"

"I'm afraid not."

"What will I do without you?"

"What will I do without you is the question. But we have to be careful."

"Then you must come every night from now on."

"And when the trial starts, you know I'll be thinking of you every minute. We'll celebrate together when it's over, just the two of us."

I would have been lost without him.

Of course, Harry and Will were appalled when I said I wanted to testify against Nick. I told them when the three of us were together, hoping at least one of them might understand.

"It's just as bad as if you'd sued," Harry yelled. "Just as public. They'll tear you *and* the Stephens name to shreds."

"They may try, but they won't succeed. I can handle this," I said coolly.

"I suppose you can. You should have been an actress," he snarled. "But that doesn't mean it's a good idea. I won't allow it."

"Well, I'm going to do it." I turned to Will. "What should we do next? I suppose you could call Larry Sloane and offer me as a witness?" I didn't tell them he had already agreed; this conversation was difficult enough.

"Harry's right. There's no need for you to expose yourself to any more mudslinging. And legally I can't imagine Larry will need you."

"He found a way to charge Nick, didn't he? I think he can find a way to use me now."

My dear Will seemed tortured, torn between his idealistic legal conscience and his desire to save me.

"You keep trying to twist the law, like it's some, some—toy or a piece of taffy. I don't like seeing anyone do that, least of all you," he said in unmistakable distress. "Or, least of all me helping you."

"Isn't Nick the one twisting the law? He's the one hiding behind it. He's trying to use it to justify his malice."

"Oh, Caroline, I'm tired of this conversation. You know better."

"And you know I would always defend honest artists, which he is not."

"When Leone is convicted, you'll be vindicated," Harry said, as if his saying so could settle things. "Leave it at that. You don't have to be any more a part of this mess than you already are."

"I *won't* be vindicated, don't you see? If he's convicted, then everyone will say he painted an obscene portrait *of me!* I have to swear in court that he didn't, that it wasn't me."

"And what pretext is Sloane supposed to use to get you on the stand, Miss Legal Scholar?" Will asked.

"Would you please do one favor for me and ask him? Call him tomorrow and ask if it makes sense for me to testify against Nick. If he says no, I'll accept that."

He looked skeptical. "Do you know something I don't?"

"Oh, Will, please, just ask him. It *is* his case."

Harry snorted, and I ignored whatever that was supposed to mean. "Let's talk about something else for a change," I said.

I didn't like keeping secrets from Will, but just as he felt he was protecting me by not dwelling on the sordid details of the case, I was protecting him by not burdening him with the knowledge of my secret meetings with Larry.

"Society Sex Trial Begins Today," the morning tabloids said.

"Sex-Crazed Artist's Day in Court."

The herd of reporters and photographers waiting outside our house were wasting their time. We all agreed I would be most effective—and seem least concerned with the outcome—if I stayed away from the trial. I would not leave the house again until the day I was to testify. Larry had made his last visit a few nights before and given me a delicate pearl bracelet to wear for luck.

Will would be in the courtroom every day—the only way we could be certain to know what was going on—far in the back, as inconspicuous as he could make himself. He would relay everything to Harry and me. They could no longer even try to protect me from the vicious words that were about to be spoken.

Will had already turned up some encouraging bits of news, though. The judge we had been assigned, Thomas Cunningham, was so new, this was only his third case; he was impossible to predict. He was relatively young, and at first Will worried that he might be inclined to see Nick as a harmless libertine, but he did some research and discovered that Cunningham had once been a member of the Society for the Suppression of Vice. He had fought especially hard against sending obscene books through the mail.

To prosecute Nick, Larry had chosen David Everett, one of his most experienced assistant D.A.'s. Will said we couldn't have done better if Larry had tried the case himself, which he was practically doing offstage. Nick's lawyer was someone named Michael Linder, whom no one had ever heard of. Will learned that he scrambled for business and in the last year had defended a few prostitutes and lost. Still, he warned me over and over, nothing was certain.

Late that first afternoon poor Will braved the photographers outside the courthouse and at home to bring word back to Harry and me. The papers didn't consider him important enough to use the pictures, but it was unpleasant for him anyway. As he walked to our door, reporters yelled questions that he politely turned away:

"How do you think it's going so far?"

"Has Caroline visited Nick in jail?"

"Is it true your sister left the country so she won't have to testify?"

When he was safely inside and settled down, he told us, "It shouldn't last much more than a week. Linder is very young, and I've never seen anyone so nervous. He sweats like a stevedore. Don't get too confident, though. That doesn't mean he isn't clever."

"How did Nick look?" I asked, and Will and Harry both stared at me suspiciously. "What I meant was, does he look worried or does he look arrogant? We want him to be smirking and hateful, don't we? That will help."

"He looked diminished," Will said. "All his hair has been cut off, and he looks gaunt, as if he's been sick."

"Guilt make him lose his appetite?" Harry asked, and they laughed together at his decline.

"Caroline's right, though, it's not good for us if he looks too ill. We don't want him to get any sympathy."

"I thought that didn't matter since it's not a jury trial," Harry said.

"I'm still worried about him getting on the stand." Even now they sometimes talked around me.

"Did he have supporters there?" I asked.

"Not that I could see. He didn't seem to have any family or friends in the room."

That, to me, was the most satisfying turn yet.

In the next days Will came and went, calmly bringing news. Harry was trapped in the house with me, and his bad temper grew, even when the word was good: Judge Cunningham ruled that all spectators, including reporters, would have to leave the courtroom when the painting was shown. The papers complained bitterly, to Cunningham and in print. The judge himself wasn't exempt from their slurs. A reporter caught Linder as he was leaving the courthouse and asked, "Do you think Cunningham is keeping the portrait hidden for his private pleasure?" Linder was foolish enough to answer, "I don't know," and the exchange appeared in several papers, one under the headline "Has Caro Caught Cunningham's Eye?" But he never wavered from what he said in court: "If Mr. Leone is found not guilty, then his painting can be shown anywhere. While that is in dispute, the painting will not be on public view in my courtroom."

There were setbacks in the papers. The *Evening Graphic*, the foulest of all, created a drawing of me—or a woman who might have been my evil twin—with flowing hair and a lascivious grin, wearing my long pearls and three fig leaves. "More modest than in life," the caption read.

"Can they do that?" I asked Harry.

"Of course they can," he snapped. "That rag is beyond our reach. Complain and they'll do something worse."

But in court, Larry's prosecutor was creating a powerful case against Nick. I longed to see this firsthand and quizzed Will so relentlessly that he said I was like a child wanting to hear the same bedtime story over and over. "Tell me again, Will, tell me the one about Mark Haskell in court."

Haskell, who had not been charged after all, had been an especially convincing witness against Nick. On the stand he sounded self-assured and wore an expensively tailored suit that made him look far more successful than he really was. The small-time art dealer appeared to be a prosperous, well-established businessman. I could guess at Larry's good advice working behind the scenes and maybe Harry's checkbook at the tailor's. On the stand, Haskell recalled how surprised he had been when he returned to the gallery an hour before the opening and saw that Nick had somehow snuck in and hung a veiled canvas he refused to let him see. "In my fifteen years as an art dealer, I have never handled, and never would handle, a work so indecent," he testified.

During the cross-examination, Linder said, "It's a large painting. Wouldn't the defendant have needed help getting it in and hanging it?"

"I suppose he could have done it on his own somehow. I have no idea how he did it. All I know is that he was alone in the gallery when I arrived and the painting was up."

"So you exhibited a painting you had never seen?"

"Accidentally, yes."

"And did you ask him about this?"

"Of course. I was angry that he had made a change without my knowledge, but he refused to let me see it and then the guests arrived. If I had known what was behind that veil, I would have turned them away and shut the exhibition down."

Three prominent dealers, including one known for handling avant-garde artists, also appeared as expert witnesses. "I could probably retire tomorrow if I handled that kind of vulgarity," one said. "But I would never be considered a respectable dealer again."

There was devastating testimony from art critics who saw genuine if minor artistic expression in Nick's other work but found no merit in the portrait.

Larry had even found some artists who had been at the opening that night and who testified that they found the painting unfit for public display, offensive by even the most tolerant social standards.

Finally it was my turn. The night before, Will made one last attempt to talk me out of it. "Things are going very well, they don't need you, Caroline. Everett will agree not to call you if we ask him. I don't think you can imagine what you'll be walking into. It will be hell. Don't put yourself through it."

But I knew what I was doing. I was ready.

The morning of my appearance in court I put on the little pearl bracelet and a simple cream-colored suit that Larry had approved weeks before; the early May weather was much cooler than we'd expected, but I wore it anyway. Harry led me through the reporters and photographers gathered outside our door as we dashed to the car. I put on a calm, impassive face, remembering not to roll my eyes or grimace or make any other expression that the cameras could freeze and distort to make me look like a madwoman. Beneath that mask I was smiling and confident.

The feeling didn't last long.

George drove us to pick up Mother and Will so we could take the long drive downtown together and walk into the courthouse united. Mother still hadn't spoken to me since the night of the opening. Will finally got her back from Newport by convincing her that if I failed to restore my good name, hers would be lost as well, that it would help save us both if her social set knew she believed in me.

Now, as George held the car door for Mother to step in, I was horrified to see that she had dressed for a funeral, in heavy black, the net veil from her hat covering her face down to her chin. Behind her, Will was insisting she turn the veil back.

"But I'll be seen," she said.

"Yes, and you will look as if you have nothing to be ashamed of," he said sternly, as if he were the parent.

She glared at me as they sat facing us and said, "But I *am* ashamed."

Harry and Will yelled together so I could hardly distinguish their voices: "Don't upset Caroline!" and "Be quiet!" Mother looked astonished. I couldn't tell if she was more amazed that they had spoken to her that way or that they agreed about something. She had obviously missed a great deal while hiding away.

"You're far too worried about me," I told them. "After what I've been through, this will be nothing." They looked at me warily. "Believe me, I'm fine."

Now that it was too late to turn back, Harry was unexpectedly sweet. He sat close to me and held my hand all the way downtown, squeezing it as we passed the corner of Thirteenth Street, where the nightmare had started. I instinctively looked in the direction of the gallery, then felt ridiculous. What did I expect to see? Crowds of people burning me in effigy? A large scarlet C in the sky? When I turned back to Harry, he was staring straight ahead.

Will kept chattering to Mother about her friends and what she had missed while she was away, anything to distract her from me.

I settled back and thought of that long, snowy drive on the night that had brought us all here, about all the naïve hopes I had carried with me as I headed out into the blizzard. What a fool I had been.

In all the months since, I'd managed to concentrate on the present, but now Nick's smile and his promise—"I did all this for you"—came drifting back to me, just when I should have been rehearsing my testimony one more time. I saw his smile, full of warmth, as he said, "For you. To repay you." I was astonished to realize how quickly we had arrived at the courthouse.

George was pulling over as close as he could to the front entrance, where reporters and photographers began shouting and pushing toward the car. The courthouse, its classical frieze and pillars designed to create a sense of import and grandeur, seemed miles away, set back from the street at the top of an enormous stone stairway we would have to climb. The crowd of men jostling each other to get the best view created a frightening obstacle course between me and the cool, reasoned justice that waited inside that building.

As we had arranged, Will and Mother got out first, forging a path through the crowd. Harry took my arm, and we walked resolutely toward the steps as voices screamed questions all around us:

"Mrs. Stephens, where have you been?"

"Mrs. Stephens, do you know where the lost Leone paintings are?"

"Caroline, do you miss Nick?"

Slowly we made our way ahead, and Harry told them, "We have nothing to say right now. My wife will be testifying, and she will clear everything up in court." I was terribly proud of him and with a rush of affection remembered how safe Harry had once made me feel. I squeezed his arm.

The reporters followed us inside, yelling all the way down the hall until we finally arrived at Room 315, already so packed we had to fight our way through. As we walked toward the front, I heard voices begin to rise and glimpsed people pointing at me; I ignored it all as I sat on a bench between Harry and Will.

The room was exactly as Will had described it, so I should have been prepared. But after the glowing sense of justice I'd felt shining from the building's façade, after the excruciating climb up the stairs toward the truth, this room was a startling letdown. It was square and dreary, windowless, with heavy, unpolished wooden tables. The ancient paint on the walls had faded to a dull gray. High on one wall was a large mural of Hudson Bay, darkened by dirt and age. On the opposite wall was another mural, of Blind Justice holding her scales; her diaphanous white robe, covered with grime, struck me as such a bad omen that I quickly turned my head away—and saw Nick.

Will had warned me not to look at him. Ignoring him would prove he was beneath contempt, and would avoid suggesting any personal connection. I was to look directly, sincerely, respectfully at Judge Cunningham at all times. But the judge had not arrived yet and Nick had. I stared straight ahead again, but from the corner of my eye could see the back of his head, the blond hair so short it was practically shaved off. He was wearing a dark gray suit I recognized as his best, but it hung loosely around his shoulders now. As he turned to look into the crowd, perhaps searching for me, I almost gasped at how he had changed. Even in my sideways glance I saw a man who was ashen and gaunt. Will was right: he looked as if he had been ill, unable to eat, barely able to drag himself from his sickbed. I wondered if his patchy-looking hair had actually been falling out. He looked as if he'd been suffering greatly; I must confess, I thought he deserved it.

Then we all stood as Judge Cunningham entered, and soon Everett called his first witness of the day, one of Haskell's artists who had been at the opening. When Nick's lawyer stood to cross-examine him, I saw what Will had meant about Linder and why this slight young man was so outmatched. His youth was the least of his problems. He created an aura of desperation even before he spoke. His suit was shiny, his shoes were run down at the heels, and he needed a haircut. During Everett's questioning, he had sat at the defense table shuffling papers as if he had misplaced his lines for the school play, and when he stood, one sheet attached itself to his sweaty palm. I was certain he was far more nervous than I would ever be.

Before long I heard my name, Will squeezed my hand, and I walked toward the witness stand. As I did, I caught sight of the sooty murals, warning me that the pristine justice I had expected might have vanished from this room long ago. I breathed deeply and reminded myself how important it was to be calm.

But it was one thing to rehearse with Larry in my cozy sitting room and another to face this crowd. As I raised my hand and swore to tell the truth, I saw all those people crammed together on the benches and standing in the back of the courtroom, staring at me as if they were a vaudeville audience waiting to be entertained; I was the act they'd been waiting for. I felt like crawling under the seat and hiding until I could be rescued, but all I could do was sit with my hands folded in my lap as they scrutinized me. I looked ahead and waited for Everett to ask his questions. When I began to answer, the judge told me to speak louder.

I had never seen Everett before that day, but he was obviously a gentleman, someone I might have met socially. His matter-of-fact, poised manner put me at ease. There were no surprises from him and no objections from Linder as I described my role as a patron of artists and of Haskell's gallery. In a temperate voice that would have made Larry proud, I told of my shock and distress, as well as the distress of the others in the room, when the painting was unveiled.

"You fainted as soon as you saw it, didn't you, Mrs. Stephens? How much could you have observed?" Everett asked.

"I fainted *almost* at once, but before that I saw the painting all too well. And I heard cries and shouts in the room. I saw a man take a woman by the shoulders and turn her away from the painting. The reaction was unmistakable. I saw it all before I fell."

"You had invited friends to join you at the opening?"

"Yes."

"Is this what you expected them to see?"

"No, not at all. I was upset and embarrassed."

"Why embarrassed?"

"Because it was shocking to see such an offensive image in a public place. I would never have invited people to see such a thing had I known."

Everett was through quickly; he only needed me to prove that the painting had violated acceptable standards. That was the easy part. I still had to face Linder—disheveled, sweaty-palmed Linder, I reminded myself, hoping he would be inept enough to help me make my case.

"Mrs. Stephens," he began, in a voice that seemed several octaves higher than it had before. When I heard that squeaky voice, I had to stifle a wave of nervous laughter. I pretended I was in my sitting room with Larry, on my Queen Anne chair, shielded from the nasty world outside.

Linder asked a few innocuous questions about my support for artists, and I repeated what I had already said. Then he took a deep breath and asked, in a sneering, sarcastic voice, "What is your personal relationship with Nicholas Leone?" and he swirled to point at Nick as if to make me look at him.

As surprised as I was by his change in tone and his theatrical gesture, I did not look. I would not let this scruffy creature—this man who was defending Nick!—unnerve me. I continued to look at Linder as I answered, "I have no personal relationship with him."

"What *was* your relationship with him on the night the exhibition opened?"

"It was professional. As I said, I had given him some financial support so he could paint, as I had done for dozens of other artists."

"But you were personal friends, isn't that right?"

"We were professional acquaintances."

"You paid the rent on his studio, didn't you? Did you do that for any other artist?"

"Yes, that is, I gave artists stipends. They could do what they judged best with the money."

"How many artists did you help?"

"I'm not sure. At least fifty, maybe more."

"You don't know? Don't you have records of those gifts?"

"My secretary does."

"And all your gifts to Mr. Leone were recorded by your secretary?"

"Yes, like any other."

"Didn't you sometimes give him personal gifts or money?"

"No."

"Not even a small gift, something he might need? Clothing? A winter coat?"

"Nothing."

"You visited him alone at the studio often, didn't you? Let's be clear—that's the studio we've seen pictures of in the papers, with his art supplies and a bed?"

Everett finally objected, but even as he was standing to speak I had quickly and adamantly said "No!" shaking my head at Linder's misleading suggestion about my visits. I had not visited Nick in the way he was implying.

Judge Cunningham asked, "Where are these questions going, Mr. Linder?"

"Your Honor, I would like to establish that by contributing to the production of the painting, as its patron, she was tacitly admitting it *was* a work of art."

"Then do that," the judge said. I looked straight at Linder and prepared myself. He was trying to implicate me in my own disgrace, but I knew that could give me the chance I needed.

"You and Mr. Leone presented the exhibition together, didn't you?"

"Mark Haskell, the gallery owner, presented it."

"But you helped choose the works to be shown?"

"I was not consulted on one in particular," I said impulsively, and the courtroom laughed. I hadn't meant for that to happen, of course, and it frightened me. I looked at the floor, embarrassed at the laughter, but remembered Larry's advice and held my head up again. Look ahead, stay calm, it's almost over, I told myself.

"You helped choose the work to be shown?" Linder repeated.

"The final decision about what to display was Mr. Haskell's," I said. "Because I had contributed some financial support, I was kept informed."

"Informed."

"Yes."

"Didn't you even discuss with Mr. Leone the possibility of showing the portrait of you?"

"Me? No, it isn't me!" I cried, my composure vanishing in the face of that awful accusation—not an accusation, an *assumption*. "I didn't even know that vile thing existed, how could I have known he was planning to show it?"

"Not you? You didn't know it existed?" he said, his voice dripping with scorn and disbelief.

"No."

"Everyone says it's you. It looks like you. It's wearing your earrings. You gave him money. How can it not be you?"

"It's not me, it's a lie, I never posed for him, not in any way," I said, as vehemently and as truthfully as I had said it in private to those I loved the most. I could feel my face turn red as my eyes began to tear, but I blinked and stared ahead. The crowd was quiet, staring; the reporters were scribbling. I didn't dare look toward the bench where I knew Will and Harry were sitting. I tried not to imagine their pained faces. I was so upset that I didn't hear Linder's next question.

"Did you hear me, Mrs. Stephens?" he was saying.

"No, I'm sorry, I didn't," I said, calmly wiping away a tear.

"I asked, what would have been so wrong about that? Posing for a nude portrait? There is a long tradition of artistic nudes."

As distraught as I was, I grasped the opportunity to say everything I had to, speaking without pause so I wouldn't be stopped. I raced ahead with the passion of someone speaking to save her own life. "This is not a classical nude, it is not a work of art at all. The woman in the painting is doing something obscene, that painting is clearly *meant* to be me, but it's not, it is *not*, I never posed for him. That is not a portrait, it is not art, don't you see? It's a vicious attack on me, on my reputation, he invented it." The judge was telling me to be quiet, someone was objecting, but I couldn't stop. "He never painted human figures, it's all a lie, something he invented to hurt me when all I did was try to help him." I heard a gavel and more voices, but they were all a swirl and I just spoke louder. "He lied, it's not true, I would *never* have posed in such a way, *never*, I *couldn't*." I began to sob and looked down toward the floor. And as I did I heard myself say, very softly and sadly, the one thing I had not meant to say at all: "I don't know why he did it."

There was a subdued murmuring in the room when I stopped speaking. I looked out into the crowd again and thought that even the reporters seemed chastened, though they kept scribbling furiously. I couldn't tell if I was only seeing what I wanted to see.

The judge banged his gavel, and I turned to look at him, expecting some reprimand. "Do you need to take a break, Mrs. Stephens?" he asked gently.

"No, thank you so much, Your Honor, I'm fine."

Linder was through. I was excused. I left the courthouse with Harry's arm around me, sheltering me as we forced our way again through the throng of reporters and photographers. Will stayed behind in court, while Harry and I drove away with Mother.

As I sat between them in the car, she patted my hand. "Well, dear," she said. "I know that was difficult. And you must need a good hot bath and a nap. But you need your strength too. Why don't you two come and have luncheon with me before you go home? I'll have Mary prepare anything you like." And even though going to Mother's and then back home would give the photographers one more occasion to catch me, I agreed at once.

"Thank you, Mother," I said. "I'm so sorry." I put my head on her shoulder and cried quietly as she patted my hair.

That's when I knew we had won.

When the evening papers arrived, I was even more certain. The last thing the gossip rags wanted was to lose their tawdry scandal, but even the lowest of them were reporting that sentiment had turned in my favor. They printed photographs of me looking dignified as I walked into court. The headlines said, "Caroline Denies Affair," "Caroline Weeps, 'Portrait a Lie,'" and "Caro to Nick: Why Did You Hurt Me?" They described me as "a moving and sympathetic witness." They called my testimony "tearstained and emotional" and said, "Spectators who had packed the room to hear more sizzling details about the love affair were surprised by her heart-wrenching testimony that she had been wronged."

I even got past my distress at the rag that wrote, "Nick stared lewdly at his Caroline." It only made him look worse.

A more respectable paper wrote, "At the obscenity trial of Nicholas Leone today, Mrs. Harrison Stephens testified against the defendant, an artist she once encouraged. In November, Mrs. Stephens fainted when Leone's allegedly obscene portrait depicting her was revealed. Today she wept on the stand as she testified that she had not posed for the painting and had not had a romance with the artist. She portrayed him as a professional acquaintance who repaid her kindness with malice and deceit. Leone, who had been subdued and serious throughout the trial, became agitated during Mrs. Stephens's testimony. He glared at her, shaking his head and sneering as if to refute her." I hadn't given a thought or a glance to Nick while I was on the stand, so that was good to know.

The trial lasted just two more days. Will said Linder presented a shockingly weak defense, even for someone with his limited abilities. He read Thomas McLaughlin's positive review from the Chronicle into the record, which Will was not happy about, but he wasn't especially worried. "It's one respected opinion against a dozen equally respected opinions on the other side. And it's not as convincing as if McLaughlin had turned up in person."

"Why didn't he?"

"He's abroad. Has been for a while. Linder hasn't really been on top of things."

I had been steeling myself for the lies Nick would tell when he got on the stand. It was a painful exercise, trying to imagine the worst he might say, and always futile. How could I begin to predict the lies he was capable of inventing, when I could hardly fathom the evil he had actually done? And he looked so changed. The Nick I knew would have been seductive and charming on the stand; this wan, strange Nick was dangerously unfamiliar. I wondered if there was a way for me to be called back as a witness after him, to counter what he would say, but I couldn't risk trying to contact Larry.

And in the end Nick didn't testify. Will said it was a curious legal move. "They had nothing to lose at that point." Harry said, "Don't look a gift horse in the mouth." I didn't tell them what I thought: he had decided not to testify because he couldn't manage the performance. Sick and weak, he must have known he would reveal himself as a fraud and a liar. Around the courthouse, Will had heard ridiculous rumors that Nick hadn't testified because he had been bought off by people working for Harry and me. As if we would have consented to give him another dime. But those rumors never made it into the papers. Linder, after all, was obviously inept; no one expected his defense to make sense.

Everett's closing argument was powerful, Will said, and the papers agreed. It was framed around a memorable line they all quoted: "Art is the truth, and that painting is a lie." He'd hammered away at the idea that Nick was a "corrupting moral influence." Linder's rambling response couldn't touch it.

The day Judge Cunningham delivered his verdict, I was at home with Harry waiting for Will to telephone from the courthouse. Harry took the phone so he could break the news to me. I could see from his face—a mere touch of relief, a relaxing of the tense grimace that had become his perpetual expression—that it was good. "Thanks, yes, see you soon," he said, then turned to me and said flatly, "Guilty. Sentencing in six weeks."

"What else did he say?"

"That no one seemed surprised."

"What else?"

"Nothing."

The doorbell kept ringing with reporters looking for comments, and though we were tempted, we knew it was best to remain aloof, to keep insisting this was not our fight. No one really saw it that way. One headline even read, "Caroline Cleared," as if I had been on trial. Which of course, in a way, I was.

We had triumphed, but no one felt like celebrating that night. We had plenty of champagne in the house, but no one suggested calling for any. We sat at the dinner table saying little—I hadn't even asked Will how Nick had reacted—drained from the ordeal and unexpectedly depressed. We had been so absorbed by the trial; now it felt as if we were staring at some vast, unknown future instead of at the happy prospect of picking up our old lives.

That sleepless vigil on the night of the opening must have been on all our minds, because we resisted going to the sitting room, as we might have. We lingered over coffee at the table until I asked Will, "What will become of the painting?"

"It will be destroyed eventually; it's officially obscene. The police will keep it for a while in case there's an appeal . . ."

"What?" Harry sprang up from the table.

"Relax, it's a formality," Will said. "If Michael Linder was the best lawyer Leone could afford this time around, do you think he has money for an appeal? Or anyone to help him? The evidence will be kept under lock and key for a while, then destroyed."

"When it is, I want to be there," Harry said. "One of us has to witness it, that's the only way to be sure it's gone."

"Let me go, I want to," I offered, and they both looked at me with such horrified concern that I could see they thought this last twist had finally cost me my sanity. "I don't want either of you to set eyes on that deceitful painting ever again," I explained,

The truth was, I wanted to see it once more. As much as I dreaded doing it, I felt the painting held all the dark secrets I needed to uncover. I had always understood Nick through his work, and in that painting he had sent me a message—a devastating, painful message—one that I hadn't had time to decipher. If I could look at it again, maybe I would be able to see beyond it, see through it to grasp what had been in his mind when he had made it. I still needed to see why.

I couldn't expect anyone to understand that at the time. Harry was sputtering at the idea that I would go anywhere near "that hideous thing from the gutter" as he called it. And Will, always the soothing voice of reason, said, "I think by now we can trust Larry Sloane to make sure things are managed properly. When it's meant to be destroyed he'll see to that. It really is out of our hands now. We've won, let's be happy."

Only Will could make "be happy" sound so mournful, but I knew what he meant. So I finally called for champagne.

Nick was given the maximum prison sentence, one year.

"That's not very long," I complained when Will told us.

"It was the maximum. There's only so much even you can do," he said.

Two weeks later Harry and I sailed to Europe for a long, open-ended visit. He had left his business affairs in such sound shape that even Mother wasn't worried. Traveling alone with Harry had never been my idea of excitement, but it wasn't excitement we needed now. It was rest and anonymity. I was looking forward to walking out the door of our hotel without being stared at.

We didn't want it to appear as if we had skulked away in the night, though, shamed out of town. So a few days before we left, Harry and I hosted a very small dinner. We told our guests it was a bon voyage party, but it was really a signal that I was back in the world, that we were welcome in society again. Mother's old friend Mrs. Copley came with Mr. Davis the banker, Milly and Dan Stoddard came, two of the opera guild ladies and their husbands, and of course Mother and Will. No one had declined. I wanted to invite Larry and Barbara but that would have looked unseemly so soon after the trial. I telephoned him to explain, and he agreed. "We'll have to postpone our own celebration until you return," he said. The society page of the *Times* carried a small notice about the dinner with no mention of the scandal, which was just right. It seemed we were putting the entire ugly affair behind us.

But as the last pieces of clothing were being packed in our trunks, the day before we left, Will appeared with unsettling news from Larry's office, proof that Nick's cruel act could send out aftershocks even if he was in prison. Someone had broken into the storage room where trial evidence was kept; dozens of items were missing or destroyed. The guard had been found that morning, bound and gagged, apparently chloroformed by someone he never saw. The police hoped to keep the break-in quiet while they tried to recover as much as they could.

In the end, none of it ever turned up. The police suspected that the thieves were after some jewelry that had been stolen from a family vault, including a famous diamond-and-emerald bracelet; all the jewelry was gone. But they couldn't rule out the idea that the motive was to undermine a different trial. So much was destroyed—and so randomly, it seemed—that no one knew whether the jewels had been the actual target or simply an attempt to throw the police off the track. Some worthless phonograph recordings confiscated from a speakeasy had been smashed to pieces. Some forged checks that would have implicated a business-man in fraud had disappeared.

All of Nick's work was gone, either cut from the frames and missing, or slashed to pieces and left on the floor in tiny bits, beyond restoration. Among the shreds of Nick's paintings, they found a narrow, silvery sliver that I assumed was from the haunted house that had once hung in my bedroom. The portrait had been slashed from its stretchers; not a scrap of it was found.

Since Nick's trial was over and the portrait meant to be destroyed anyway, the police were not concerned with tracking it down. But Harry was. He worried for the rest of his life that it might surface; finding it became an obsession. He hired people to search across the country and in Europe. He discreetly offered a reward. For years he sought out the most disreputable dealers, hoping it would turn up. He had no taste or feeling for art, and I could just see poor Harry trying to describe that painting without seeming like a dirty old man. He was torturing and humiliating himself, and I tried so hard to discourage him for his own sake. "You'll never find it, it's gone," I reassured him. "If not we would have heard something. There's nothing more you can do." But he wouldn't listen. Sometimes I could tell when he had returned from another pointless visit to one more shadowy dealer. "It's got to be somewhere," he would say, shaking his head as if he still couldn't believe it had simply vanished.

He never found the portrait, but he did find and destroy a few of Nick's other paintings, early works Nick had sold even before I knew him. Harry didn't tell me that until much later, and it's just as well. Whatever I thought of Nick as a man, he was a dazzling artist, and I couldn't have agreed to destroy such brilliant work. Harry must have known that.

We were still abroad when Nick was released from prison; then he vanished too.

We were in Paris when I got the cable from Will telling us that he had married. I remember standing alone for what seemed like hours at our hotel window, staring across at the Tuileries. We had not been gone two months. How could he have done it without me?

Will had hardly known Rose before we left, and had not seemed interested at all. They had been introduced the year before by one of my old school friends, who told him they would make "a darling couple." Will mentioned her to me at the time and said she seemed awfully young, even prim—which coming from my proper Will made her seem positively Victorian—and that she didn't have much to say for herself. He saw her a few times, then quietly let it go. Of course, none of us had a real life after the scandal broke, we were all so caught up in dealing with it. So he must have seen her again soon after I'd left and made up his mind quickly. I had never even met her when they married.

As I stared at the gardens and the traffic on the rue de Rivoli, I suddenly saw myself back in my girlish bedroom on the night of my engagement party. I thought about Will's impassioned warnings to me that night, about his selfless, unquestioning support ever since. I wondered if I might have warned him against this hasty marriage if I hadn't been so far away. Such an impulsive move was so unlike him. And I wondered if he would have listened any more than I had.

His cable made him sound content, though, so I cabled back at once to Will and Rose that Harry and I were happy for them. I added that it was just as well Will hadn't given in to my pleading that he come along to Europe—I had tried because he deserved and needed a rest as much as anyone—or they might not have found each other. But privately I was fearful about his future with a woman he scarcely knew and had once found dull. I couldn't possibly express that fear to my own dull Harry.

And boredom with Harry was not always the worst of our time together. From the day we boarded the ship, Harry never mentioned the scandal, but I felt the subject always hovering between us. We went to London first, arriving unfashionably in August, and were thrown back on each other's company a great deal. We went to the theater, we strolled through Kensington Gardens, we passed the time and spoke about nothing that mattered.

By September we were in Paris and busier. We shopped, we walked on the Champs-Élysées, we were invited to elegant dinners. I was beginning to enjoy myself again. Then Will's cable arrived. I had rarely felt so alone.

That night I tried to talk to Harry about what had happened, or not happened, with Nick. The weather had turned warm, and we had dinner sent up to the suite, where a breeze came through the open windows. We were drinking our coffee, Harry was smoking a cigar, and we could see the evening lights sparkling across the city as darkness fell over the Tuileries. So many people happily in love under that romantic sky—well, I had long ago stopped expecting that for myself, but I would be sorry if Will had missed it.

We had been talking about Will, of course, deciding on a wedding present to send. Harry seemed carefree and relaxed, so I said, "You know, Will has assured me many times that he believes what I've told both of you about that painting. You never have. Do you have any doubts?" If he had even the slightest doubt, I wanted to explain once and for all that I was innocent. I was sure he blamed me for bad judgment, I deserved that. But I didn't know if he secretly held any suspicions about my dealings with Nick, and I wanted it all behind us.

He didn't let me say more. "The incident is over, Caroline," he broke in. "We will not speak of it again." He said it with a stiffness that led me to believe he had prepared his lines, just as I had prepared mine, had been expecting that moment to come. He was resolved and would not be budged.

So we did not speak of it again as we went on to Florence. Sometimes Harry trailed me to churches and listened as I chattered about the frescoes, and often he stayed behind drinking coffee in the piazzas. Then on to Rome for the winter (we never considered Venice). On New Year's Day 1929 we were in Rome; as festive as the scene was, we were ready to come home. We booked our passage. We had been away six months; it seemed like six years.

Will met us at the ship, alone. He knew I would want to talk. I hugged him and was delighted to see him looking happy and rested. But as soon as we were in the car, I asked what I had been burning to know: why had he married in such a rush?

He and Mother had both sworn in their letters that Rose was not expecting a child. By now everyone could see that was true, though Mother was still humiliated by the idea that people had assumed so at first. Will fumbled for an answer. "I had a hard time getting her to agree to move that fast, and it wasn't easy to plan a wedding and find a place to live in a month, but we were too eager to wait."

That didn't sound like my Will at all—impatient, eager, insistent?

"You might have wired us to come home. We could have made it in a month," I said.

"You needed the time away."

"Would you have been embarrassed to have us there?"

"Oh, Caroline, don't be silly."

"Then how could you have done it without me?" I asked.

"How could he have done it with you?" Harry mumbled, and Will changed the subject.

"We're going straight to Mother's if that's all right. She and Rose are waiting there," he said.

As soon as I met her I could tell that Rose was a sweet thing, as dear as Will, and she has stayed that way ever since. She had a constant, lovely little smile, blond curls, and a girlish voice. Her flowery dresses always reminded me of spring no matter what the season. She was good for Will and quite easy to be around. I liked her and soon got over my fears for the marriage, though she and I never had much in common.

I still saw Will often. We remained each other's closest confidants always, but of course things changed. And by the end of that year the world around us had changed so incredibly that my problems and Will's quick marriage seemed petty.

Many of our friends lost vast amounts of money when the market crashed. We lost some, though not very much. Harry got all of us—including Mother and Will and Rose—through the Depression in excellent shape. When things were back to normal, he made all of us even richer. He truly was some kind of idiot savant about money.

For years, though, poverty was everywhere around us. We did what we could privately to help friends who were hurt. We donated money to charities that ran soup kitchens and gave out clothing, but it seemed so little to do. That was when Will started the family foundation.

By the time the country bounced back, my little scandal had faded away to nothing. Harry and I traveled in the same circles as before; our friends were so polite that no one mentioned my ordeal, at least not to my face. And if, on occasion, I encountered someone indiscreet enough to bring it up, however sympathetically, I would respond with a blank stare as if I had no idea what they were talking about. Soon everyone knew it was a subject I would not discuss.

I went on collecting art, but the Museum of Modern Art and the Whitney had both been established in the meantime and were taking care of new artists, who needed me less than before. I had spent a lot of time looking at Old Masters while we were in Europe, and my taste was changing. That's when I sold many of the works I had bought so frenetically while waiting for the trial; even the ones I liked were reminders of a sad period, and I was happy to move on. Rembrandt became my new passion.

Soon after we returned from Europe, Larry Sloane showed up one afternoon unannounced, when he knew Harry would be at his office. He asked if we could go up to my little sitting room, but I thought we'd be more comfortable in the sitting room downstairs. He looked unhappy. "We need to talk privately," he said.

"I'll make sure the servants don't interrupt." I gave them instructions and closed the door. Almost as soon as I sat by the fire, Larry fell on his knees before me, put his arms around my waist and his head on my lap. He was ready to leave Barbara now, he said, she had agreed to a divorce. If I began proceedings against Harry on grounds of adultery—surely Harry would play along—we could be married within a year. If Harry resisted it might take longer, but we would be together soon. It wasn't a proposal or even a question. He acted as if we had discussed this and were simply working out the details.

No such thing was true, and it was not at all what I wanted. Of course I didn't want to hurt Larry's feelings, either. He had been such a good friend to me. So I took his hands off my waist as I stood, walked a slight distance from him, and said as sincerely as I could, "My darling Larry, it will always mean so much to me that you asked. But you must see that anything between us is impossible, however much I might want it? Harry has stood by me, and I can never turn away from him." I walked to the door before he could say anything more and opened it. "Please stay for tea and be my dearest friend," I told him. "I want to catch up on everything you've been doing while we've been gone."

Larry did remain our friend through the years, Harry's and mine. He never left Barbara, and after she died he never remarried. He proposed to me again decades later, a few weeks after Harry died in '62. I always remained grateful to him. But I never stopped experiencing that moment of surprise when I saw him—the shock that he wasn't, after all, very good looking.

Besides, even if I could have left Harry, why would I have married someone who would bring to mind those terrible days? I settled into a comfortable life. My gifts to the Metropolitan Museum were not anonymous, but I insisted they be handled without fanfare. The last thing I needed or wanted in my life was more public scrutiny.

I've sometimes wondered if I brought on the next burst of notoriety myself, by tempting fate. Maybe I created another round of unwanted fame by trying all those years to avoid it.

THREE

Caroline: Nick's Ghost

You think when you haven't heard from someone in forty years, he is powerless to touch you.

I had come home from meeting a friend for tea that darkening day in 1968—a late afternoon in November, threatening to snow, not unlike the afternoon of the opening. I rarely thought of the scandal anymore; and although it would be convenient to say I was thinking of it then, I wasn't. I did have an ominous feeling as I was driven home, but I blamed the weather, the fact that I was tired, and an atmosphere I have always found haunting, even sinister—when darkness has fallen too soon, like a black veil over a winter afternoon. A relaxing bath and a quiet dinner at home were all I needed.

At tea my friend had talked a great deal about her husband's fragile health, and I suppose that's why I was thinking once more about Harry as I headed home. Since his death my life had settled into a pattern even quieter than before. I rarely went out in the evenings, except to see a few close friends at small dinners, and spent most of my days considering grant requests to the foundation. I wasn't collecting much art anymore, but I took my role as a trustee of the Met seriously and helped them raise quite a lot of money.

As we drove through the falling darkness I was thinking, as I often did, that I missed dear old Harry more than I ever imagined I would. I had taken his solid nature for granted all those years, was so often annoyed by his density that I hadn't realized that was what I loved him for—his unchanging, immovable presence. So I had become a bit nostalgic and sentimental as I walked in the door, emotions I resisted because they made me feel old. I tried to shake off this foul mood while John, who had been with us for a dozen years by then, took my coat.

"I'm very sorry, ma'am," he said, "but we have an unusual problem, a young man who came to the door and refused to leave. He says he has to see you urgently on a family matter. He says his name is David Leone, that he is the great-nephew of Nicholas Leone, and that you would know why he was here."

I did not know why he was here. I did not know he existed, if in fact he was who he said he was. I'm sure my face gave that away.

"Why hasn't Julia dealt with him?" I asked. No one saw me without making an appointment through my personal secretary; she looked like a timid little thing with pixieish brown hair but could be ruthlessly efficient when she needed to be.

"She tried, ma'am. She came to the door and explained that he would have to apply to her for an appointment, but he insisted he had to see you at once and that you would want to see him. We were all suspicious, and we haven't been able to reach Mr. Will, so we thought it best to keep him in the kitchen, where the staff could keep an eye on him if he got violent. Would you like me to call the police?"

I could imagine the staff buzzing—of course they'd heard about the long-ago scandal, which was why they hadn't slammed the door against this stranger—but I knew they'd be buzzing to protect me.

"Does he seem *violent*?" I asked.

"Not yet, ma'am, but he is scruffy. If you want to know what I think"—and I nodded that I did—"I think he's a hippie. I don't trust him."

Neither did I—after all, he had lied about my knowing why he had come—but I didn't feel in danger. It wasn't the first time someone had appeared out of nowhere wanting to discuss the past. Students and scholars would sometimes try to contact me, wanting to talk about artists I had known. If they were serious, I invited them to view the collection in my absence but always turned down requests for interviews. Maybe this young man was simply more inventive.

And to be perfectly honest, if he *was* Nick's nephew, how could I not be curious?

"Tell him I'll see him in the sitting room," I said and settled myself by the fire that had been prepared for me.

In a few minutes John led him in and said, "David Leone, ma'am."

He did look scruffy, but all men in their twenties did then. He wore old jeans and heavy climbing boots, a tweed sports jacket that seemed two sizes too small, and what looked like a purple T-shirt underneath. I suspected he had borrowed the jacket and pulled his curly dark hair back in a ponytail to look respectable for me. It seemed sort of touching.

"Should I stay, ma'am?" John asked, but I let him go. This young man seemed more pathetic than threatening.

Still, it was upsetting to be sitting in this room, in this chair on the very spot where the old chaise had been, thinking about Nick again. I did not intend to let my guest stay long.

He sat in the chair opposite me—he didn't wait for me to ask him to sit—and dropped a dirty Army knapsack at his feet. He was swarthy and dark-eyed, nothing like Nick, not the slightest family resemblance. Even so, for a moment I thought he might have come to apologize for his great-uncle.

"Mr. Leone," I said, waiting for him to explain himself.

"Right. Listen, I won't beat around the bush. They told you Nicholas Leone was my great-uncle?"

"Yes, I've been told that's what you said."

"Do you know what happened to my uncle after you were through with him?"

His tone was belligerent; there would be no apology from him.

"I have no idea what became of him after he was sent to prison."

"You ever try to find out?"

"I had no reason to. I don't know what your family might have told you, but he treated me very shabbily. Why have you come here, Mr. Leone? I don't mean to be abrupt, but I'm afraid this is not a convenient time."

"There's no convenient time for you to hear what I have to say." He looked pleased with himself, as if he had made a joke. Yet he seemed nervous too as he said, "I'll tell you what became of him. You destroyed him, you know it and I know it. When he got out of prison he moved to Chicago to try to start over, but all he could do was scrape by doing manual jobs. He couldn't even get work doing illustrations anymore. After a while he gave up and stopped painting altogether. He just wanted to survive. Sometimes I guess he didn't want to do that. He got out of touch with the family. We were only in Pennsylvania, but I think I saw him once in my life, at a funeral when I was a little kid."

"I'm sure you love your family, but you can understand I have nothing to say about all this. It doesn't concern me."

"That's what you think. I know different. Did you know he died?"

"No." And I shuddered. Somehow the idea of Nick dead upset me, left me feeling light-headed and unmoored, as if I were tumbling down a dark well—it was the disturbance you feel when a part of your world crumbles away. The Nick I knew was young and handsome and golden—how could he be dead? "I'm sorry," I said, something I never expected to say or to feel after all the years of hating him.

"Yeah, I'll bet you are," the nephew snapped. "Well, he's dead. He died a few months ago, and my father sent me to clean out the crappy little apartment he rented. It was a shithole. The furniture was falling apart. He ate out of cans. He probably drank more than he ate. There wasn't even a pad of paper with a doodle on it, he was so broken down by then. But I found some real interesting things anyway." He reached into the dirty knapsack at his feet and pulled out two large manila envelopes.

"These were way back in a closet behind a bunch of old magazines. I'm not sure he knew he still had them."

He reached into one envelope and pulled out a cheap dime-store scrapbook with an imitation leather cover and coarse gray pages. He flipped the pages in front of me, and I could see that Nick—or someone—had pasted in newspaper clippings about the scandal and the trial. The words "Artist Convicted" flew by.

"This is what people know about him," he said. "What they think they know." He reached into the other envelope and pulled out a handful of envelopes. "This is what I know. Letters. Your love letters to him."

"That's impossible."

"Don't lie anymore," he said, raising his voice, and I could see the angry look that might have made John think he was dangerous. But he calmed down and actually chuckled. "Lady, I've got you, I've got you good. You lied at his trial. You made it seem like you were some great, snooty art lover helping a poor little artist," and he made a simpering face and softened his voice to mock mine as he said, "Oh, I'm so innocent, how could he do this to me?" Then he went on in his normal voice, sneering. "Look at you all nice and neat. You were fucking him. You two were fucking the whole time. You were slumming, getting a few cheap thrills like you were sleeping with the handyman or the gardener or whatever it is you have. It's all here," he said, waving a fistful of envelopes up and down.

I held out my hand. "Let me see."

He gave me some letters. "I think there are some good ones in this batch," he said. "But they're all pretty heavy."

Some of the envelopes had faded postmarks from 1926 and '27. Others had evidently been delivered by hand. I saw my writing, faded and antique looking, but definitely mine. I took a letter out of an envelope, and there was my monogram engraved on the stationery; it had held up exceptionally well.

I read quickly.

March 6, 1926

Dear Nick,

I am sending this note to remind you that the sketch you showed me at our studio yesterday was extraordinary, truly divine, despite all your doubts. You are reaching for something no one has ever done before, and I know you will achieve it. It may seem tiresome now, making the false starts that so discourage you, but one day everyone will recognize your brilliance. You will give the world an experience it has not had before—and it will adore you as I do.

Yours,
Caroline

I could see David Leone's game now; he would take an innocuous message and give it some wild misinterpretation. It was no secret that I had visited Nick's studio or that I thought he was brilliant.

I read another; if this was a love letter, it was only about my love of his work.

May 11, 1926

Dear Nick,

As I promised, here is a check that should cover the materials for the larger version of Sunray, plus a bit more for framing. You know how I love your large canvases. Do you know how much I also love the small, intimate ones? The ones I can hold in my hand, that I embrace and take to my heart, the ones that only you can create.

Until tomorrow,
Caroline

Then I read a few more.

Friday

Dearest N,

You did not answer your phone, and I may not have a chance to try tomorrow, so I am sending this note with George to say I cannot meet you after all. H. is insisting I go with him to Saratoga, and if I tell him I have a sore throat once more he will send me to the Mayo Clinic. I long to see you and will let you know when I am free.

Your,
C.

Palm Beach
January 30, 1927

My darling N,

I am just back from the most glorious swim, alone as always. I imagined you were with me, and that we held each other and let our bodies meet as the waves swept over us—so far from shore we might do anything without being seen. I have never had such a pleasurable swim. If only my fantasy were real. I miss you more than I can say. I think of you always and will write again soon.

C.

January 14, 1927

Dearest,

I don't know how I will bear not seeing you for an entire month, not feeling the exhilaration I always feel the minute I step into the warmth of our little room, crowded with the evidence of your genius and the memory of every experience we have shared. I will try to return early but cannot promise. I do promise you will be in my every thought. Although I am in a sunny climate, it is my vision of you and the memory of our moments together that warm me. The sunlight cannot touch me as tenderly as you do.

My love,

C.

How could I ever have been so silly? Or so reckless?

"Take your time, read them all if you want," David Leone said when I looked up at him.

"Did he keep copies of his letters to me?"

"If I'd found any they'd be here."

"I thought maybe he had made drafts. He must have planned very carefully to ruin my reputation."

"Oh, I guess *you* had nothing to do with that."

"He used me."

"You're still lying," he said, and he smacked his hand against his forehead in amazement. "You're unbelievable. You got balls, lady, I'll give you that. Read those letters again and tell me if they don't prove you had a fucking affair and lied about it and railroaded him into prison. He didn't ruin you, you ruined *him* so the world wouldn't know you were fucking. Then you fixed it so he couldn't even get work. For all I know you killed him."

Such outrageous lies and accusations did not deserve a response, so I stood silently and reached to ring for John.

Leone stood too and practically grabbed the letters from my hand. "Wait," he said, as he stuffed them back into the knapsack. "Before you have that penguin throw me out, let me tell you why I'm here. My great-uncle, he didn't have a cent. You, you'll leave your millions to your relatives, right? My uncle had nothing to leave me except these letters. These are my inheritance, as good as cash. For $150,000 they're yours. I'll throw in the scrapbook for free."

In all those years, even during the scandal when so many false rumors were swirling around, no one had ever tried to extort money.

"You are his nephew after all," I said. "Tell me, is Leone really your family name? I always suspected he had made it up. He liked it when people said his leonine name suited his leonine mane of hair—it all seemed so calculated and false."

"It's real all right. Listen, I'll give you overnight to read the letters and get the money. I'll come back tomorrow, same time. If you don't want these letters, I'm sure there's other buyers who will."

"You'll find you're mistaken, Mr. Leone. No one knows your uncle's name anymore, and no one will care about these ancient letters."

"He's a nobody, but you're a somebody. I think the public will want to know about how a great society millionaire lady lied about fucking somebody then made sure he never worked again. I'll go somewhere else, I'll go to *Life* magazine, I'll go to *Time*, I'll go to *The New York Times*. Somebody will bite, you know that."

"Not for $150,000."

"That's chicken feed to you. Here," and he reached into the knapsack, pulled out a third envelope, and handed it to me. "These are Xeroxes of the letters. Did you think I'd be stupid enough to leave the originals here? You get the originals tomorrow when I get the money." He put the scrapbook in the knapsack and hoisted it over his shoulder. He waved as he headed for the door and said sarcastically, "See you tomorrow."

He was halfway down the hall before he turned and rushed back as if he had forgotten something. "And make that cash, unmarked bills, don't try to screw me." Then he made his much diminished exit. I would have thought he'd been reading too many bad novels if he'd shown any sign of having read at all. I suppose he'd seen too many bad movies.

I read the rest of the letters that night. I took a hot bath and crawled into bed and faced them. They were a wrenching reminder of the young woman I had been, so gullible, so ready to believe what I wanted to believe. At the time I thought I was being clever and cautious, and over the years I must have convinced myself that I had never written a word I might regret or that might come back to haunt me.

As I read late into the night, sitting up with the letters and envelopes strewn all around me on the blankets, I didn't berate myself for so many foolish mistakes. I didn't feel sorry for myself—not for the woman I was then or now. But I did feel pulled back in time, to a moment when I had believed in Nick. Part of me read with cold calculation as I tried to gauge how much the letters might damage me and the family—not to mention Mother's and Harry's memories. My heart was engaged for a different reason. I pored over every one as I had searched my memory all those years ago, looking for clues to Nick's betrayal. Why had he been so eager to hurt me, why had his malice taken so hideous a form?

I came across letters that I'd had no memory of, and that reminded me how completely I had given myself to him, how certain I had once been that we understood each other profoundly, with no dark corners we failed to share.

November 3, 1927

Dearest,

I missed you today immensely, but I know how frantically you are working to get ready for the opening, so maybe it was just as well. You understand I could not break this date with Mother (especially if we want her support). It seems absurd to say how much I missed you when you know every thought I have—but maybe you'll like to hear me tell you anyway, the way you like to hear me say how glorious you make me feel, even when it's perfectly obvious.

I got your note about Mark but had already spoken to him; he agrees. And since we can read each other's minds so well on even the smallest details, you'll know exactly what I am thinking as I write this now, and what I will be imagining as I lie alone in my bed and drift to sleep tonight.

Your C.

There were letters that reminded me of how giddily happy he had once made me, and of everything I had missed since then.

May 19, 1927

My dear, handsome Nick,

I adore you, I want you, I love you. Is that a tempting enough offer? I am inviting myself to come by tomorrow afternoon—it seems I am free after all, so unless I hear otherwise I will visit you in our cozy place. I will bring wine. I will rush in, tearing off my cloak on the stairs, my shoes on the landing . . . imagine . . .

Your Caroline

I found only one letter that even hinted at anger or disagreement.

September 29, 1927

Dear Nick:

Here it is—less than you wanted but more than I expected it to be. You know how devoted I have been to this exhibition, and I continue to be. But we don't want H. to ask for an accounting. I'm sure this will do.

C.

Even those people who thought Nick was only after my money—and I have never been one of them—would not find much evidence in that one brief note.

I had never wanted the slightest mention of Nick to intrude on my life again. But that night, I knew that if he had been alive I would have found him wherever he was and asked him, no matter how painful, "Why?" If he were alive I could have looked him in the eye after all those years and said, "Tell me the truth, whatever it is. Just tell me why."

But he was gone, so I searched every syllable of those letters, looked between every line, as I did for years to come, fruitlessly.

In the morning, though I dreaded what he would say, I had to call Will. I couldn't keep something that explosive from him, especially when it involved the family name. Through all the years and changes, he had remained my soul mate, the baby brother who loved and protected me, the person I loved and depended on more than anyone else alive. We could still look at each other across a dinner table and share some wordless joke no one else would have laughed at, as if we were children hiding from the roaming gaze of

Mother's eyes in the Sargent portrait. Rose was lovely, always, but at times she must have felt left out. There was simply nothing we could do about that.

Will was as handsome as ever, or as handsome as anyone could be four decades after his youth. He was a bit heavier, his hair a bit thinner, but he had the same soft, lamblike features.

His personality, however, was considerably crankier.

I phoned early and said it was important for him to stop by before going to the office. He complained a bit and arrived in a grumpy mood. I sometimes thought Will enjoyed looking burdened; it gave him an air of carrying the most important issues in the world on his shoulders.

I gave him the simple details of what had happened the day before and handed him the worst of the letters to read. He flushed bright red, whether from anger or embarrassment I couldn't tell. When he was through reading he tossed them on the floor and said, "Let me ask you something, Caroline. Why did you never mention that there were incriminating letters floating around? Did Harry know about this?"

"Don't be angry. Of course Harry didn't know. I didn't mention them because I didn't think they *were* floating around. All Nick's work disappeared, and I naturally assumed the letters had too. As a matter of fact, I forgot they ever existed."

"You forgot?"

"Yes. I've tried hard to put this behind me, as you know."

"Obviously not hard enough." He shook his head as he bent slowly and picked up the letters from the floor. He kept staring at them in his hands, not looking at me as he said matter-of-factly, "They are authentic, aren't they? They're not fabricated, they're not some trick?"

"No, they're real. I remember them now. I'm sorry."

He looked up at me and seemed almost as sad as he had on that awful night forty years before—which shocked me and broke my heart. All that time, I thought he must have understood about Nick and me somehow, must have absorbed it without my having said a word.

"I thought you must have known," I said gently. "You never did ask about my relationship with Nick. I would have answered if you had."

"You said you were innocent. I thought you meant it."

"I meant innocent of posing for the portrait. I *was* innocent of that."

"Well, I suppose I must have known on some level," he said, smiling at me like a little boy bravely pretending to be more grown-up than he is.

"It was so long ago," I said, "I hope it doesn't matter now."

I was talking about us, about Will and me, but he heard it differently.

"Not matter?" he said, sounding angry again. "You are being blackmailed, do you understand that?"

"Oh that, I can handle that. But I couldn't bear for you to be disappointed in me. I never did lie to you about Nick."

He handed the letters back to me and said coolly, "Isn't it a little late to be falling back on a technicality? You always were good at finding loopholes."

"Please forgive me?" I asked. "For everything. For being careless, for not telling you, for all of it. I did think it was behind us forever. I can't stand the thought of hurting you again." I truly felt I couldn't live with that.

Without hesitating for a second, Will gave me his tender smile and said, "Of course I forgive you. I've always loved you more than anyone, Caroline."

More than he had ever loved anyone else? Or more than anyone had ever loved me? I didn't ask.

"I have to go to the office soon," he said. "Let's be practical. If you give in to this, they'll bleed you forever. How do we reach this Leone character?"

"I have no idea where to reach him. He said he'd come back this afternoon."

"What time? I'll be here."

"No, dear, I'm not asking you to do that, in fact you mustn't. I wouldn't want to drag you into this. I just wanted you to know what we're up against. And I need a little advice. If I *were* going to buy the letters—don't argue, just hear me out—if I *were*, shouldn't I have some kind of contract for him to sign, to make sure that after he turns them over he won't be free to speak about them publicly or release copies or something?"

"Have you lost your mind? You are not going to pay him for the letters, it's a horrible precedent, I won't let you."

"They're my letters, and I need to have them back. Oh, it's so hard to explain. I feel as if Nick has reached out from the grave and grabbed me by the throat, and I'll never be free unless I deal with him one last time."

"You haven't been free? Whose fault is that?"

"I *thought* I was, of course."

"Be reasonable," he said impatiently. "We can't afford for you to be emotional and self-indulgent about something this damaging."

"I know you're thinking of my best interests, but I have to deal with Nick in my own way."

"You're not dealing with 'Nick.' And by the way, you're awfully fond of saying his name all of a sudden, do you realize that? You're dealing with his filthy, blackmailing nephew."

"It feels the same to me! I have to do this for my own peace of mind." I didn't add: for the peace of my soul itself.

Will sighed and looked at his watch. "Why are you being this way? At least let me check to make sure he's really dead. For all you know this is part of a bigger scam. Give me time to do that much and we'll talk again. I'll call Chicago this morning and check on the death certificate."

Somehow the thought that there was a certificate, some piece of paper bluntly stating that Nick was dead, unsettled me all over again. Through the night I had been visualizing Nick as he was when I knew him; even in his ghostly state he seemed to reach toward me from some gauzy past where we were all young. Now the image came to me of what he must have become. Not my golden Nick but a Nick who had died old and beaten, his hair gray, his blue eyes clouded, his face lined with wrinkles—the Nick who had brought all this on himself and deserved to die that way.

I would let Will confirm the death, but I didn't have to wait for the answer. If Nick were alive and behind this, I would have known. "Go ahead and check," I said. "But hurry. The nephew will be here at five."

"Anything else I should know?"

"Well, Leone had a scrapbook of Nick's that I didn't have a chance to look through completely, but it seems it only has newspaper clippings about the trial. I'd be astonished if there were anything in it we hadn't already seen."

"Don't astonish me any more, please. I've had enough surprises."

I smiled and kissed him good-bye. "Have a good day, baby brother. Thank you. And don't worry about me."

He laughed and shook his head. "Why would I worry about you?"

At nine, I phoned my banker and arranged for a cashier's check for $150,000 to be drawn. I would indulge David Leone's melodramatic fantasies only so far; getting that much in cash was out of the question. I sent John to the bank to pick up the check and gave him some other private instructions. I had never been more grateful for his loyalty.

Will cut through some red tape in Chicago and phoned me midmorning with the news I expected, and I asked him to draw up the document I needed. He fought me bitterly; he yelled, "I won't let you do it" into the phone; he accused me of slipping into early senility.

"I've thought about this all night, and I've made up my mind," I told him. "Now we're running out of time, so if you won't help me I'm afraid I'll have to go to another lawyer."

"Good luck explaining that you want a contract you can use to blackmail someone if he reneges on the terms of the original blackmail."

"Well when you put it that way, it doesn't sound quite so simple anymore," I agreed. "But I'll have to try. Do you *want* me to try to explain all this to an outsider?"

"I doubt that you really will."

"You *know* me, Will. And I am as determined about this as I have ever been about anything. Please help me, dear. You *are* the only one I trust."

"Then trust me when I say this will only be the beginning. Once you start giving in to something like this, it never ends."

"That's why I need you to write me a foolproof contract."

And of course when he saw how adamant I was, he didn't refuse to help me. He drew up the legal document I needed for the horrible nephew to sign and came by to drop it off. "Don't say I didn't warn you. And don't forget to have Julia notarize it," he reminded me as he left, mumbling, "I'm glad I don't have to be a witness to this catastrophe."

Around five o'clock David Leone arrived, and I had him shown into Harry's old study, which had not been used since he died. His papers had been cleared away, of course, but the room was the same as he had left it, with his big green leather chair and the mammoth polished oak desk with brass handles. Years ago I had sat outside this very room in my Queen Anne chair, eavesdropping as he and Will schemed to save me. This time I sat behind the mammoth desk.

When John led Leone in, I could see he was wearing the same clothes as the day before, carrying the same filthy knapsack, as well as a larger, empty one.

He stood before my desk. "Got the cash?" he said, and at last I saw the family resemblance. His smirk brought to mind that look on Nick's face when the police had led him away, the one that had appeared in all the papers, the one that exposed his true evil. David glanced at Julia, sitting quietly off to the side, and nodded his head as if to gloat that he'd gotten past her the day before.

"May I have the letters?" I asked, as we played out a trite scene that he seemed to think he'd invented. I was as gracious as if he were a dinner guest.

He reached in the knapsack, pulled out the two manila envelopes, and withdrew one letter. He waved it in front of me. "The cash?" he said.

"Please show him the check," I told John, who took it from my hand and held it in front of David's face so he could see but not touch it.

"A cashier's check, don't worry, your name isn't on it. You can turn it into cash immediately, and it's much easier to carry," I explained.

He frowned and reached toward it, but I said, "Not yet. I need to examine the letters first. And I need the scrapbook. Please, why don't you sit down?"

He sat in a hard chair across from me and looked around the room, tapping his foot nervously as I slowly, carefully matched every letter against the photocopies he had left, to make sure nothing was missing. Julia and John refused to meet his eyes, and the more bored and impatient he seemed, the more slowly and methodically I matched the letters.

"Now, how do I know you don't have more?" I asked when I was through.

"You'll have to take my word for it."

I laughed, as if he had, finally, made a very funny joke. "I'm sure you'll understand if I need more than your word."

"Listen, I emptied that apartment and I need all the cash I can get. I don't have time to hold anything back. This is a one-time thing for me."

"What we need is a contract," I said, and I opened a folder in front of me and handed him the agreement Will had drawn up. It said that David Leone would turn over to me all letters in his possession from or to me, or referring to me in any way, as well as all copies of those documents. That he would turn over all scrapbooks or clippings or other material that was in any way related to me or my life. That he would not sell or make public in any way, verbally or in writing, any information he had about me, or about Nicholas Leone's relationship with me. It said that if he violated any part of this agreement he would owe me $500,000.

"I don't have $500,000," he said, as if that were the point.

"I know you don't. That's why it really is to your benefit to keep the terms of this agreement. If you were to violate them in the smallest way, any money you happened to make would be mine and it would take you a lifetime to pay this off. And if you resisted, you'd be in for a very long, expensive court fight. You'd never be free; it would be awful for you!"

"Are you threatening me, lady? I'm not stupid, you know. Why don't you give me $500,000? Maybe the price just went up."

"This is not a negotiation. We've agreed on $150,000. The document is simply a kind of insurance for me, to make sure you keep your word. That's fair, isn't it?"

"Like you care about fair," he said, but he was looking over the agreement as he said it, sweating as much as Michael Linder had while defending his uncle. "Look, I just need money. What about $200,000?"

"I think we're through," I said to John.

"No, no, okay, okay," David said. "I sign this and you give me the check, right?" His foot was tapping faster than ever.

"If you don't sign, you don't get a penny."

He shrugged, leaned over my desk, and signed. John witnessed it; Julia notarized it. And I knew in my heart again that Nick was truly dead. If he were alive, no matter how old or ill, he would certainly have come up with a more efficient plan than this clumsy nephew had. I could almost hear the wind rattling through David Leone's empty skull.

The letters and the scrapbook were in my hands. John was standing next to David's chair, holding the check. David stood and smirked again, and as he reached for the check John handed it back to me.

I have never wanted to be onstage, and I have never thought of myself as a vengeful person. But I must say I enjoyed the theatrical moment when I calmly tore the check in half, then in quarters. David Leone had set off this shoddy melodrama, but I would see it through to the end. The minute John had handed me the check he had also signaled to Francis, my chauffeur, who was waiting outside the door. Even as David yelled, "Hey! What the hell . . . ?" John and Francis were taking him by the arms. They were both at least twenty years older than David, but they were bigger and there were two of them. He struggled and squirmed, yelling, "You can't do this. I have more copies, you know."

"I'm sure you do," I said serenely as he was hauled toward the door. "But think of what that document will do to you. Think of how it will make you look and how long it will take you to pay me. And think about this—it didn't promise you anything, did it?"

He kept yelling, "You haven't changed. You bitch. You rich old bitch," as John and Francis took him away.

The thought of rewarding yet another vile Leone had been, of course, unbearable. But my decision had nothing to do with money—in fact, it cost me nearly as much to thank John and Francis and Julia. No, as I watched the dreadful nephew being dragged away, what I kept reminding myself was: This is my story and I must be the one to tell it. I had left it to others too long.

Deciding how to tell that story was a different, quite urgent matter, and I began brooding about it while David Leone's voice was still fading down the hall. He could cause trouble with his copies of the letters despite the agreement; even the slow-witted nephew would soon realize that. If those letters were bound to become known, I didn't want him to let them out; then I could only look defensive. I had to find a way to bring my story to the public again, the whole story this time.

I'd assumed that the need to do that had disappeared along with the painting. Oh, if that vile painting hadn't vanished, I would have gone on doing everything I could, everything on earth, however public, to refute Nick's lies and make sure the world viewed the work as it should have been seen—an act of great malice. I was glad that hadn't been necessary. But now David Leone had forced my hand, and I had bought myself just a little time to figure out what to do.

Poor, dear Harry must have been spinning in his mausoleum to think of me going through this once more. I was happy he wasn't here to see it, yet part of me wished he was; he had always stayed in touch with his publishing cronies and would have known where to turn. I asked myself what Harry would have done, and the next morning called Ned Robertson, who had remained one of his most loyal friends.

Ned had grown enormously fat, with a quaint walrus mustache that made him look like Teddy Roosevelt, and he was more blustery than ever. But I had learned over the years that his old-fashioned look and buffoonish manner worked as camouflage. Ned was as shrewd and forward looking as anyone around—Harry refused to play chess with him—and though he was no longer publisher of his paper, he still knew everyone in power and could advise me well. I asked him to come by that afternoon to help me on a delicate matter. He said, "I'll be there for lunch."

I had the cook prepare a feast on short notice—lobster, pheasant, champagne, all the luxuries I knew he would like—and as he ate I confided in Ned about the letters and what I needed to do.

Dear Ned never said a word about my dealings with Nick; he was simply furious at David and indignant on my behalf. "How dare he! I wish you'd come to me sooner, but it's done now. Don't concern yourself about a thing. Planting a story? Nothing easier, you've come to the right man, just as Harry would have done. He's probably smiling down at you right now." We had never talked about how Ned had helped in the old days, about how respectfully his paper had treated me throughout the scandal, and we didn't mention it now. He did say, very cheerfully, "Good to feel useful again."

Between the soup and the fish courses, he pulled a small notebook out of his jacket pocket and began listing names of reporters he trusted, at his paper and others. "You have some options," he said. "Let's say I find a society columnist to do a profile of you: the reclusive Mrs. Stephens gives a rare interview to promote her favorite charity. You have a favorite charity, don't you?"

"The family foundation."

"Oh, yes—the reclusive Mrs. Stephens gives a rare interview to drum up interest in the good works of her family's foundation. Along the way, you casually mention your girlish past, even a couple of long-lost love letters that have turned up. You laugh charmingly, you spill the beans about some ancient affair. 'Oh, we were all so young and foolish, such flibbertigibbets.' You say what you want, then go right back to discussing charity. You make sure they agree up front that the interview will only be about the foundation, so you can refuse to go into anything personal if they press you for more. Don't worry, they won't. They'll think they've wormed something out of you and be happy with that. Let them think you've let it slip out accidentally and they'll use it. It's all about control." He checked off the first two names on the list.

"I'll get in touch with the right people for you when it's time. Now, here's another option. You go to an art critic and guide him through your collection: the reclusive Mrs. Stephens gives a rare interview and a tour of her private art collection. There'll be great photographs, magazines will jump at it. You'll have to open the house to photographers, but it'll be worth it. And along the way you casually mention how you've been thinking of the old days because some long-lost letters reminded you of silly youth, flibbertigibbets, et cetera, et cetera, same idea. Here are the pros and cons." He leaned forward as his empty fish plate was cleared away. I've never figured out how Ned managed to eat and talk at the same time without seeming crude, but he did.

"The society page is nice, I like the altruistic angle, makes you look like a do-gooder, but it might not get such big play. The art tour is splashier. You'll get plenty of space because they'll want to publish those photos. Problem is, you could come off like a rich dilettante when you want to look like a nun, or at least a noble widow. Tough call."

"I can see that," I said, worrying that there was no ideal way to accomplish what I needed to do.

"You don't look anything like a nun, of course, you're as lovely as the day we met," he said. "You haven't changed in forty years." Another man would have thought to flatter me first and tell me what to do later; I suppose that's one reason Ned and Harry got along so well. They were both so focused on the business at hand that everything else—like sexual attraction—was an afterthought.

"Everyone changes in forty years," I said. "But you're as dashing as you ever were."

We laughed, and he said, "You've given me another idea, since we're talking about age."

"We are not talking about age."

"Oh, no, I'd never ask a lady her age. But here's a thought. Why don't I call my grandson Adam, my oldest son's boy? Everything does change, and I've found it's useful to get the young genera-tion's opinion nowadays, even if you decide to ignore it. He started off at the paper, then gave it up for television, couldn't talk him out of it. He's producing some news thing on CBS now; loves it. And he says they reach millions. Adam's a smart kid, not like the other grandson. Let me see what he thinks about this."

"But you won't tell him that David Leone asked me for money? I've told you that in the strictest confidence, as a dear, dear friend."

"Never fear, I know a thing or two about discretion. Let me call Adam."

Everything happened so quickly after that. Adam phoned the same afternoon and arranged to come by the next day. I was struck by how different he looked from David Leone, though he couldn't have been much older, maybe in his late twenties. Adam was the pic-ture of success, for his generation at least: thick hair to his chin, but beautifully groomed; a crisp blue shirt and colorful flowered tie, loosened and askew at his neck. And his manners were impeccable;

I expected no less from Ned's grandson. He was effortlessly full of youth and confidence—a most appealing, reassuring combination.

I explained that I had recently recovered some letters and told him the story behind them—of Nick's betrayal, the trial, and what I had to say about it now. I told him quite a bit more about that part than I had told Ned.

He listened and nodded quietly as I talked, and when I was through he leaned forward in his chair. "Wow," he said. "Here's what I'd like. I'd like you to come on our program. This is a great story, and you'll be great telling it on camera."

That was not at all what I expected. "I'm sorry, maybe you misunderstood. I was thinking about a newspaper or magazine interview, I thought you might help me decide what to do or where to go. And I'm afraid I've never seen your show." In fact, I had never heard of it.

He shook his head. "Don't worry about that, hardly anyone has, it's only a few months old, but it's real. It's called *Sunday Magazine*, and it's like a magazine but on television. A few news stories on every program, some serious, some light, but they're all done by our top reporters—Jack Tyler, Lewis Edmonds, Jonathan Knowle, they're the regulars."

Well, of course that kind of thing is commonplace now, but it was quite new then. And although I had heard of those reporters, I must have looked skeptical.

"I can tell you this," Adam said. "Even a low-rated TV show will be seen by more people than a newspaper, and our ratings are going up all the time."

"Why would your television audience be interested in my story?"

"It's a terrific human interest story! Think of it as a forty-year-old mystery being solved. A woman whose reputation was attacked speaks out and tells the truth, the whole truth, for the first time. It's got a trial, it's got missing paintings, it's got the dead painter. Best of all, it's got that great forbidden love story. I guarantee this will get people's attention."

"You're not just being helpful for your grandfather's sake? I'm grateful for the offer but . . ."

"I'm doing this for my own sake. It will be fantastic."

"But I've never been on television."

"I have a feeling you're a natural."

He sat back and looked thoughtful for a minute, then said, "I can understand why you'd hesitate. I know my grandfather looks down his nose at what I do sometimes. He considers television dé-classé or second-rate. Sure, he's proud of me, but he can't understand why I left the paper, he doesn't get it, he doesn't see that I want to be on the edge of what's next. Well this is what's next, and it's just what you're looking for—one interview, you'll reach millions of people, and you're done. You know those reporters, they're serious, they've covered the White House, they couldn't be more respected. It will be painless and you'll come out of it a heroine. Will you at least think it over? Please?"

Then he said something that I'm sure was simply meant to be playful but that kept me awake all night. He had a gleam in his eye as he looked at me and said, "Take a chance, Mrs. Stephens. I know you can do it."

I had no intention of taking his offer seriously, but there was some vague quality in this dynamic young man that made me agree to consider it.

After he left, it took hours of thought before I realized what that quality was—the gleam in his eye reminded me of Spencer. Oh, Adam didn't actually remind me of Spencer, but he brought me back to a time when I had wanted more than anything to be daring and reckless. I wondered what I had to gain by choosing the safe news-paper interview Ned had proposed; I could see it would hardly make a ripple. And I thought of Mother, so tied to her old, fading world.

I doubted that Adam's solution would be as painless as he promised. None of this would be painless for me. But what he said made such sense. And I couldn't deny that the world had changed; the new world had walked down my hall in an old purple T-shirt.

If Adam was wrong, then no one would notice my little TV appearance. But if he was right . . .

The next morning I called him and agreed.

I decided to approach the interview in the spirit of my old days with Spencer—it would be an adventure, something risky and thrilling, something with the power to save my life.

Will said I was a fool. But Adam was wonderful from the start, and made things as easy as they could be. He produced the piece himself, explained every step along the way, and took care of me just as carefully as his grandfather had all those years ago.

A few days before the interview he arrived with a camera crew, and they filmed me walking up Park Avenue—though I insisted they not reveal my address—then up Fifth and into the Met.

When we were through, he and a few others came home with me, as we'd arranged. "We're going to look around and find the best place to shoot with Jack," he said. "Then I'll do a preinterview—no cameras, we'll just go over a few more things so I can figure out what he should ask. And that's it, you'll be ready. We're lucky Jack was free, he's the best."

"Are you certain he's the best choice for me?" I wondered. I trusted Adam, but Jack Tyler was famously difficult. I'd admired his radio broadcasts from London during the war; that was how he made his name. But since moving to television he had gotten a reputation as a shark; recently he had asked the British Ambassador how it felt to represent a has-been empire.

"It's terrific for you," Adam assured me. "People know him and pay attention to him. That's what you need. He's tough, no question about it. He'll be very direct, maybe blunter than you'd like. But that will work in your favor; you'll look more credible by standing up to tough questions. There's no need to worry. I'll run you through the whole thing, and by the time we're done you'll be able to breeze right through the interview. But first let's see where we can shoot."

I took him into the sitting room, which I thought would be perfect. I could see myself in front of the dramatic Art Nouveau fireplace. He ran a finger over the gray moiré fabric on the wall, but one of his colleagues shook his head and said, "Let's not even try to light this."

Adam turned to me. "The wallpaper's too shimmery, it might glare on camera. Let's look at some other rooms, okay?"

I took him to Harry's study. "Too heavy and masculine, this doesn't look like you," he said. "We want something personal. Where do you spend most of your time?"

I took him to the private sitting room in my suite. I'd had the furniture reupholstered several times over the years, but it looked much as it had when Larry had coached me there, with an ivory carpet and a black settee. I had always liked it too much to change anything.

"This is it, we can make this work, don't you think?" Adam asked one of the men trailing him. "Simple but dramatic. You should wear something colorful so it will stand out against the black sofa. We'll take a look in your closet before I go. These sculptures, what are they?"

"Brancusis."

"Perfect. They'll look incredible on camera, too. We can move them around so we can see a couple of them behind you." He was walking around the room examining the paintings on the walls. Then he asked a question that made me wonder if he had been listening at all. "You don't happen to have anything by Nicholas Leone around here, do you? Maybe some small painting, a drawing?"

"No, not one. Not anywhere."

"Right, you told me, I remember. I was hoping you'd saved some little thing, maybe some memento he gave you? Some trinket or a note, any piece of paper with his writing on it or a drawing?"

"Not a scrap. I have nothing of his."

"Okay, so we'll play that up, the lost Leones, that's probably better. We're on our way, Mrs. Stephens."

"Please call me Caroline," I said. If he was going to pry into the intimate details of my past, we might as well be on familiar terms.

He sent the crew away and said, "Let's sit somewhere and I'll ask you some questions and you tell me what you want to say. You'll see, it will be easy. We want you to be comfortable and relaxed."

"Let's talk here," I said, and he sat next to me on the black velvet settee. "Would you like some tea or coffee?" I thought of Larry and wondered if Adam would like champagne. I smiled to myself but didn't offer him any; I didn't want him to think I was an eccentric old lady who drank champagne at noon. The fleeting thought of Larry was comforting, though. I had been through an ordeal far worse than this. After testifying in court all those decades ago, facing Jack Tyler should seem like a lark.

On the day of the interview, while Adam and his crew set up their cameras, I stayed out of their way in my dressing room, getting ready. I put on the royal blue dress he had chosen, then sat in a chair while someone put what seemed like pounds of makeup on me, more than I had ever worn in my life. When Adam popped his head in, I called him over and whispered, "This is too much. I look like a clown."

He laughed. "You won't, don't worry. You'll look entirely natural and beautiful on camera. If you weren't wearing so much makeup, the lights would make you look unnatural, like a ghost."

I'd been only vaguely aware of the sounds in the next room, so I was shocked when Adam let me in. My beautiful sitting room had been turned into a war zone, a horror of lights and white screens and wires. The Brancusi bronzes were arranged behind the settee, creating a graceful backdrop, each Bird at a different, perfectly adjusted height; I looked to see how the crew had managed that and realized the sculptures were on metal equipment cases precariously stacked up.

I waited on the settee for ages. They clipped a microphone on me, and attached it to a wire they ran under my dress; they played with the lights again. All this gave me far too much time to be nervous. And when everything was ready, the doorbell rang and Jack Tyler appeared. His face, already in its mask of makeup, was craggier than it looked on television; his thick black hair, his trademark, had less of a shoe polish shine in real life. But even off camera he had the same dramatic air. He complimented my clothes, my hair, my art collection and my courage in a great rush that was clearly meant to disarm. But I had been around as long as he had, and I saw from the way he treated the crew—snapping his fingers to get their attention, grabbing some papers from Adam's hand, shooing away someone who offered him water—that he was a tyrant, not to be trusted.

He sat in a chair across from me, smiling and making cheerful small talk for a few seconds, then said, "Are you ready?" He had been in the house all of ten minutes.

I caught a glimpse of Adam standing against the wall behind

Tyler, looking thoroughly at ease—his arms folded, a smile on his face. He nodded his encouragement when he saw me glance his way, so I smiled too and said, "I'm ready."

Two hours later, I wanted to run screaming from my own house. I was so worn and confused I had no idea what I had said, but we were finished. "That was terrific," Adam told me. "We got great stuff. You'll be really pleased when you see it, Caroline, I know you will."

I did not know anything of the sort. Later I wondered if the British Ambassador had cried in frustration after Tyler had gone; I thought we might have that in common. I managed a polite good-bye to Tyler, then fled to hide in Harry's old bedroom, leaving the crew to take down the lights and do God knows what to my Brancusis. Why hadn't I listened to Will?

Most of Tyler's questions had been the same as Adam's, but they seemed different when delivered in a bullying tone. And I had done everything wrong. Adam had coached me to be natural and straightforward, to give simple answers. I had been tense and convoluted, and it was all on film for the world to see.

I fell into my own bed at six o'clock, unable to face another minute of that day. Will called to ask how it had gone, but when John told him I was asleep, he said not to wake me. For once I was glad to miss his call. I didn't want to tell him it had been a disaster.

And as wonderful as Adam had been, he refused to show me the edited tape before it was on the air. I kept trying to convince myself I was only imagining the echo of Nick's words when Adam said, "You'll be happy with it, Caroline. Let it be a surprise."

A few weeks later, on that Sunday when the interview was to be shown, I watched at home with Will and Rose, and Ned and Adam. I couldn't go through it alone. I had bought a large color television set, which was put in Harry's study—not a gracious place to receive guests but the only place I could bear to put such an ugly piece of furniture. And the setting was oddly appropriate. I had last seen David Leone being dragged from this room and now could almost hear his derisive laughter in the air. Through him, his great-uncle was about to destroy me a second time.

I sat on a sofa between Adam and Ned, with Rose in the green leather chair nearby. Will obstinately sat behind Harry's desk, where he could only see from a skewed angle. "Partial view seating is fine with me," he growled. I had told him after the interview that I feared the worst and he had gone to Ned and Adam to try to call it off, but Adam explained it was far too late for that. Will knew that if he went higher up at the network and tried to squelch the story, word was bound to get out and might call more attention to it. I was trapped, and this time I had only myself to blame.

Mine was the first story on the show, and I was appalled when I heard Tyler's booming voice begin his introduction. "Forty years ago, New York high society was shocked by a sex and art scandal that made lurid headlines for a few months then quickly died away. Caroline Holbrooke Stephens was at the center of that scandal." I must have gasped because Adam put his hand on mine, patted it and whispered, "Don't worry. It will be fine."

On the screen I saw my past flitting by: newspaper clippings about the opening; photographs of Mother, Harry, Will, and me walking into the courthouse; the vicious *Graphic* drawing of me in fig leaves. Will groaned and put his head in his hands as he leaned on Harry's desk.

Then I was walking up Park Avenue as Tyler went on, "Nicholas Leone was convicted of public obscenity and spent a year in Sing Sing. While he was in prison, every bit of his work disappeared amid accusations of bribery and theft—never proven—leveled at the Holbrooke family, at jealous artists, even at the late, revered district attorney Lawrence Sloane." Tyler reported on Nick's life after prison; David had told the truth about the pathetic decades he had endured after he was released. And Adam had found one of Nick's brothers and his sister, but all they said was that he had distanced himself from the family.

"Did you find his nephew?" I whispered to Adam.

"A few great-nephews and nieces; they never knew him much."

"Was there one named David?"

"Oh yeah, he refused to talk. Nervous guy, seems to have some kind of problem."

Mercifully for me, they had no photographs of Nick in old age.

Then I was standing in the Met looking at a Rembrandt as Tyler said, "Now the mainstay of her family's two-hundred-million-dollar charitable foundation, on the Board of Directors of the family shipping business, and a Trustee of the Metropolitan Museum of Art, Caroline Stephens is a pillar of New York society. She is also a woman with a decades-old secret she has at last agreed to reveal."

Finally I saw myself on the settee, before the perilously balanced Brancusis. I looked older than I would have liked but at least appeared poised and dignified as I answered questions I thought I had buried forever, questions that had risen to haunt me as surely as if Nick had put a curse on me as he left this world.

"Take me back to that night in 1927, when you first saw the portrait," Tyler said, and I did, more clearly than I thought I had on the day of the interview.

"I told you so," Adam whispered, apparently reading my mind.

"Did you, in fact, pose for that portrait or any like it?" Tyler was asking me.

"No, I did not," I said.

"Did you have a love affair with Nicholas Leone?"

The camera was close on my face, looking into my eyes, and I seemed to return its gaze as I said softly, honestly, "Yes. He was my great love until he betrayed me."

"Which you have never admitted before," Tyler said, a tone of accusation creeping into his voice. "In fact, you denied it at his trial. You lied on the stand under oath, didn't you?"

"I didn't tell outright lies, but I suppose I evaded the truth by pretending I was no more than Nick's patron. At the time, I believed I was getting at a deeper truth. He had lied about me with that painting, and I wanted the world to know. Maybe that was wrong of me. But you see, things were so different then. It seemed so important to preserve my reputation, the good name of my family, my place in society—that was all so ingrained in me, shallow though it seems today. And for some reason Nick Leone was trying to destroy me with the painting. I have always told the truth about that."

"How did the affair begin?"

"We met at his gallery. I fell in love with his work, and then I fell in love with him."

"So this was truly an affair of the heart, as well as the body."

"For me it was. Before that night of the opening, I loved him completely and passionately. I had made the kind of safe, appropriate marriage my mother approved of. Nick seemed like a gift. He and I understood each other so deeply. We spent afternoons at his studio, and when we were alone the differences between us in background and social class seemed to evaporate. We simply merged, as if we were one."

Watching the screen, I suddenly saw myself as others would: I seemed like a woman still in love.

"Why come clean about all this now, after all these years?"

"Some old letters I wrote to Nick were returned to me after his death, and I realized how important it was to set things right."

Tyler reached his arm out, and an assistant off camera handed him a copy of one of my letters. "Will you read one for us?" Tyler asked as he handed it to me. I had loaned copies—selected copies—to Adam, but he had not prepared me for that. I was sure it would look bad if I refused, though. So I took the letter—I knew most of them by heart—and kept my eyes on it as I read in an unembarrassed voice:

"My darling Nick,

These days apart are torture. I am sitting in bed looking at your painting of the silvery house, imagining us inside it, alone together, our lives transformed as magically by your touch as that house was transformed by your genius and my life has been changed by your love. I long to be in your strong arms, in our own private places together. Until we can be in each other's arms again, I will live in the light of your art.

Your Caroline"

"If you loved him as deeply as this letter suggests, why didn't you leave your husband to be with him?" Tyler asked. "It must have crossed your minds."

"I'm ashamed to admit it now, but I couldn't see myself running off with Nick and living the life of a struggling artist's wife, or even worse, a disreputable mistress. I couldn't. He begged me to, over and over, but I guess I wasn't as unconventional as I thought."

"And while you were together, he painted and displayed that shocking portrait." Tyler gave a dramatic, skeptical sigh. "You say without your knowledge?"

"Absolutely without my knowledge."

He raised his eyebrows with enough exaggeration so the camera wouldn't miss it. "Then it was from memory?" he asked.

"Well, he knew my body from memory," I said, and the face I

saw on screen looked mischievous, a look I certainly hadn't intended to display.

"And the pose?" Tyler pushed. "That pose—excuse me for being indelicate, but it can only be called masturbatory."

I shook my head. "I never posed for that portrait."

"But you admit you had a sexual affair and your role as his patron was a ruse."

"Oh, no, my role as his patron was real. It was what brought us together in the first place. We were just as passionate about his art as we were about each other. Remember, women were entirely dependent on their husbands in those days, so I used my husband's money to buy art and help artists. That was what I could do. I did believe Nick was a brilliant artist. I still do."

"But you thought his painting was obscene?"

"I knew that one painting was a lie."

"But not obscene?"

"Maybe it's the same thing."

"What did you and your family have to do with his prosecution?"

"Nothing at all."

"Oh, come on now, there were always rumors, you've heard them over the years, about bribery, about your family using its influence with the judge and the district attorney. You socialized with Lawrence Sloane."

"Yes we did, my husband and I, but those rumors about our influence were just that. I assume they were started by friends of Nick's to try to discredit me and to help him."

"How did you feel when he was sent to prison?"

"I thought he deserved it."

"So what went wrong with this perfect love affair?"

"I don't know."

"Why do you think Nick did it? Resentment? Jealousy?"

"I don't know," I said, looking infinitely sad and wounded. How had Tyler gotten me to look that way? "I'll never know," I said, shaking my head slowly, sounding wistful, looking straight ahead beyond Tyler, as if I could see all the way into the past, my baffling, impenetrable past. "I don't know," I said again, and the camera lingered on me, staring silently, for what seemed an eternity. I felt more exposed than Nick had ever made me feel. The image seemed frozen on the screen, and I nearly jumped when I heard Tyler's voice break the silence.

"Do you think he was getting back at you for refusing to end your marriage and be with him?"

The camera had stayed on me, and I saw my eyes focus on Tyler again as if returning from a great distance. "I couldn't say. I never spoke to him again after the night of the opening."

"Well, you've admitted to lying about the affair back then. Forgive me, but how do we know you're telling us the truth now?"

"Mr. Tyler, the only reason I am here is to tell the whole truth at last. Those letters made me realize something more important than my own past or my own embarrassment." And as I once had on the witness stand, I now spoke quickly and intensely, yearning to make my point. "The reason I'm here is to say that I wish society had been different when I was young and I'm glad it's changing. I'm not ashamed of my passion for Nick anymore, though I *am* ashamed that I didn't have the courage to live by my passions instead of my fears. Young people today have so much more freedom—economic and, yes, sexual. Especially young women. I want them to know they shouldn't make my mistakes. They should love whom they want and follow what their hearts tell them to do, and not pay attention to outdated social rules. That's why I agreed to tell the truth after all these years. I want to tell young people: Don't let society tell you what to do, don't waste that passion as I did." They hadn't cut a word.

What they *had* cut from the interview was Tyler trying, persistently and unsuccessfully, to get me to give him details about sex with Nick. I couldn't remember exactly what he had asked, but I remember politely deflecting the questions, saying they were too personal, even as my mind was flooded with memories of the glorious things Nick and I had done together.

They had kept what truly mattered.

At the end Tyler asked, "Would you be ashamed of the portrait today?"

"Oh, I would still blush. I would still consider it a lie and a betrayal."

"Do you know what happened to it?"

I shook my head again. "How would I know that?"

I believed everything I had said, about love and sex and freedom. But I never meant to be a crusader. I simply wanted to tell the truth.

Adam was right, though. I became a heroine. Nothing had shocked me so since the night I saw that painting.

Minutes after the show ended, the phone was ringing—I'm not sure how so many reporters got my number so fast—with newspapers and magazines and television networks begging for interviews. I turned them down, but they wrote about me anyway, praising my courage and my honesty. My picture was everywhere. I was called a social revolutionary, a radical, a groundbreaking feminist. Women's groups wanted to give me awards. Jack Tyler sent me flowers and a note with an open invitation to appear again. "We could tour the Metropolitan Museum, or your own art collection. We could tour your shoe closet if you like, just please come back!"

It was all quite amusing. This time when I read about myself in the papers, I didn't have to be afraid, even if some of the headlines did sound as lurid as they had in '27. They were everywhere. They came from respectful publications: "Art World Grande Dame Admits Affair." They came from trashy ones: "Caroline Says: 'I Did It with Nick.'" But however tawdry the headlines, the articles were on my side.

"Socialite Caroline Stephens told Jack Tyler she has no regrets about her long-ago love affair with a young artist, Nicholas Leone, who served a prison term for obscenity after painting an explicit nude portrait of her," said the *News*. "Mrs. Stephens, who had long denied the affair and still insists she did not pose for the portrait, said she was appearing on CBS's *Sunday Magazine* to voice a plea for social change. 'Young women should love whoever they want and do what their hearts tell them to,' the sixty-six-year-old philanthropist and art collector declared, sitting primly in front of her collection of phallic sculptures by the famous artist Brancusi. Her heartfelt words have been embraced as a rallying cry by women's groups across the country."

It was the sixties, after all. I was being labeled a wild Bohemian all over again, only this time it was meant as a compliment. A couple of conservative papers attacked me, but even they admired me for "confessing" about the past, as they put it.

For weeks after the interview, every day I received phone calls and letters about it. One letter was outraged at my "whorish Jezebel ways" and begged me to "seek God's forgiveness and mercy." Another chided me for not going far enough: "Marriage is a corrupt institution, which you have it in your power to undermine." Most were full of praise.

People found out where I lived and turned up at the door, where John quickly shooed them away. Julia had to hire an assistant to help her with the calls and mail. We ignored the cranks, gratefully turned down many requests for interviews and a few extravagant offers to publish the letters, and directed appeals for money to the foundation. I appreciated the irony: that poor, unwitting nephew had made up for his uncle's malice. He had helped me burnish my reputation.

Will was much less amused. He stopped by one day with a copy of a weekly magazine he had just picked up at the newsstand. There I was on the cover, in a photograph from the *Sunday Magazine* interview, under the headline "The Grandma Moses of Free Love."

"Well, I hope that label doesn't stick," I said. "I don't look anything like Grandma Moses. And I'm not nearly that old! In fact, I think I'm insulted."

"You're not taking this seriously enough," Will said. "Nothing good will come of this."

"What am I supposed to do? I haven't given one more interview, this is all happening without me."

"I wish you hadn't gone on TV in the first place."

"I know you do. But it worked. I saved myself from David Leone. There was no blackmail money, and now there's not even a scandal anymore."

"You're enjoying this."

"Why shouldn't I?"

"Because it's a dangerous game. This kind of public attention exposes you too much."

"Exposes me to what? How much more exposed can I be?"

"More blackmail and extortion."

"Oh, Will, there is nothing more I can be blackmailed with."

"Lunatics, then. You'll be prey to lunatics."

"What do you mean? Everyone has been very good to me. The press has actually been kind, even though I haven't talked to them."

"You're feeding their interest by playing Garbo now, and you know it. Tell me you're not planning to do another interview."

"I'm not, you know better. And I don't see why you're so upset. You know, it could help the foundation if I *were* better known."

"The foundation doesn't need any help. Promise me you won't give any more interviews."

"I promise." It was the last thing I wanted to do anyway. "You're worrying for nothing, as usual," I said. "And as usual I love you for it, my lamb."

He grumbled.

And as usual, he was right.

I wasn't alarmed at first.

One morning soon after Will's visit, when Julia brought me the mail, she handed me a letter that had a small pencil drawing of a staircase, no more than an inch high, next to the signature. "Does this mean anything to you?" she asked. Written neatly in pencil, the letter said:

Dear Caroline,

I hope you remember me, I could never forget you. You probably know my name now as a painter. I was Nick Leone's assistant all those years ago, and I have a very clear memory of events you will want to discuss. You can reach me at MU5-6711 to set a time for my visit. Please call as soon as you get this note. It will be grand to catch up on old times, I've missed them so much.

It was signed "Raymond Mahoney," next to the drawing of a tiny, disembodied staircase ascending straight up to nowhere.

When I saw the signature and the drawing, I did remember Mahoney's name, not as someone I had ever met and certainly not as Nick's assistant—he'd never had one, I would have known—but as a minor, long-forgotten painter. He had once shown some promise with graceful, mysterious drawings of staircases. I'd even bought one decades before. But his promise was never fulfilled, and he quickly faded into obscurity when it turned out that all he could do was stairs.

I guessed that Mahoney was struggling, that he wanted to sell me some work. I asked Julia to answer him as she had all the others, directing him to the foundation.

He responded by sending her a rude note:

> Tell Mrs. Stephens I do not want money. I want to discuss the missing Leones. Here is proof that I am who I say I am. I know what I'm talking about.

And he included another drawing on a piece of folded-up paper torn from a spiral notebook, a pastel that looked both delicate and ominous. It was an unfinished view of a woman's legs; a purple cape with black fox trim swirled around her knees as she climbed a zigzagging wooden staircase outside an old tenement building. It was unmistakably the staircase that led to Nick's studio, and the cape was identical to one I'd had back then. The drawing ended so abruptly at the top of the paper that the woman's torso was cut off and the unfinished stairs—like those in the first letter—seemed to be leading eerily into empty space. This sketch seemed new and rushed, as if it had been dashed off the day before, but the building had been torn down years ago.

The drawing unnerved me a bit, but when I showed the letter to Will he dismissed it. "This is a fraud. There are no missing Leones, Caroline, we know that."

"How can you be so sure?"

"You remember how hard Harry searched."

"But what if there are some he never found? Maybe this man is a lunatic, or a fraud who has done a lot of clever research. But that is the staircase to the studio, and if he knows something, we owe it to ourselves to find out, don't we? I feel I owe it to Harry's memory. It's what he would have done."

"Have Julia give him an appointment with me," Will said, and I happily agreed. This was one situation I did not believe I could handle alone. But Mahoney insisted on speaking to me, so Will reluctantly arranged for the three of us to meet at his office in two days.

Mahoney was ten minutes late. Will and I were waiting in his private office, the small one off the large office where he usually held meetings and did most of his business. There was a bar and big easy chairs and a sofa I had settled into. It was his comfortable inner sanctum, and as I ran my hand over the sofa's drab tweed fabric, I said, "If you insist in keeping this, you might at least have it reupholstered, Will."

He was standing at the bar and asked, "Would you like a drink while we're waiting? I'm not offering him one when he gets here."

"No, thank you."

"Well I'm having a Scotch. You know, a shrewd con man would have the sense to be on time."

"We don't know that he's a con man."

"I know he is. What are you hoping for? Do you want there to be more Leones in the world? Are you that reluctant to give this whole thing up?"

"Of course I don't want to find any, I just want to be sure. I want to know."

Will's secretary buzzed and said Mr. Mahoney had arrived. "Send him in," Will answered through the intercom. "And did you make sure security is standing by in case we need them as I asked?"

"Dear," I said, "you're being so dramatic."

"Let's hope so."

Mahoney was a short, wiry man with a florid face, a fringe of wispy gray hair, and a rumpled gray cotton suit whose pant cuffs stood in puddles at his ankles. He bounded into the office so smiling and energetic that he looked like an aging elf, yet from that first moment he frightened me. I was sure I had never seen him before, yet he ran up to me as if we were old friends. He carried a tattered leather portfolio held together with masking tape, which he dropped on the floor, then reached out both hands and grabbed one of mine between them. I was still sitting on the sofa, and he kept pumping my hand as he leaned over me and said, "Ah, Caroline, we meet again, so good, so good to see you. After all these years. So good." I hoped I didn't show my revulsion.

"And Mr. Holbrooke," he said, almost leaping across the room to where Will stood by the bar, one hand in his pocket and the other holding his drink. "We've never met but I feel I know you." He stuck out his right hand, and Will slowly, very slowly, took his out of his pocket and shook briefly without saying a word.

Mahoney turned back toward me and must have caught my puzzled expression. "You don't remember me, do you?" He looked sad but not entirely surprised.

"I'm sorry, I don't."

"You never did notice the help," he said, in a teasing voice. "But I don't hold that against you. I was just an aspiring artist then, a kid, about sixteen—too young even for you." No matter how rude his words, his tone remained confidently cheerful.

I glared and opened my mouth to speak, but he held up a hand and said, "Let me remind you who I am. I became Nick's assistant after he got the studio. I guess you were paying for me too, but maybe you didn't know it. I did all sorts of menial jobs for him, swept the floor, cleaned the brushes. Who do you think helped him carry your portrait that night? All the time, I was watching and learning from him, watching and learning, watching and learning. Eventually he let me stretch and prime his canvases now and then. But whenever he knew you were coming—almost every day for a long, long time, I know that—I was sent away before you got there. More than once I had to run down the front stairs while you were coming up the back. You must have seen me sometimes, didn't you?"

"The front door of that studio was painted shut," I said.

"Oh no it wasn't."

Will came and sat next to me but did not ask Mahoney to sit. "You claim to know where to find some missing Leones?" Will asked.

"Did I say that, Mr. Holbrooke? Whatever gets your foot in the door, right? Well, maybe I do, maybe I don't. Maybe I don't know where they are but I know somebody who does. Or maybe I don't know where they are but I know who took them."

"Can we get to the point?" Will said.

"I'm getting there, I'm explaining," Mahoney said and turned to me. "I didn't really go away all those times Nick sent me out. I was too shrewd for that. I would go around to the back and hide in the toolshed. Didn't you *ever* see me? Nick and I had keys to the shed—where do you think he kept that painting?—and I would hide inside, and if I left the door open a crack I could look out and see that big back staircase that led up to the studio. I think that's when I first became interested in drawing stairs. They're my signature work, you know."

"There was no toolshed," I told Will.

"It was hidden behind some trees," Mahoney said. "Anyway, I could see you hurrying up the stairs, you were always in a big hurry. I got a good look at your legs from that angle, and you had this purple cape with all this black mink on it, and it was always blowing around your legs. Great legs then." He paused to take a long look at them now and nodded. "Still pretty good."

Will broke in sternly. "Mr. Mahoney, do you have information for us or not?"

"I am *talking* to your *sister*," he said, getting angry. "I thought you people were supposed to be so polite."

I glanced at Will and could see that he was thinking the same thing I was: we didn't know whether to be relieved that Mahoney was a fraud or terrified that he seemed more and more unhinged.

Mahoney stood in front of me and started bouncing up and down on the balls of his feet as he kept talking. "I sketched you hundreds of times," he told me. "Not your whole body, not like Nick"—and he actually snorted—"but your legs while you were climbing those stairs. One of my favorite paintings, in fact, one I've never sold, comes from those sketches: your legs running up the stairs with that black mink blowing around your knees. Let me show you." He picked up the portfolio and began to unzip it.

"I'm not buying anything right now, Mr. Mahoney," I said.

"Wait, wait. Take a look."

And he took out a small oil painting, about six inches by four, and dropped it into my lap. It looked remarkably like the pastel he had sent, but older and more polished—and I have to admit, not bad. The top was also unfinished—he clearly meant for me to walk off the top of that zigzagging staircase into a void—but this version was more evocative. The fur on the bright purple cape gleamed, suggesting wealth, making the unpainted wooden stairs seem even shabbier. The bare legs, in thin black pumps with high heels, were, in fact, very shapely. Like Nick's old painting of his silvery house, the image seemed haunted—yet this one meant nothing to me.

"We're not in the market for art right now," Will said, taking the painting from my lap and handing it back to Mahoney.

"Don't you see what I'm getting at?" Mahoney asked, waving the painting under my nose. "I know the truth about you and Nick."

"Everyone knows the truth," Will said, tired and annoyed. "She went on *Sunday Magazine* and told the world. I'm afraid we have no more time for you, Mr. Mahoney."

Mahoney didn't even look his way. He stood in front of me earnestly and said, "Not that truth, the real truth. You lied on TV, but you don't have to lie with me, Caroline, I'm on your side. I'm here to help you through this, we can get through it together. I want you to come clean all the way this time, the whole truth and nothing but, as they say."

"I think you may be a little confused," I said calmly, not wanting to inflame him.

"You lied," Mahoney went on. He started pacing and clutching his fringe of hair as if he were trying to pull it out, still holding the painting in one hand. His eyes seemed glazed. "You said on the television you had this great love affair with Nick. Maybe once upon a time. But what about the big fight and the breakup? What about the fact that you were keeping Nick and were about to stop the money coming? He confided in me, he did. He got a letter from you once, that you were going horse racing somewhere with your husband, but he knew you were really off with some other man. Come on, even if you don't remember me, you have to re-member those fights."

I could only stare. This man *was* insane.

"I took notes!" he cried, and he reached into the portfolio to pull out a gray, cloth-covered accountant's ledger, the kind he could have gotten a few years or a few decades ago. From the corner of my eye I saw Will creeping toward the edge of his seat, as if he were dealing with a mad dog and knew better than to make any sudden moves. Mahoney flipped through the pages of the ledger and went on pacing as he read. "Here, I wrote this down. Nick said to you, 'Who were you really with in Florida? I deserve to know!' And you said to him, 'Harry, of course. You know I have to be with him.' And Nick says, 'No, you were with somebody else.' And Caro-line says, 'No, there's only you, darling. Why don't you trust me all of a sudden?' "

He stopped and looked at me, as if I would be convinced by this fiction that sounded not the least bit like Nick or me. I looked sideways toward Will, which only set Mahoney off. "Don't look at him. I know why Nick was so upset!" He was yelling now. "I know! I overheard the fights. I heard him say you treated him like the hired help, like you owned him the way you owned everything else. He didn't like that. He hated it! When you broke things off and told him the money would stop coming after his show, he took it worse than you knew. Oh ho, much worse than you knew. He got drunk and ran around the studio banging on the walls. You didn't know that, did you? He told me everything: about how you were keeping him like a gigolo, and cheating on him the whole time, or almost the whole time, and you were finally going to dump him for another man, and he would get even. He told me never be an artist. I should have listened too. Look where it got me."

"That's what he believed?" My voice came out in a whisper.

But either Mahoney hadn't heard or decided to ignore me, because he went on in a much more rational tone. "You know, I hadn't decided on being a painter then. I thought about being a playwright or a novelist or a jockey. That's why I kept notes, in case I needed it for a play. I told Nick about this diary"—and he waved the ledger in the air—"when I went to see him in jail, down at the Tombs. Boy, they didn't call it that for nothing. I thought he could use my diary to prove his case, I offered to help, but he said no." Mahoney was standing still, staring above my head, apparently remembering. I saw that Will had somehow, silently, gotten across the room to his desk. Mahoney seemed not to notice. He simply rambled on about Nick.

"He looked sick. I asked how he felt, and he looked like he was going to cry. He didn't, though. All he would do was look toward the guard, like he didn't want him to hear. He mouthed a word I couldn't understand. I thought maybe it was *noisy*, meaning he couldn't talk freely until there was more noise to drown us out. I asked how I could help him, get some friends to raise bail or get him some food or something, but he told me to keep quiet and stay out of sight. He said I would mess up his deal if I talked, but he wouldn't say what deal. What deal was that?" he asked, looking down at me again as if I knew. I shook my head slowly, said nothing, and he went on. "I shut up 'cause Nick asked me to, but now I'm sorry I did. I've been torn up with guilt all these years. He got out and I never heard from him again and it wasn't until ten, twenty years later I figured out the word he was trying to tell me in jail: it wasn't *noisy* it was *poison*. He mouthed the word *poison*. He must have looked sick because he was being poisoned and he was trying to send me a silent message and I didn't get it. It was a scream for help and I let him down."

Mahoney looked as if *he* were about to cry for a minute, then became more businesslike. "You let him down, too, Caroline," he said. "Now he's gone and you've been lying about your love affair like it was the greatest romance in history. We need to set the record straight this time, straight and narrow. If you don't want to—and I have an idea you don't or you would have done it by now—I will." He stepped closer to me and said, "It's all here in my diary. I'll show your pal Jack Tyler."

So he was more than a lunatic after all; he was, as Will had feared, another bumbling would-be blackmailer.

Will was picking up the phone, and I could see he was controlling himself, careful not to upset Mahoney any more than he had to. "I'm afraid we can't help you, Mr. Mahoney, but thank you for coming," he said, the phone still in his hand. "Shall I call someone to see you out?"

"Oh, I haven't gotten to *you* yet, I'm still dealing with her," he told Will, then turned to me again. "Here's what I thought you could do. To make amends."

"We said, we can do nothing for you," Will told him, sounding tougher. "Now, you must go."

"But she can do something. You can, Caroline. You can take this painting—I'll give it to you. Here, take it, it's a gift," and he held the small oil painting toward me. "Get it hung in the Met. You can do that. They listen to you. Give it to them and make them hang it."

I was appalled, and now that I could see Will calling for help, I became less cautious. "I'm afraid I can't," I said. "And even if I could, why would I?"

"Because you don't want Jack Tyler to see my diary. Maybe he'll believe it, maybe not. That's not my problem, that's yours."

Will had spoken softly into the phone and now said, still polite, "Thank you for coming, Mr. Mahoney, but we have no business with you and nothing left to say."

"Don't you want to know what I know about the famous missing Leones?" he asked, turning to Will. "Now it's your turn. You think all I saw from that toolshed were her legs? I saw those other paintings going out of the studio after he was arrested. I was sleeping in there that night, I did that sometimes. I saw two guys carry them out. They were covered in tarps, but I knew what they were. I didn't see you personally, but I know they must have worked for you because Nick didn't know anyone with that kind of money."

Will said nothing, buying us time.

"What do you have to *say* for yourself?" Mahoney yelled.

"Mr. Mahoney, I'm going to be generous and say you're mistaken. We know you could not have seen any such thing. That was all investigated long ago."

"Come on, you both know what I'm talking about," he said, looking from one of us to the other. "Or maybe not." As if something had just occurred to him, he went on, "Maybe only one of you knows." Three security men walked in and surrounded him. "Oh, what are you going to do to me?" he sneered, looking back and forth between Will and me. "You going to do to me what you did to Nick? You going to get me too? One little painting in the Met, that's all I ask. And then I won't say anything. Why do you let them treat me like this, Caroline?" The guards had led him to the door, and he yelled, "Let me get my stuff!" as he tried to shrug them off.

"You okay, Mr. Holbrooke?" one of them asked.

"Yes, just give him his portfolio. Put that little painting and the ledger in it, please, and take it away with him."

Mahoney took his tattered portfolio, the guards close by his side as they led him out. "You know where to reach me if you change your mind," he told Will. "And I'll see you again, Caroline," he said cheerfully. He looked toward me and said in a stage whisper, "I'll see you when you're alone and we can really talk. Maybe you can't talk now 'cause there's someone you need to protect," and the guards closed the door behind them.

"Are you satisfied?" Will said. "He was dangerous, Caroline."

"I know."

"Now I have to take care of this." He was not angry or accusing, just exasperated. "Now I have to make sure he doesn't try to get to you again. We're going to have to hire security people to stay at your house for a while."

"Yes, I'd appreciate that."

"You know, you're lucky you haven't had hundreds of these crackpots at your door. You opened yourself up for it."

"I know." I was trembling now that the danger had passed, at least for the moment.

He sighed as he poured himself another Scotch and one for me. "I'll call some friends. I'll call Ned and a few others and tell them the publicity is attracting threats. They'll put out the word not to write about you anymore."

"Thank you."

All of a sudden he grinned. "You sound abashed, Caroline. Could it be I was right?"

I smiled too. "Yes, you were right. I was wrong, and I should have listened to you. Don't get used to hearing me say it, baby brother."

"Let's go. Come home with me and join us for dinner. Rose would love to see you."

"Thank you, I will."

"And stay out of trouble from now on," he said wearily, as we walked out arm in arm. "I'm getting too old to keep bailing you out."

A year or so later I received a phone call from a doctor at Bellevue. He said he had a patient named Raymond Mahoney who had been picked up on the street, walking in circles and babbling. When they calmed him down, he claimed to be a friend of mine. He also claimed to be a friend of Ginger Rogers's and asked the hospital to call one of us. He said he used to have money but had spent it all and one of us would help him get back on his feet. The doctor wondered if I could help sort this out.

I told him about the visit and about Mahoney's ravings. I explained that Mahoney had so frightened me that we had hired security people to protect me for months afterward, that I had never known Nick to have an assistant, and that I had no memory of ever having seen Mahoney before that day. "That's what I expected to hear," the doctor said.

Mahoney was just a poor, crazed little man, but he had scared me. He scared me back into private life, where I belonged.

FOUR

Philip: The Painting

$\mathcal{I}$ had no idea how much Grandfather had bailed her out until years later," Philip told Alessio.

While he had been talking the heat had become intense, the sun glaring and reflecting off the steel sculptures on the roof. The champagne had left Alessio's mouth sticky and dry. Midway through Philip's story he had taken off his jacket, and his shirt was now clinging to his back. But he had listened quietly, afraid that if he stopped to ask a single question or get a sip of water, he would break the momentum of Philip's performance. There would be time later, Alessio hoped, to ask all his questions; he began compiling a long list. As wilted and passive as he might appear, there wasn't enough sun or cheap champagne in the world to cloud his sense of how important this information was and how lucrative it might be.

He took out a handkerchief to wipe his face, and Philip, who had seemed cool and oblivious to everything during his monologue, finally looked at Alessio's handkerchief and asked, "Is it getting too hot up here?"

Alessio had been silent for so long and become so thirsty that his voice was hoarse when he tried to speak. "Did you talk to Caroline about the painting again? Did you ask her any questions after the day she told you the story?"

"No, I left on a cloud that day, so enchanted that no questions even occurred to me. She died that spring, before I ever saw her again. All the obituaries mentioned the scandal, they couldn't ignore it, but they treated her respectfully. Most of them said she had been the subject of a lewd painting and had denied an affair at the time, then recanted in the name of sexual freedom and equality, that sort of thing. They said much more about her role as a collector and philanthropist, as they should have. And of course everyone assumed the painting had been destroyed. I thought her story only mattered to me."

Philip stood from the bench and said, "Let's make our way down to see Aunt Caroline."

They took the elevator to the ground floor. Alessio hid a satisfied little smile at this reminder that Philip's dramatic trek up the grand staircase hadn't been necessary. Let Philip underestimate him, think he could be controlled. Alessio followed as Philip led him on another meandering route, this time toward Caroline's exhibit, taking a path that made her seem the culmination of centuries of art, Caroline as the center of the world. Philip walked slowly but told no more of the story as they passed through galleries of eighteenth-century French furniture, fifteenth-century Florentine sculptures, immense medieval tapestries. He stopped briefly in a room where suits of armor sat on horseback, wooden lances in their hands. "I always loved this room as a boy. I never miss a chance to walk through it," Philip said. He glanced around as if smiling at friends. "Now I like to think they're Aunt Caroline's knights, protecting her. She's very nearby."

Then he quickly turned left out of the armor room and stepped into the peaceful courtyard of the American Wing, with bright but cool sunlight shining through glass walls onto flowing fountains and gilded sculptures. Philip walked straight to the center of the courtyard, where a large sculpture of a golden Diana stood tall on a column of green marble, naked and graceful, pointing a bow and arrow into the air. "Caroline's ancestor," he told Alessio.

"Really?"

"Not literally, of course, metaphorically."

"They're both very beautiful," Alessio said cautiously. He was willing to play along and say whatever Philip wanted, if only he could guess which question or compliment Philip was hoping for.

"Yes, but that's not what I meant," Philip said, pointing to the label next to the base of the sculpture. Alessio read about the Diana. She had been made in the late nineteenth century, a reproduction of a Saint-Gaudens, and set on the tower of what was then Madison Square Garden. At first, she had been modestly covered in cloth drapery, but when the cloth blew off in the wind she became a scandal. "The sculpture was severely criticized for its nudity," the label read. "But even as a campaign was launched to remove it from the tower, Diana was becoming one of New York's most popular landmarks."

"I think Aunt Caroline would have appreciated the company and the irony, don't you?" Philip asked.

To his right, Alessio saw the exhibition poster, reproducing one of Caroline's sleek Brancusi Birds, above an arrow pointing toward "Nicholas Leone and the Stephens Circle."

"That way?" he asked.

"Not just yet, let's sit here for another minute," Philip said, heading for a bench that faced Diana. "We can look at her while I tell you how Grandfather led me to the portrait." Alessio followed, wishing he could begin to take notes. He would have to find a quiet place the minute he was alone and write down everything he could remember—every question, every fact, every detail that could possibly be a clue. They sat so Diana was pointing her arrow above their heads.

"When my grandfather first mentioned the painting, I hadn't thought about it in years. I hadn't even thought about Aunt Caroline much. More than fifteen years had gone by since that afternoon, and her story had become one of those memories you store away, something precious to turn to when you need to remind yourself what's good in your life. I still feel incredible when I think that she chose *me* to tell her secrets to.

"The day Grandfather called me so urgently I believed I was going to his deathbed. He had been ill for some time, and I prepared myself to say good-bye. He sent Grandmother Rose from the room. That's when he said, 'I'm going to tell you where to find that old portrait of your Great-Aunt Caroline.' I'll never forget it, how he looked so frail yet sounded so intense. 'Try not to judge her. It makes her look like a whore.' Well, you knew Grandfather, he never used that kind of language. He never had much flair for the dramatic in his lifetime, but he absolutely made up for it at the end.

"He fell asleep or became unconscious, I'm not sure which, right after he said it. Of course, I assumed he had been delirious. He was taken to the hospital that night, and we all thought it was the end, but he rallied. I decided not to mention his remark about Aunt Caroline. If he *had* been delirious, bringing it up would only upset him. But a week or so later, when he was a bit stronger, he phoned and told me to come to the hospital at four o'clock the next day to continue our conversation. He said he had made sure he would have no other visitors.

"I found him alone in his room, waiting in a wheelchair. When I had seen him a few days before, he had been ashen and unshaved, dazed with drugs. Now he looked more like himself, freshly shaved, his white hair neatly combed, wearing a new wine-colored silk robe and velvet slippers. He still looked gaunt, and he grimaced from time to time as if in pain. He was obviously not being given as much pain medication as usual, and was more alert than he had been in weeks.

"He asked me to wheel him down the hall to the hospital's solarium, which was like entering a different state of delirium entirely. I don't know if they do this in Italy, but here the best hospitals are something like spas. In the wing where Grandfather was being treated, patients who were well enough could go to a little tea dance every afternoon. There's not much dancing, as you can imagine, but there is tea, and that day a pianist was playing show tunes, Gershwin and Cole Porter. There were enormous flower arrangements everywhere, and waiters passed by with carts of cakes and juice. It was quite elegant except for the bathrobes. This was where Grandfather insisted on talking. 'Secrecy in plain sight,' he said as I wheeled him in.

"So while the pianist played 'I Get a Kick Out of You,' I sat at a table next to Grandfather's chair, beneath a skylight, and called for a waiter to bring him some apple juice and me some tea. When the waiter had left, Grandfather said, 'Keep an eye out. If you see him coming back, give me a signal to stop talking. I don't want anyone to overhear what I have to say. We have some arrangements to make. I have to tell you Caroline's story.'

"I didn't want to tire him, so I said, You only have to tell me about the painting, if it exists. I know the rest of the story—the unveiling, the trial, all of it—Aunt Caroline told me.

"He looked astonished. I said, She did, one Christmas when I was in college. She confided in me, she wanted me to know what happened. Don't trouble yourself with it, Grandfather. I understand. Aunt Caroline told me everything.

" 'She couldn't have,' he said. 'She didn't know everything.' He paused, then said almost to himself, 'I hope she never knew.'

"That can't matter now, I began to say, and he snapped at me, very angry. 'Can't matter? It matters more than you can possibly imagine, Philip.'

"Then he smiled and said warmly, 'Can't matter? You sound so like her when you say that, you have her charm. But you must understand it matters to me more than anything. Caroline is gone and I will follow her soon, and all I can do is trust you to go on protecting her good name and the family's, as I have tried to do all my life. I've done things I never wanted anyone to know, least of all Caroline. I want to tell you so you will know she was innocent— not only of the original event but of everything that happened after. I did what I had to do to protect her, and I don't regret that. Judge me harshly if you like, but you must always remember that I, and I alone, was responsible for my actions. Not Caroline, not ever. And certainly not dear old, deluded Harry.' Grandfather chuckled then. 'He even bought a racehorse he didn't want because it was an easy way to pad expenses and get cash. He got me all the money we needed, but he didn't want to know the nasty details. But you must know the details. It's the only way you can prevent other people from learning them.'

"His words and his sudden bursts of emotion made me very uneasy for his sake. He seemed consumed with some desperate need to assume any blame, all the guilt, that could possibly attach itself to Aunt Caroline. Knowing him as I did, I suspected he was just being noble by taking it all on himself, protecting her from any taint to the very end and beyond. He would have done anything for her, that much had always been clear.

"You don't have to protect her anymore, Grandfather, she's safe, I said, trying to free him from that weight.

"He gave me a withering look and went on. 'There were very few people we could trust back in 'twenty-seven. Lawrence Sloane, the district attorney, was the main one, and Philip, you must protect his reputation as well. He was known all his life for being incorruptible, and he deserves to keep that reputation. He helped us enormously.'

"Yes, Aunt Caroline implied that. He found a way to charge Leone and oversaw the prosecution.

" 'There was more. Did your aunt tell you that Leone's paintings disappeared from the evidence room?'

"Yes.

" 'Did she tell you how?'

"She said the guard was knocked out and everything was missing, no one knew why.

"Grandfather smiled. 'Sloane found out which policemen would be guarding the evidence room on which night, so we knew whom to get to and when to go in. It was awful to watch that man being chloroformed and gagged, but he had named his price like the others.'

"You and Sloane were there?

" 'I was,' Grandfather said. 'Not Sloane, he just helped arrange it. He'd sent me a client, a bank robber who came to the firm under the guise of having an inheritance problem, and he took care of what I suppose you'd call the heavy lifting. Sloane had to keep his distance, but he made things possible. It was Sloane who made it possible for me to meet with that damn Leone in jail. The idea made my skin crawl. It had made my skin crawl just to be in the same room with him that night of the opening, to see him at Caroline's elbow, drooling over her. You can imagine how disgusting it was for me to meet him in jail.'

"As he recalled this, Grandfather seemed to shiver, and I asked, Are you cold? Do you want me to get you a blanket?

" 'Oh, Philip, please, let me go on,' he said. He was very impatient. 'I will be much colder than this for a long, long time, so do let me go on.'

"Of course, Grandfather. Whatever you say.

" 'I did not want to set eyes on Leone ever again, but there was no one else we could trust to do it. We couldn't ask Sloane to do such a thing. It was Harry or me, and that was no choice at all. A few weeks before the trial, Sloane arranged for me to slip in to see Leone in his cell. I arrived at the Tombs around three in the morning, met with him alone, and left before anyone knew I'd been there. He was sitting on the edge of a filthy cot when I was let in, as if he never slept. He looked seedier than ever; his hair was greasy and falling into his eyes. He sneered at me. *Well, look who she sent, the baby brother, the lamb*, he said. *What do you want? Whatever you're offering, it's not enough.*

" 'I sat next to him on the cot so I could speak in a low voice. He stared at me. He was so close I could smell his rancid breath. I thought I was going to vomit, but I steeled myself and said: I think you should be quiet. You should be quiet about this visit and about everything I am going to say. And you should be silent at your trial. You will not speak a word at the trial or for the rest of your life if you want to have any kind of life at all.

" 'Leone said, *You can't threaten me. I haven't done anything wrong.*

" 'The judge will disagree, I said.

" '*You don't know that.*

" 'Yes, I do. As a matter of fact, I do.

" '*You're bluffing.*

" 'Do you want to take that chance?

" 'Leone looked at me for a second, then became sarcastic. *Any message from my precious Caroline? Is she dreaming of me?* I thought I might hit him, but somehow I controlled myself and said: You have to deal with me now. I don't know much about you, but I know you like money. I'm here to buy that obscene painting.

" '*You like to look at it, baby brother? Well, I don't have it anymore, and when I get it back it's not for sale, not to you.*

" 'I am going to buy that painting. I don't care where it happens to be right now. I need to own it.

" 'He smirked at me. *You think you can buy anything, don't you? That painting will make my name, and I'm not going let you take it so you can hoard it and satisfy your sick fantasies about her and do whatever you like to do in private while you're looking at it.*

" 'I walked to the bars of the cell and grabbed them so hard I thought they would break in my hands. I knew he was trying to provoke me, and I looked out through the bars until I was calm. Then I turned and walked back toward the cot and stood looking down at that creature with his sickening grin. I said: You have a choice. Money and a new life somewhere else, or poverty and obscurity for as long as you live. If you do not sell that painting to me, you will not find work or patrons no matter how hard you try, anywhere you go. You will not find work sweeping streets, in any city in the world. We can make sure of that.

" 'In truth, I wasn't sure we could stop him from earning a living anywhere in the world, but I knew we could take care of things at home.

" 'Leone stood up and laughed. He was still mocking me. *The kid brother gets tough. You don't know what you're saying.* He thought he could overcome us, both of us. He said, *Let me explain a few things about your goddess of a sister. Caroline and I were lovers. She did more for me and to me than I could begin to suggest in that painting, things you don't even know exist. Imagine that, if you can, put your pathetic fantasies to work trying to picture your sister naked on top of me, imagine her mouth . . .'*

"Grandfather sounded as if he were about to sob, and he paused for just a second before he went on. 'I remember wondering if I should kill him right there, I thought if I smashed his head against the concrete wall hard enough I could do it. Then I wondered if we could arrange to have him killed a slow, painful death, worse than anything I could do to him alone. I didn't believe him about Caroline, not then. How could she have been with such an animal?'

"Grandfather, I said, don't upset yourself this way.

"He turned to me but was staring furiously ahead as if he were seeing Leone. 'He thought he could get away with it, that he could malign Caroline, take advantage of her generosity, humiliate her and become rich and famous for it.' There was a violence in his eyes I'd never seen before. I think that look was much more disturbing to me than anything he'd said. All around us in the solarium I could see patients being wheeled by or walking with their IVs rolling alongside. I could hear the pianist playing "Cheek to Cheek." Grandfather seemed to see and hear nothing. He said in a voice so cold and menacing I could imagine how well it convinced Leone, 'I'll be back in a few days with a bill of sale for that painting. You will sign it.

" 'And I left the cell,' Grandfather said, sounding like himself again. He took a sip of apple juice and looked around as if to remind himself where he was. 'When I went back to the jail a few days later, Leone looked so sick I was surprised they hadn't moved him to a hospital ward, but there he was in the same cell, lying on the filthy cot. The cell reeked, as if the toilet in the corner had overflowed. He wasn't smirking anymore. I promised him money. I showed him a bill of sale that proved we had bought the painting for a hundred dollars. We didn't want to give him even that much, but we didn't want it to look too suspicious.

" 'Sick as he was, Leone resisted. He said, No, you can't have it. He sounded like death. It was my turn to laugh at him. I said: You really don't have a choice, do you?

" 'He said, You did this to me, as if I could have made him sick, as if being in that damp, rat-infested place wasn't enough to make anyone sick. I laughed again. I took out a pen. I had to help Leone sit up, though it repulsed me to touch him. I put my own briefcase on his lap with the agreement on top of it and put the pen in his hand, and he signed.

" 'Stop doing this to me now, he said as he fell back on the cot. I don't *want to die in here.* But I didn't have another word to say. I walked out and never spoke to him again. As sick as he looked at the trial, he had recovered a lot by then.'

"Grandfather leaned forward and gestured for me to come toward him so he could whisper in my ear. He said, 'There is a small wall safe in our bedroom that only your grandmother knows about, behind some shelves in her closet. She will open it for you after I'm gone, but she won't know what you're looking for. There are many papers in there, but they're useless. I put them there to make it look convincing. The only valuable papers are the bill of sale for that painting and the document that proves I have given it to you as a gift.' He leaned back in his wheelchair. 'That's all you have to worry about, that one painting. There are no other works by Leone. I was very thorough at the time, and Harry was relentless afterward.'

"You never found any? I asked. Aunt Caroline told me Uncle Harry did, and destroyed them without telling her.

" 'Years later he found a couple, but they weren't dangerous. Leone stopped painting after he was arrested, and there wasn't much of his earlier work around. Remember, he was young when he went after Caroline and not a success, so we didn't have much to take care of.'

"We? You and Uncle Harry or you and Sloane?

" 'Me,' Grandfather said, sounding annoyed again. 'Me.'

"Do you know how the rest of his work disappeared?

" 'That wasn't even difficult. The robber Sloane sent me knew what he was doing. I'm not sure how he did it. He said it was better if I didn't know. But he and his men made Leone's work disappear from his room and the studio and later from the evidence room. Every piece of it was burned so there'd be no trace left, all except that one. It was the only way. You never know what people might pay for. We had to make sure Leone was totally crushed, you see, with no money, nothing to sell, no hope for the future. You do see what I'm saying, Philip?'

"Yes, I do. But weren't you worried that your client might have kept something to sell? He *was* a bank robber.

"Grandfather shook his head as he looked at me and sounded weary. 'Philip, have you learned nothing about the way of the world? Haven't I taught you better than that? We protected ourselves. Besides giving them a trunkful of cash, I mean. These men were easy targets for the police, we knew who they were. We made it clear that if any work of Leone's ever turned up anywhere, through them or not, they'd all be back in prison in a minute. As long as no Leones turned up, Sloane's office would forget those men existed. They were, you might say, meticulous in their work. There were certain pieces of evidence Sloane needed to keep for important cases, and they weren't damaged at all. Caroline's portrait was another matter. I arranged to have that delivered to me later so I could destroy it myself, Harry and I agreed on that. There was too great a risk there; it would have been too tempting for someone to slip it to some pornography collector who might be willing to pay a fortune for it.'

"He sounded gentle, even wistful as he said, 'You have to pay attention to these things, my boy. You need to know how to handle such matters, know whom to trust. I had a hard time over the years explaining to Harry just how much he owed Larry Sloane. I'm not sure I ever convinced him. Harry seemed to have a grudge against him, maybe he couldn't bear to be that much in his debt. Caroline always understood, or at least as much as we told her. I never told her about destroying Leone's work, she never knew we had anything to do with that part of it. Even though she hated him by then and wanted the rest of his life ruined, she still thought he was some kind of genius. I did tell her—and I've regretted it ever since, more than anything in my life—I told her I had arranged to get the portrait after the trial to destroy it. I thought it would put her mind at ease to know that no one would ever see that evil thing again.'

"Grandfather sounded amazed, as if he still couldn't believe what he was about to say. 'She refused to let me get rid of it. She would not let me destroy that piece of filth. She said I need to see it, just once. We argued terribly. I always hated arguing with Caroline, but it was for her own good. I didn't have the painting in my hands yet because we were still under too much scrutiny from the newspapers. She and Harry were sailing for Europe soon, Harry had decided on it, and I would stay behind and get the painting while they were gone. She was frantic. She cried and threw her arms around me and held me so tight I thought I'd suffocate. She made me swear on everything that was sacred to me, she made me swear on her life, that I would not destroy the painting while she was away. She made me swear not to tell Harry I'd kept it. Well, in the end I never could deny her a thing, not when she threw herself in my arms and pleaded like that. She kept begging me to go to Europe with them, too, I don't know what she was thinking. How could I have guarded the painting and protected her if I were away? I thought that was a sign she wasn't seeing things clearly anymore and told her so. But she wouldn't be moved, and it was her life, not mine.'

"Then Grandfather abruptly began speaking in a completely different, quite happy tone. 'Did I ever tell you how your grandmother and I met? Not how we actually met, but how we fell in love?'

"I'd always heard a cousin introduced you. And you didn't get along at first.

" 'It's not that we didn't get on. We liked each other well enough, but it's true there were no fireworks at the beginning. We were young, and I guess I wasn't ready to be serious, so we went out once or twice and that was that. But when Caroline and Harry were away I had time to myself; I'd always spent so much with them. And I thought of Rose and called her again, and this time there were fireworks. It hit me so strongly that she was the girl of my dreams, I couldn't believe I hadn't seen it before. She says she felt that way about me from the start, but I'm not so sure. Anyway, everything happened fast, much faster than usual in those days. She was so pretty and sweet and innocent, I couldn't resist her. She was my happiness and my refuge from everything, and she has been my refuge to this day. I wasn't sorry I'd protected my little sister, but Rose made me feel good again. I've never told her anything of what I'd done.'

"Grandfather turned to me and grabbed my hand, upset again. 'Whatever you do, Philip, promise me you won't tell your grandmother about this. I have tried to shield her, as I shielded Caroline. Promise me she'll never know.'

"I promise, I'll protect her.

" 'They required such different kinds of protection,' he said, grabbing my hand more tightly. 'You may think I'm a foolish old man now, but I did try to protect her, I tried to save her, I tried to warn her. She was even more persuasive then than she is now. She was incomparably beautiful, the most beautiful woman I had ever seen. She'd look at me with those eyes and call me her lamb and I'd do anything. She returned from Europe with Harry and insisted on looking at that vile painting. She knew I had it. I said: Why hurt yourself this way? And she said: I have to, I have to know.'

"He stared into space as he talked but never let go of my hand, and he sounded more anguished as he went along. 'We arranged to meet at Mother's one afternoon when we knew she and most of the staff would be out. The canvas had been delivered to me rolled up inside a large carpet, and I had my own servants drive me to Mother's as if I were bringing the carpet as a gift. They carried it to the room that had been Caroline's, the room where I

had tried to stop her from marrying Harry. I had seen the painting briefly at the gallery. And I had made myself look quickly
when it was delivered to make sure I hadn't been cheated, but
God knows I never wanted to see that thing again.

"'When Caroline arrived, we unrolled the carpet together. At
first we only saw the edge of the carpet, and even that I'll always
remember—an Aubusson, blue and gold on a beige background.
Then there it was, that painting, laid out on the floor. It was horrible. It looked as if Caroline were lying there with Leone leering
over her, watching her, waiting for her, telling her what to do to
herself and she did it. I always knew he was filth from the minute I
saw him, the way he looked at her in public, as if he had some
right to her. He didn't deserve to have a career afterward, he didn't
deserve to survive in the same city as Caroline, even in the lowest
way, and I do not regret anything I did. I'm glad I never gave him
the money I promised. I never meant to. He deserved that. He deserved worse, I should have done him real harm when I had the
chance and it would have been over.'

"Grandfather stopped and let go of my hand. He looked at me,
and I saw the expression Aunt Caroline had described, as sad as any
I have ever seen. His voice was calm and quiet now. He said, 'She
stood looking at that thing he had made, no expression on her face.
Without saying a word, she got down on her hands and knees to
get a closer look. Then she sat on the floor for a long time, it must
have been twenty minutes, staring at it. I wouldn't look at it again.
I kept my eyes on her face. I knew better than to speak or disturb
her, she seemed lost in her thoughts. Finally, I saw tears roll down
her cheeks, though her face remained still. And she said, very softly,
without taking her eyes off it: *Please do this for me. I want you to hide this
painting so no one will ever find it in my lifetime. Do not damage it, but do not let me
or anyone else ever see it again while I live.*

"'Then she stood and left the room. I rolled up the carpet, not easy to do alone, and by the time I got downstairs she was gone. We never mentioned that day again. I took that awful thing back home; the servants must have thought Mother didn't like it. I hid it in my study for weeks while I figured out the details.'

"Grandfather reached into the pocket of his robe and handed me a slip of paper. 'I memorized this long ago, and you should too,' he said. It had the address and phone number of a place called Miller Storage in Goshen, Connecticut. 'We have furniture stored there. It's all yours now. I've made it over to you. And there is an Aubusson carpet, rolled up. When you unroll it, be certain you have complete privacy. Look at me, Philip, this is extremely important. You have the discretion to do what you want with the painting. I promised Caroline I would not destroy it, but you have made no such promise.'

"What do you want me to do? I asked.

" 'What you know is right,' he said, still sad. After the long afternoon he sounded so weak it seemed a great effort for him to speak at all. 'I want you to think well of her. Think badly of me if you like, but please do not think badly of her. She asked nothing of me that I was not willing to do. I wish I could have spared her more pain, but I didn't know how. I never knew how to please her enough and now she is gone.' He closed his eyes and grimaced, giving in to his own pain at last.

"The pianist had stopped playing. The sun coming through the skylight had faded, and the room was nearly empty. The waiters were clearing the tea things away, and a nurse came to ask if she could help me wheel Grandfather back to his room. I shook my head and stood behind his chair so she wouldn't come any closer. Then I bent over him and whispered, Is there anything else you need to tell me before we go back, Grandfather? 'No,' he said. 'That's everything you need.'

"I got him to his room, then drove home repeating the address and phone number of Miller Storage out loud, wondering what, if anything, I would find there, thinking about what else I might need to ask Grandfather while I could. He got much worse the next day, and from then on was so full of morphine he was hardly himself. I was alone with him one afternoon when Grandmother was at home resting. He was groggy and in pain, but a bit more lucid than usual, so I took the opportunity I knew might not come again.

"I need to ask you something about Aunt Caroline, I said, and he looked at me without speaking. What about Mahoney? I asked him. Was there any truth in what he said?

"Grandfather looked puzzled. I reminded him, Mahoney, Raymond Mahoney, the artist. Aunt Caroline told me how he came to you and claimed he had been Leone's assistant. He said he knew what happened to the missing paintings. He came to your office and tried to blackmail her, and she was frightened.

"Grandfather nodded then and gestured toward the cup of water by his bed. I helped him drink and he said, 'Crazy. Crackpot.'

"Did he ever contact you again?

"'Yes,' Grandfather said, his voice thick. 'Gibberish letters. To me. A few. He didn't know anything.'

"Did he contact Aunt Caroline again?

"'Didn't know anything,' Grandfather repeated, sounding lost. 'No link to us.'

"Grandfather, it's me, Philip, please concentrate. Did Raymond Mahoney ever contact Caroline again?

"He focused his eyes on me, his voice tired but clear. 'No. I asked, and she said No.'"

"Grandfather died a few days later," Philip told Alessio. "It hit Grandmother Rose very hard, as you might expect. We thought we were prepared, but you never are, are you? When I thought Grandmother was finally up to it, I asked her to open the safe in her bedroom closet. It took a while to sort through the papers, but eventually I found this. Or rather, this is a copy of what I found." He reached into his jacket pocket and handed Alessio a bill of sale stating that on November 17, 1927, William Holbrooke had bought an untitled painting by Nicholas Leone for one hundred dollars, a life-size nude of a woman wearing gold filigreed earrings. Sitting on the bench before Diana, oblivious to her as they bent their heads over the document, they looked like two businessmen who had decided to work out some highly sensitive and possibly irregular deal in the last place anyone would find them.

"He thought of everything," Philip said as Alessio examined the paper. "This must have protected them in case Leone was found innocent and the painting was given back to him. It certainly gave Grandfather the right to destroy it free and clear. I have to hand it to him. I always respected Grandfather's judgment, but when I realized how he managed all this, I was more impressed than ever. He was pretty young and inexperienced in those days, and there was no one he could turn to for help. I guess Aunt Caroline was right when she said he learned fast."

Alessio handed the paper back to Philip and turned his head conspicuously in the direction of Caroline's exhibit. He had seen more than enough of Diana.

"I've just thought of something," Philip said. "Maybe if you write the biography you would like to have some of the furniture the painting was stored with. As a gift, naturally, no strings attached. To inspire you. Maybe the antique desk the painting sat on all those years."

"The desk?" Alessio sounded intrigued; he couldn't help himself.

"Yes. The painting was still rolled up in the carpet when I found it, and the carpet was stored on top of a magnificent eighteenth-century mahogany desk. I don't know where it came from but it's a beautiful piece. It's still there, with Mrs. Miller. I found her about a month after the funeral when I called the number Grandfather had given me. There was so much to take care of, and I didn't see how to leave town for even a day before that. And, I can admit it now, I was a little afraid of being disappointed.

"When I finally called, I heard this faint old woman's voice say hello, and I was sure I had the wrong number. Or worse, that Grandfather had misremembered it, or the company had gone out of business. I thought the painting, even if it had survived, really was lost forever.

"I said, 'I'm trying to reach Miller Storage,' and the old woman answered, 'I suppose that's me,' but she didn't sound sure. 'Who are you?' she asked.

" 'My name is Philip Holbrooke and—'

" 'Ah, Mr. Holbrooke,' she said. 'We've been expecting you for years. Would you like to come see your things?'

"We settled on a day and time, and she gave me such elaborate directions I knew no one could possibly stumble across this place accidentally. 'When you get here, you won't see any sign for Miller Storage,' she told me. 'There will be a sign at the start of the drive that says Miller Studio, Art Lessons. You're looking for Adele Miller, that's me.' This time she sounded sure.

"I drove there alone as Grandfather had ordered and got lost a few times before I found the right turn, onto a dirt road almost hidden in the overgrowth. Eventually I found a tall post with a weathered wooden sign made of three planks, one on top of the other: the upper one said Miller Studio; the middle one said Art Lessons next to a faded painting of a palette; the bottom said Antiques Restored, with a painting of a spinning wheel. I turned into the driveway and went past a shingled barn to a white farmhouse. It all looked old and picturesque and deserted, with no sign of human life, not to mention crops or animals. I knocked at the door, waited a minute, then knocked again and eventually heard the old woman's voice say, 'I'm coming. I'll get there. Don't go.'

"Mrs. Miller was a tiny woman who looked as if she was in her eighties, though she must have been even older. She wore a fresh, flowered dress and had thin gray hair pulled back in a ponytail that reached almost to her waist. She didn't ask me in but pointed toward the barn I had passed. 'We're going over there, that's where your things are,' she said. 'Been there for years.' She tottered along a gravel path toward the barn, carrying a huge ring of keys. 'You know, I always wanted to meet your grandfather, but never did. I was sorry when I read in the paper about his passing. My husband met him once, when he first came to bring the furniture, that one time. We read everything about your family after that. My husband would have liked to meet you, I know. He's been gone a few years now.'

"She unlocked the barn door, and I pulled it open for her. She stepped in, turned on a light switch, and I saw a room filled with paintings of orchards, all uncovered and leaning against a wall, and reproductions of Early American furniture. 'My husband was the painter. I kept signing those checks your grandfather sent him, I hope that was okay. I never sent word he died. It didn't seem to bother the bank.'

"Mrs. Miller saw me looking around—pieces of furniture were stacked on top of each other, canvases were on the floor, all unprotected—and she laughed. 'Don't worry, this isn't yours, yours is in the next room.' She led the way to another door that had to be unlocked. This smaller room was insulated against the weather. There were about two dozen pieces of furniture, or I assumed it was furniture, covered in heavy tarpaulin. 'This whole room is yours. Take your time, take what you want. I'll be sorry to see it go. Your family has been very good to mine over the years. Well, I'll leave you alone to look around. Head back to the house when you're through, and I can get our handyman to help you carry anything you want. Can I send you out some lemonade?'

" 'No, thank you, that's very kind. I think I'll just look around on my own, as you suggested.'

" 'Suit yourself,' she said. 'I'll be back at the house when you're ready.'

"It took a long time for her to totter to the main door of the barn. I waited until I thought she had reached the house, an excruciating wait at that point, then closed the door to the small room and tried to absorb what I saw. It seemed so innocuous. I don't know what I'd expected. I must have imagined I would walk into some replica of Haskell's gallery and find Aunt Caroline's portrait staring at me. Part of me dreaded seeing her like that; I suppose I picked that up from Grandfather. But I was more afraid of not finding the painting at all. Anything could have happened to it.

"I forced myself to start. I pulled back one tarp and found a green horsehair sofa. Under other coverings there were chairs and tables, a few that looked like fine antiques, but most of them well-made pieces that might have been new in my great-grandmother's day. Then I lifted a tarp off a large, ornately carved desk and saw a rolled carpet sitting on top of it. I turned back one corner of the carpet and saw a blue and gold pattern on beige. I stuck my hand farther inside and touched something—it felt like a linen sheet covering something thicker, possibly canvas.

"I almost ran to the farmhouse, and I did have some lemonade. Mrs. Miller had a pitcher and glasses all set out on the porch with cookies, and it would have been rude not to. Then her handyman helped me load the carpet, two small chairs and a small table in the car, all that would fit but enough to disguise what I was really after. I broke the speed limit going back to New York.

"I learned from Mrs. Miller how well she had been paid to store the furniture and decided to let her go on storing the rest. No wonder she didn't have to run a farm. That's where the mahogany desk is now. It might inspire you as you're writing about Aunt Caroline, Alex; she did sit on that desk for quite a long time."

"No one has called me Alex in years," Alessio said. He sounded amused. "You haven't called me that in years."

"It must have come from all this reminiscing, all this family feeling. I do still consider you part of the family," Philip said. He stood from the bench abruptly and headed toward the exhibit, saying, "Well, let's go," as if it took some burst of will or courage to do it at last. Alessio trailed after him.

Philip paused in front of a sales counter loaded with Caroline paraphernalia: posters and postcards, exhibition catalogs and DVDs, reproductions of her gold filigreed earrings and her favorite pink cashmere shawl. He picked up a postcard, then put it down, saying, "This is good for the Met, but no reproduction does her justice. There's nothing like the first time you see the portrait." He quickly walked ahead.

When Alessio had once again caught up and was walking by his side, Philip said, "I remember the first time I saw it. When I got home with the furniture, I had the carpet carried into a guest room and placed on the floor, still rolled up, as if we were going to consider putting it down there. Olivia was the only person I trusted to help me, and we waited until the servants were asleep. We snuck into the room in the middle of the night, the two of us in our robes, and untied it. When we rolled it out, what we saw was the Aubusson with a large white sheet in the center. I began pulling the sheet down, slowly from top to bottom, and as I did Aunt Caroline's face emerged."

That besotted tone was creeping into Philip's voice, Alessio noticed.

"The face was unmistakably hers, the face of an angel. She had the most beautiful, enigmatic smile, more dazzling than the gold earrings that caught the light. I kept pulling the sheet down slowly, revealing more and more of the painting, more of her body, and I must say, I could see why a woman of her generation would have fainted. When I looked back up at her face, her smile seemed different, more knowing. It is an extraordinary work of art."

"What did Olivia say?" Alessio asked.

"First she said she understood why the family had guarded it so carefully. Then she said"—and Philip raised an eyebrow slightly— "to tell you the truth, since you're my oldest friend, she said it was sexy. I guess she had a point, though it's a strange thing to think about your great-aunt. And when I consider what Grandfather might have thought—well, you'll judge for yourself."

Philip had led them out of the courtyard into the next gallery, which re-created a dining room from the Federalist period, with a large, polished table under a crystal chandelier. As they passed through the room, Alessio imagined the ghosts of Caroline's dinner guests sitting around that table—Harry and Spencer and Will and even Nick, improbably gathered together as in a dream. He followed Philip up a short flight of stairs to a mezzanine, where straight ahead he saw Sargent's *Madame X* in her plunging black dress. Her haughty eroticism had once been considered brazen, too. Had everything in this museum once been a scandal? Maybe everyone had overreacted to Caroline's portrait, Alessio thought. Maybe the entire New York art world on one wintry night in 1927 had been in the grip of some St. Vitus' dance of the mind that made them believe they had seen something lascivious in a perfectly tame nude.

He turned to the right, where the Stephens exhibit began. And in the center of a white wall, in the simplest golden frame, there she was, standing before him: Caroline, life-size, beautiful, enticing. Her soft brown hair gleamed as it curled and fell on her right breast. Her skin was ivory, and somehow you knew it felt like rose petals. Her left hand was hidden behind her head, and the fingers of her right hand reached down in front of her, mysteriously. Her smile was small and enigmatic, her lips slightly open. And her eyes, her guileless blue eyes were life itself as she looked shamelessly out, at every man in the world, with love and honesty and the whispered promise of unspeakable pleasure.

"She is magnificent," Alessio whispered to Philip, who was standing proudly beside him, beaming with ownership. They stared for a long while.

At last Alessio turned away to look at the rest of the exhibit. It was an old trick; he would then return to Caroline and appreciate her with fresh vision.

The entire show was contained in two modest rooms. Caroline's portrait stood alone on one wall. Facing it was Sargent's portrait of Edith as a young woman, leaning awkwardly against the mantel, eternally glaring at her daughter with disapproval. It was, Alessio thought, an excellent Sargent, as Caroline had said. It seemed to him that the portrait revealed Edith to be a person with no curiosity, someone who would have her nose buried in her teacup. But then Alessio always worried that he just didn't understand Americans.

The other works were by Leone's contemporaries, most of them from Caroline's own collection. The Marins were there and the Sheelers, and of course her prized Brancusi Birds. But while each work was exquisite in itself, from realistic to Cubist and abstract, together they simply highlighted Leone's originality; his magnificent portrait had broken with every school. The critics had not overstated that.

Alessio was about to turn back to Caroline when he glanced through the crowd into the gallery beyond the Stephens exhibit and saw a small, vaguely familiar painting almost hidden in an alcove. He dashed toward it. This time Philip trailed after Alessio.

Tucked away in what might have been the least important position in all of the Met was an oil painting, barely six inches by four, of a zigzagging wooden staircase with a woman's legs ascending, a purple cape with black fox trim swirling around her knees as if she were in a great rush. It was signed "Raymond Mahoney," and the plaque beside it read, "Gift of anonymous donor, 1969."

"Mahoney," Alessio said.

"Yes." Philip was standing calmly at his side. "Mahoney," he said, as if he had never heard the name before.

"But this painting, this is the one he tried to blackmail her with."

"Oh no, of course it's not. He made dozens like that. Those staircases *were* his signature. But it's a minor work, don't you think? I have no idea why it's hanging here at all."

"But . . . the date. Wasn't 'sixty-nine when Mahoney tried to blackmail her?"

"Yes, as it happens. Obviously a coincidence."

"Where did this come from?"

"I don't know, it's anonymous."

"But we must find out," Alessio said. "We . . ."

Philip put his arm around his friend's shoulder and gently but firmly turned him around. "Never mind that, come with me," he said, leading Alessio back toward the portrait. "Caroline is waiting. We can't disappoint her."

EPILOGUE

Caroline's Last Words

lessio did not have the Holbrooke flair for storytelling, but he was a scrupulous researcher. Before he wrote a word of *Immortal Caroline: The Life and Influence of Caroline Holbrooke Stephens*, he interviewed nearly a hundred people and in the end was satisfied that he had created as comprehensive, objective, and authoritative a biography as there could be.

True to his word, Philip had turned over Caroline's papers, given him access to her art collection and entrée to all the Holbrooke intimates and associates. And he never asked his old friend to change a thing. Philip even gave Alessio the use of an apartment in New York and an office down the hall from his own, where the eighteenth-century mahogany desk did seem to inspire him.

Caroline herself seemed to be a vivid and helpful presence in the room, a muse or a guardian angel. The unedited version of her famous television interview had been cleaned out of the network's vaults long before, but Alessio had a tape of the final version, and he watched it often as he worked at her desk. He could understand why she had been so surprised by the public reaction. The Caroline he saw on screen was an astonishingly beautiful older woman who had retained a look of pure innocence, her soft blue eyes gazing directly into the camera even when she spoke of her most embarrassing memories. Her honest beauty had made the public adore and embrace her. From her side of the camera, she could not possibly have seen what they did, what Alessio did.

There was one moment on the tape he returned to again and again. It came after Caroline had said, as she had so many times in her life, that she had not posed for the portrait, had no knowledge that Nick had painted it, no idea why he had done it. She sighed and sat very still, her hands folded serenely in her lap, looking straight ahead. It was the briefest lull, but in that quiet second Alessio thought he saw in her eyes, beneath her innocence, the look she had in the portrait, promising endless revelations and pleasures. He paused the tape and looked at the frozen image over and over. What had she been thinking? What was she telling him? After many months he realized he would find no hidden message in her look; he was simply captivated by her beauty. Yet he went on playing the tape and freezing that moment, because he wanted his book to be worthy of her eternal promise.

When the biography was published, Philip hosted a party at the Temple of Dendur, and Alessio was dazzled by the people who came to celebrate him—painters and sculptors, art critics and collectors, Wall Street moguls and Hollywood stars. All night long, actresses in 1920s-inspired dresses sipped champagne in the shadow of the Egyptian temple, touching Alessio's hand while telling him how they adored his book and, by the way, longed to play Caroline in the movie.

Alessio was pleased with the book's success; it sold well and was generally praised. Even the few negative reviews, from academics who quibbled jealously about his qualifications—they saw him as a mere dealer, a lapsed scholar—acknowledged that Caroline's warm, seductive personality came through despite his sometimes stiff writing.

Yet it had been with excruciating disappointment that he had written, at the last possible moment, the final words to his epilogue: "Despite the most thorough searches throughout the United States and Europe, no evidence has been discovered of any other surviving works by Nicholas Leone."

Alessio had used every contact available, searched almost as hard as Harry had, but turned up nothing more than false leads. This was difficult for him to admit. For the longest time Alessio had believed that Philip knew more than he was letting on, that he was waiting for the right moment to reveal that he had a secret cache of Leones, or at least a theory about where to look.

At the beginning, Alessio dreamed that Philip would make this grand announcement after he signed the contract with the publisher. When that didn't happen, he told himself that Philip was still testing him, waiting until he thought Alessio was ready, perhaps after he had become more familiar with Caroline's papers and collection. Hadn't Philip insisted on dragging him through the Met as if it were a labyrinth on the day he first saw Caroline? Naturally, he would do something similar now. Whenever he saw Philip, Alessio was half-expecting to be handed a treasure map, but the map never materialized, and at last Alessio decided that his friend had told all he knew.

Philip, of course, was a major source for the biography and the only source for Will's deathbed confession. Alessio held nothing back in reporting Will's tale, but he was cautious, emphasizing Will's weakened state of mind when he spoke to his grandson about those faraway years.

Alessio himself had found no proof that Will had done anything illegal or the least bit underhanded. But he couldn't disprove anything Will had said either, and he *had* led his grandson to the supposedly missing portrait. So in response to the book, a widely shared interpretation of the entire affair took hold, a view in which

Caroline was seen as the wronged heroine, Nick the malicious genius, and Will the villain who had destroyed the genius's future.

Nick's name, Alessio learned, really was Leone, but his family couldn't offer much more. His great-nieces and -nephews, those who would talk, had little memory of him and no artifacts at all—not even a baby picture, much less any childhood doodles. David Leone, whom Alessio had tracked to his new home in Arizona, had not responded to his many letters and calls.

Even without any new Leones, though, the book was beautifully illustrated and designed. There were photographs of Caroline's collection as it had changed over the years, her black velvet settee a constant through it all. There were newspaper photos from the trial, and reproductions of Caroline's love letters to Nick. And there was a color plate that reproduced four Mahoneys from various private collections, all depicting the same zigzagging wooden staircase with a woman's legs ascending, each with a different fur-trimmed cape—violet, royal blue, red, and deepest black—swirling in the wind as she dashed up. The paintings were undated but seemed to come from the same period as the one that had hung in the Met near Caroline. The presence of that Mahoney had to mean something, Alessio thought. But the gift remained a mystery, wrapped in layers of legal documents that confirmed its authenticity while shielding the donor's identity. For all Alessio knew, the donor could have been the crazed little artist himself.

He discovered that Mahoney had died in Bellevue in 1983, a forgotten old man who had been there for years. Alessio wrote that Mahoney's accusations were the ravings of a seriously disturbed mind. While in Bellevue, when not properly medicated, he ranted at the attendants to help him reach his important friends. Ginger Rogers was starring in one of his plays on Broadway, he said, and if he sold his secret diary he could raise the money for a ticket. He left no trace of any diary or ledger.

Near the end of the biography, Alessio reprinted the letter Caroline had written to Philip, not long after she had told him her story, not long before she died.

January 7, 1979

My dearest Philip,

As you sat with me by the fire the other day, you looked so like your grandfather that I could hardly believe it was not Will as he used to be, young and dear as a lamb, with all his life before him and all his ideals intact. It was a gift to me to see that innocent face again. He did everything I ever asked. I fear I have damaged his life.

Thank you for listening to my secrets as only you could. Those secrets have often been a burden to me, and it brought me the greatest joy to look into your comforting eyes and know that you understood the truth at last.

Perhaps one day you will have a reason to tell my story as honestly as I have told it to you. If that day arrives, dear Philip, I know you will rely on your own impeccable judgment. And I hope you will always hear the sound of my voice as it spoke that day and speaks to you still, with immeasurable love.

Aunt Caroline

The book did not mention the envelope found by her bedside when the maid entered that spring morning and saw that Caroline had died in the night. She lay on her side, still beautiful and serene. On her bedside table was an aging envelope, never addressed, of the finest stationery; inside were two yellowed scraps of paper.

One was torn from an ordinary notebook and had pasted on it a single line, apparently cut from a magazine:

I won't sue you, for the law is too slow. I'll ruin you.

The other was a fragile newspaper clipping: the photograph of Nicholas Leone being led away between two policemen on the day he was arrested, the smirk on his face as monstrous as ever.

At first these fragments seemed to Alessio to hold some secret meaning, but eventually he concluded that, as he had done with Caroline's image on the tape and with the missing Leones, he was merely hoping to find treasures where there were none. He quickly learned that the magazine clipping quoted a notorious old threat by Cornelius Vanderbilt, but he could never determine where that version had appeared, where the notebook paper had come from, or why Caroline had it. He was certain, though, that the graceful handwriting beneath the newspaper photo, in faded ink, was hers. She had written, "Nick—I did all this for you."